MW00678978

THE PRAYER AMENDMENT

THE PRAYER AMENDMENT

A Humorous Novel of Southern Politics and Religion

S. DENNIS HALE

To Rob –
Happy Reading
7/17/05

S. Dennis Hale

COURT STREET PRESS
Montgomery

Court Street Press
P.O. Box 1588
Montgomery, AL 36102

Copyright © 2003 by S. Dennis Hale
All rights reserved under International and Pan-American Copyright Conventions.
Published in the United States by NewSouth Books, a division of NewSouth, Inc.,
Montgomery, Alabama.

Library of Congress Cataloging-in-Publication Data
Hale, S. Dennis.
The prayer amendment : a novel / by S. Dennis Hale.
p. cm.
ISBN 1-58838-118-8 (trade paper)
1. Prayer in the public schools--Fiction. 2. School
children--Fiction. 3. Alabama--Fiction. I. Title.
PS3608.A5458P73 2003
813'.6--dc21
2003007253

ISBN 1-58838-118-8

Design by Randall Williams
Printed in the United States of America

To Judith,
my best friend

You may give [children] your love but not your thoughts,
For they have their own thoughts.
You may house their bodies but not their souls,
For their souls dwell in the house of tomorrow,
which you cannot visit, not even in your dreams.
You may strive to be like them,
but seek not to make them like you.
For life goes not backward nor tarries with yesterday.

—Kahlil Gibran

PROLOGUE

EMMA'S ROOM SHUDDERED as the six p.m. freight train rumbled into Orchard Hill.

"Emma, Emma, come ou—"

"Good timing," said eleven-year-old Emma to herself as the hungry whistle gobbled up the words rising from her back yard.

As the echoes died, Emma, wearing shorts and T-shirt, shouted toward the window without rising from her desk. "What?" She knew who was calling and why, but she was not ready to go out just yet. The whistle had jarred loose a little plan. She waited.

"Come—"

Again the whistle chewed and swallowed Susie's words.

"Darn that whistle! Come on out! Let's play before it gets dark!"

Emma went to the window. "Give me a few minutes! I got a couple more problems on my homework. Go swing!"

"Okay," said Susie. "But hurry! I can't stay long."

Emma moved back into the shadows of her room and watched Susie mount the plank seat of the rope swing hanging from the sycamore tree in the back yard. She slipped on her thong sandals and left her house by the front door, careful not to let the screen door slam. She circled to approach Susie from behind. With cat-like stealth, she closed in. She crouched and watched as Susie pumped higher and higher—red hair flying, bare legs spearing the air. Then, at the moment the swing reached the apex of the back stroke, Emma pounced and grabbed one of the ropes. The swing stopped but Susie didn't.

"Emma Wedgwood!" Susie jumped up and brushed herself off. "You do that again and I'll never come over to play no more."

"Well, since you're already here, let's play chase."

Susie looked at her elbows and rubbed them with her fingers. "That hurt. Ain't you sorry?"

"Yes, I'm sorry. Let's play. I'll give you a head start to that lawn chair. Run!"

"No. Just because you're a year older than me you want to choose first every time," Susie frowned. "Besides, if you're really sorry, you'll let me choose. Let's play hide-and-go-seek."

"No. We played that yesterday. How about school? I'll be the teacher."

"Nah. I'm tired of school. How about church?"

"Play church? Don't you get tired of that, too?"

"It's been a long time since we played church," Susie said.

"All right. I'll pray and you preach," said Emma.

"I'll pray," said Susie. "I want to pray."

Emma started to protest, then saw the scrape on Susie's elbow. "That's fine. Let's get started before your mother calls."

Emma sat down in the swing, her long auburn hair falling on her shoulders and framing her narrow face. Susie sat on the ground and partially crossed her plump legs, yoga style.

"Bow your head and don't look." Susie closed her eyes.

"Let's pray with our eyes open."

"Won't that make God mad, peeping?"

"No," said Emma. "God peeps. Daddy said he's got insomnia—never sleeps. Go ahead!"

Susie brought the palms of her hands together under her chin and looked up. She paused then dropped her hands.

"I see a squirrel!"

"Susie! You're supposed to see God."

"Maybe it is God. Our preacher said he came down one time as a pigeon."

"Not a pigeon, a dove."

"Whatever."

"Now, get on with the prayer."

"Okay." Susie looked up again, then closed her eyes. "Oh, God—"

"Wait! That sounds like cussing. Why don't you start with 'Our Father?'"

"Our Father?"

"'Our Father, in heaven,' you know. That's the prayer we do in the Unitarian church about once a month," said Emma.

"That's a memorized prayer. Baptists don't do 'em."

"Well, do what you do."

"Okay. We make up new prayers every Sunday. Now be quiet."

Susie began again. "Oh, Father, we stand in your humble presence this morning—"

"Wait a minute! We're not standing; we're sitting. And it's not morning, it's evening."

Susie squinted and focused on Emma's forehead. "The scar over your eye is bright red."

"Quit changing the subject. We've got to get the prayer right or God might not understand. Tell it like it is."

"God knows everything even before we say it."

"Then say, 'Oh, Father, Amen,' and let me preach!"

"No! We do long prayers in church; people like to pray."

"Then, get on with it. We're running out of time."

Susie jumped to her feet. "Emma, you're my best friend but you sure get on my nerves. Now, close your eyes. I think it's irrelevant to look around."

Emma raised a hand then lowered it. Maybe she ought to let Susie pray. She closed her eyes.

"Oh, holy Father, Emma sits and I stand in your humble presence this evening, like dirty rags—"

Emma couldn't let that pass. "Like dirty what?"

"I said, 'like dirty rags.' It's in the Bible somewhere."

"Why tell God what he's already said in the Bible?"

"I don't know. They do it at church."

"Well, I'm not a dirty rag. I wash every day. Why don't you pray it with plain words?" Emma pushed off with her feet. The swing began a gentle arc.

"Like what?"

"Like talking to God."

"Oh, yeah. Our preacher said praying is like a phone call to God."

"That'll work."

Susie closed her eyes. Emma kept silent as the swing moved back and forth.

After a long pause Susie broke the silence. "I overheard Momma and Daddy talking about something that sounded serious."

"Go ahead. Pray about it," Emma said.

The methodical creaking of the swing ropes on the tree limb metronomed the silence.

Suddenly, Susie blurted out, "Hello, God, are you listening? If you are, help Brother Marvin's prostrate organ. Mrs. Marvin's worried about it. I ain't got no idea what else to say, but since you know it all, you figure out the rest. Amen. No, wait! Not thy will but our will be done. Amen, again."

"Susie!" called a voice from the house next door. "Time for supper."

"Gotta go."

"But I haven't preached yet." Emma pumped higher.

"We'll start with preaching next time." Susie moved in front of the swing barely beyond the increasing arc.

Emma extended her legs and pulled back hard on the rope. At the moment the swing reached the apex of its front stroke, Susie leaped, and before Emma could react, grabbed her feet momentarily and then let go. The seat dropped and Emma, clutching the ropes, was dragged back to the bottom where she lost her grip and rolled on the ground. Susie ran laughing toward the safety of her house.

Emma lay on her back for a long moment watching the rolling clouds. Then she looked toward the sound of an approaching airplane. A Piper Cub appeared trailing a waving banner not far above the sycamore tree. Emma squinted to read the message against the background of the fading sunlight. "For-be-for-Go-ver-nor." She mouthed the syllables then assembled them. "Forbe for Governor. Hmmm." *Must be headed for a football game at Auburn or somewhere to fly around and get votes.* She picked herself up and checked her elbows for scratches. *Daddy said that with all the church people's votes he's going to get, even God can't sink his ship . . . or was it . . . crash his plane? Whatever. Sometimes I wonder about the things grownups say.*

1

DARK CLOUDS TUMBLED across the sultry Montgomery sky above Tabernacle Baptist Church and its ten acres of lawn and parking lots. The pure scent of distant rain wafted under the upturned nostrils of several hundred perspiring Forbe followers who searched the burdened sky for signs of approaching relief.

James B. Forbe, wearing a plaid shirt and gray Nautica trousers, and sweating profusely, surveyed his constituents from the podium. "If I'm elected guvnah—"

He paused and looked up at the small plane circling overhead. *Too damn close,* he thought. *Gotta see about that.* As the engine's drone faded, he tried again. "If I'm elected guvnah of this great state, I'll change our constitution so our school children can pray. In 1962, the communists and secular humanists kicked God out of our schools, and I'm going to put him back—"

"You got God in your pocket, Jimbo?" came a voice a few feet from the platform. The crowd rumbled.

"The courts have been relentless in attacking prayer and Bible reading," Forbe continued. "We can't even post the Ten Commandments in our courtrooms, let alone in the classrooms. With God on the sideline—"

"Whose bench? Auburn's or Alabama's?" the heckler teased.

The crowd rumbled again. Heads turned toward the anonymous voice. Several news cameras found and focused on the well-dressed old man, slight and fragile in an outdated fedora.

Forbe followed the pivoting cameras and sighted the elder looking straight at him. Like a magnet in reverse, the old man's demeanor had pushed back the crowd until he stood alone. When Forbe locked onto the gadfly's eyes, his momentum faltered. The ensuing pause echoed across the church grounds. Forbe pulled a white handkerchief from his pocket and quickly wiped the sweat from his forehead. He looked back at the crowd, and spoke: "Homosexuals teach our children, counselors give condoms to adolescents, and the murder of unborn babies is skyrocketing. In Alabama, we're going to draw the line."

"Like you draw flies, Jimbo?"

"We'll no longer allow the forces of evil to set the educational and moral agenda for the children of our state."

"Then you better drop out while you're ahead."

Forbe paused again. An irritated follower waved a baseball cap and shouted, "Quiet, old man! Let Forbe speak!"

News technicians moved microphones closer to the old gentleman.

Forbe watched the red light go off on the camera pointed at him and light up on a camera pointed at his adversary. He took a deep breath and reasserted his ownership of the gathering, speaking quickly and without pause.

"Listen you ACLU meatheads, black-robed intellectual dwarfs, and foreign religious freaks; you will no longer run our schools. We'll take control for the sake of Jesus. Hallelujah. Three cheers for Jesus. Hip, hip . . ."

"Hurrah!"

"Hip, hip . . ."

"Hurrah!"

"Hip, hip . . ."

"Hurrah, for Jeeeeeesus!" roared the crowd. Many wore Christian T-shirts and some held hand-lettered banners aloft: "GOD LOVES YOU, JIMBO," "LET'S DO IT FOR JESUS," and "JESUS WANTS BACK IN SHCOOL." Forbe waved his WWJD baseball cap at the crowd as he backed away from the podium.

"Keep that goddamned heckler away from my rallies!" Forbe hissed between clenched teeth to campaign aide Dick Little, then flashed a smile at Brother Johnny Carroll and the other ministers on the rostrum. He reached for his handkerchief and wiped his forehead. As he stepped down from the platform and made his way through the crowd, his toupéed head submerged in a sea of microphones. State troopers swam between Forbe and the media, who threatened to swallow the paunchy aspirant to the Alabama state house.

"Mr. Forbe, Mr. Forbe," shouted the scavengers—each maneuvering for a chunk of the candidate to round out an enticing tabloid menu to be served on the 6 o'clock news to a hungry but overfed audience. Forbe stretched to his full five feet eight and gestured to the attractive blonde waving a pencil and writing pad in his direction.

"Thank you, Mr. Forbe. I'm Barbara Willis of the *Atlanta Journal-Constitution*. Question: Can you pull it off?"

"Pull off what, dearie?" Forbe blinked his eyes and flashed his teeth even before seeing the flush on the newswoman's pretty face.

Reporters within earshot laughed. Microphones recorded the sound bite.

She spoke again. "Can you ride into office on the back of this religious spirit?"

"Barbara, that is, Ms. Willis, you got it right. This 'religious spirit,' as you call it, is gonna bear me right into the guvnah's mansion."

"Aren't you afraid it'll come back to haunt you? You're playing with some powerful spirits."

Forbe smiled. "Here in Alabama we believe in the *Holy Ghost*. It don't haunt." Forbe listened to his faithful supporters applaud and chant: "Praise the Lord! Hallelujah!"

As Willis folded her pad and turned away, Forbe motioned to another reporter.

"Yes, you, Billy," he pointed to a familiar face. But before looking into the WSFA camera, his eyes strayed to the swaying of shapely hips as Barbara Willis hurried toward a BMW awaiting her on the street. Those were hips he would never forget. Forbe turned away and sneezed into the air.

"Mr. Forbe, would you tell us . . ."

FROM THE PLATFORM, John William Carroll, better known as Brother Johnny, beamed as James Forbe worked the crowd. Thinning brown hair sprinkled dandruff on the collar of Carroll's navy blue Goodwill suit. His mournful eyes watched with pride as the excited news reps pushed mikes and pointed cameras at the noble man who, in his humble opinion, was destined to move this great state toward God.

"God bless you, Mr. Forbe," Carroll formed the words with his lips. 'As thou hast sent me into the world, even so have I also sent them into the world.' Oh, Jesus, help me get this man of God elected as governor of Alabama."

Lightning jerked heads skyward and thunder pushed them down. Pellets of rain baptized the assembly. Brother Johnny joined the rush to escape the shower's welcome relief.

2

FORBE SCANNED HIS wife's immaculate kitchen. Every utensil was in its place. White counter-tops glistened. He looked at his wife across fried eggs, bacon, biscuits, and grits. Steam spiraled from freshly poured coffee.

"No, Betty. I can't go to church with you today!" he said. She wore just the right amount of makeup—every brush of mascara precisely in its place.

"Brother Johnny Carroll's the visiting preacher at Tabernacle Baptist. I thought you might like to hear him again."

"I don't care if *Jesus* is preaching. I've got important things to do." Forbe sipped his coffee, and glanced out the window.

"I'd love to have you sit beside me, Jimmy."

"You can sit with your friends today," Forbe said, reaching for the *Montgomery Advertiser.*

"Then you're not coming?"

Forbe turned away from the table and sneezed. "Ah . . . ah . . . ah, choo! Aaah. That's better'n sex." Forbe looked at Betty, smiled and winked.

"You've said that before," said Betty. "You're definitely not coming?"

"I don't feel like it. May have a cold coming on. Besides, I've got preachers up to my— ah, my neck."

"Is that what you want me to tell Brother Johnny when he asks about you?"

"Hel—heck, no! Tell 'im I'm doing some thinking. And be

sure to ask him to pray for me from the pulpit. I need those darn votes."

As Betty's car pulled out of the drive, Forbe moved to his La-Z-Boy recliner, took a deep breath and stretched. He switched on "Baywatch" and laid the *Advertiser* on his lap. Hasselhoff jogged onto the screen flanked by three shapely lifeguards in bright orange, high-leg swim wear. As the scene switched to rolling surf, Forbe closed his eyes and floated down onto a deserted isle covered with palm trees swaying gently in the cool, ocean breeze. Salt air caressed his countenance. He rolled his head back to inhale the aroma of the sea. Suddenly, he discerned movement around the side of a distant sand dune. He did a double-take. A dozen curvaceous blondes jogged toward him, clad in topless orange bikinis, breasts bouncing like basketballs in slow motion. *Wow! This is for certain the Kingdom of Heaven*, he thought. *I've never witnessed anything—*

The doorbell rang, snatching him back from paradise. He shook his head.

It rang again.

"Shit!" Forbe rubbed his eyes then hit the mute button on the remote. He rose to answer the door. The *Advertiser* fell to the floor. He closed his robe around him and turned the knob.

Three people stood in his doorway, behind the screen door. A middle-aged man in a dark brown suit, white shirt and tie, his sweet cologne mixing with perspiration in the humid Alabama heat, spoke first. "Hello. We're from the Kingdom Hall of Jehovah's Witnesses. I'm Brother Jacob and this is Sister Leah and Sister Rebecca. Could you spare us a moment of your time?"

Forbe looked toward Sister Leah and Sister Rebecca who stood in stark contrast to the dreamy blondes they had replaced in his consciousness. Brown-headed Leah wore a navy blue knee-length dress with a white collar and black-headed Rebecca had on an ankle-length dark brown skirt with a beige blouse. Both held pea-green Bibles—swords of the Spirit—offensive weapons ready to be used if needed.

"How do you do, ladies," said Forbe.

Both women smiled, nodded, then frowned again. Neither spoke.

Forbe looked back at the chief Witness. "I'm really quite busy. Could you come back later? My wife isn't home right now."

"Do you mind if we talk with you a few minutes? We have a message from Jehovah God."

"I'm up to my neck in work. Could you come back when my wife is here? She'd love to talk to you about God." Forbe half turned as if to leave the door.

The Witness stepped closer. "We'll return, but we'd like to leave you some literature of the Watch Tower Bible and Tract Society. Jesus is coming back soon. Are you one of the elect?"

"Well, I'm running for guvnah and, God willing, will be elected come November."

"Oh, you're Jimbo Forbe. Nice to meet you, sir."

Forbe turned back, opened the screen, and shook the extended hand.

The Witness pulled the screen farther open and wedged it against the back of his shoulder. "Mr. Forbe, you need to know that Jehovah doesn't have much use for the government. His kingdom is not of this world."

"I'm only running for guvnah of Alabama," said Forbe. "Maybe I'll try for the Kingdom next time."

"Oh, that's very funny." The Witness smiled and turned toward Leah and Rebecca who did not smile. He looked back at Forbe. "This is no laughing matter, Mr. Forbe. Please take this pamphlet and read what Jehovah says about the world's governments."

"Okay. Let me have it. Is that all?"

"Mr. Forbe, Jehovah's kingdom is supported by voluntary contributions. Generous people like you give after receiving free books and literature."

"How much would a voluntary contribution be?"

"A dollar or two would help further the Kingdom, but who am I to say you cannot contribute more?"

"Let me get my wallet," said Forbe. Returning to the door, he fumbled for a dollar and finding none pulled out a five.

"Oh, what the hell. I'll buy a few votes," he muttered under his breath.

"What was that, sir?"

"I said I'd appreciate your votes." He gave the five to the Witness. "I hope you'll remember me when you go the polls in November."

The Witness took the bill and handed it to one of his silent partners who placed it in a small bank-bag. Then he turned back to Forbe.

"Thank you very much, sir. We will remember you, but not when we go to the polls. We Jehovah's Witnesses don't vote. We don't believe in it. Have a good day."

As the three Witnesses walked toward the next house and the smell of sweet cologne and sour sweat followed them like dogs in heat, Forbe tried to remember the joke he'd heard recently at the country club. *What was it? . . . Oh, yes. What do you get when you cross a Jehovah's Witness with a Unitarian? You get a religious fanatic who goes around knocking on doors but doesn't have anything to say.*

He sat back down and noticed "Baywatch" was at a commercial. His fingers hovered over the remote control, finally landing on the channel change.

As he settled again in his La-Z-Boy and focused on "Face the

Nation," he said out loud, "I hope Betty's having fun. The morning's been a bust for me."

3

BETTY FORBE STRUGGLED to keep her eyes open as Brother Johnny rambled on. She regretted having stayed up to the end of the late Saturday night movie. Jimmy had barely lasted through the first commercial.

"'And Noah was six hundred years old when the flood of waters was upon the earth,' Genesis 7:6. 'And Abraham was a hundred years old, when his son Isaac was born unto him,' Genesis 21:5. God has anointed me to preach . . ."

Betty adjusted her glasses hoping the lens would hide her sagging eyelids from the preacher. *I've got to sit further back when I stay up late.*

"'And Abraham was ninety years and nine, when he was circumcised in the flesh of his foreskin', Genesis 17:24. Circumcision cuts away the flesh—a symbol of sin. 'Arise and be baptized, and wash away thy sins,' Acts 22:16. We don't have to cut it off anymore. We can wash it away. Blessed . . ."

Betty roused with a start. *What did he say? Oh, well. If Brother Johnny could only preach as well as he ministers to the elderly . . .*

"'He that believeth and is baptized shall be saved,' Mark 16:16. We had forty baptisms in the rest homes last month. Forty precious new babes in Christ now ready for glory."

Just hold them under a couple of minutes and they'll float right up. Betty suppressed a chuckle.

"Thanks to your generous offering last year, new souls have been baptized and floated into the open arms of Jesus. 'Bring ye all the tithes into the storehouse,' Malachi 3:10. 'God loveth a cheerful giver,' Second Corinthians 9:7. When the deacon passes the offering plate, God will deposit heavenly riches to the eternal account of every saint who gives freely. Let us pray."

He circles and circles. I thought he'd never land. Must have quoted the whole Bible. Betty looked at her watch.

BROTHER JOHNNY DID indeed have forty baptisms last month in his rest homes, more than all the Baptist churches in Montgomery. He always had lots of baptisms. He knew how to get the old folks into the purifying waters.

He preached later that week at the Valley of the Shadow Rest Home, in Dadeville. "'He that believeth and is baptized shall be saved,' Mark 16:16. God saith in his Holy Book, 'Remember the days of old,' Deuteronomy 32:7. Do you remember? If you do not remember the day you were baptized, how can you be sure you were?"

As Johnny preached, he saw heads nod and fall forward while others tilted back with mouths open. A loud snore rose from the corner of the room.

"Sister Margaret, would you please come to the piano and lead us in a song?" he said to a matronly resident sitting on the front row. *If the singing doesn't wake everybody up, the piano will. Sister Margaret plays like Edith Bunker.*

Johnny announced the hymn number but few of the elderly residents opened the songbook as they raised their weathered voices, "'Tempted and tried we're oft made to wonder, why . . .'"

Johnny closed his eyes to rest them for a moment. The old folks would think he was praying. He thought about his trials—trials he would like to forget—especially his father. His thoughts drifted back to his childhood in Monroe County.

"Get your skinny ass out of here!" his drunken father cried. "I'm tired of looking at your ugly face."

Johnny started for the door.

"Where you think you're going, you worthless turd? Get back here. Who told you to leave?" his father yelled. Johnny ducked as his father swung wildly. "Get your ass into that corner you shithead, and don't move till I tell you."

Johnny seldom knew what to do. Even when his father was sober, which was increasingly rare, he still ordered his family around. "'Children, obey your parents,' Ephesians 6:1," his father quoted with frequency during his dry periods. When Elijah Carroll drank, alcohol was his master and when he didn't, God was. And, whoever his master, the Bible was the weapon of choice. "'For the word of God is quick, and powerful, and sharper than any two-edged sword . . .' Hebrews 4:12," he quoted whatever his state of sobriety.

Sister Margaret struck a discord. Johnny opened his eyes as the dissonance yanked him back to the rest home.

"' . . . while there are others, living about us, never molested, though in the wrong. Farther along . . .'" The septuagenarian, octogenarian, and nonagenarian voices droned on.

Johnny again closed his eyes and drifted back.

"Woman, get the food on the table!" Elijah Carroll demanded.

"I didn't have time to cook today. We're going to Kentucky Fried," Johnny's mother replied. Johnny knew what was coming.

"We're not going anywhere and spend my fucking money on somebody else's shit. Turn that stove on, woman, and get some food on the table. You're not going to bankrupt this family."

"I don't feel like cooking today."

"But you will. The Holy Book says, 'Wives, submit yourselves unto your own husbands,' Ephesians 5:22. Now do what God says. I'm gonna feed the dogs. When I get back, supper better be on that table."

Johnny knew that the fight had ended and Momma had lost. It was not his father who had spoken but God. Momma would turn on the stove. She said that God, our Heavenly Father, was good, but Johnny did not understand. If God the Heavenly Father is good, why is my earthly father so bad? Ain't they kin? Maybe I'll understand by and by.

The dissonant harmony of off-key singing brought him back to the Valley of the Shadow Rest Home once again.

"'... Cheer up my brother, live in the sunshine. We'll understand it all by and by.'"

"Praise the Lord. One day Jesus will tell us all about it." Johnny clapped his hands above his head. "My, how good y'all sing! God says, 'Make a joyful noise unto the Lord,' Psalm 100:1. God says again, 'Singing with grace in—" Johnny cut himself off. He knew the verse but squelched the compulsion to quote it. He was as addicted to quoting scripture as his father was to alcohol and the Bible put together. How he wished he could stop!

"Now, where was I? Oh, yes." Johnny returned to his sermon. "If you remember not your baptism, then maybe you were never baptized. Sister Margaret, stroke that piano again and lead us in singing, 'Shall We Gather at the River.' As we sing, I want all you dear saints that haven't been baptized or maybe you forgot if you were, to come right down here and take my hand and say, Brother Johnny, 'I want to follow Jesus in baptism.'"

Several pushed themselves up from their seats and shuffled down to where Brother Johnny stood. He took the hand of each and whispered words of encouragement before gently nudging them back toward the group.

Johnny baptized some of his aging parishners repeatedly. Their short-term memory was gone. They could be baptized yesterday and forget it today. So they responded again and again and Brother Johnny re-baptized them. He sometimes thought about changing his approach but the baptisms might decrease. He couldn't afford that. Baptisms were like ratings for the

Baptist churches. They brought donations to Johnny's ministry and he needed all he could get.

Brother Johnny always closed his visits by inviting all who were going to be baptized to be ready next Saturday. "We'll have running water like the River Jordan. Now all that's gonna be baptized, be ready at 3 o'clock."

"Where we going, Brother Johnny? I can't swim," asked one lady.

"Why, honey, we're going to a nice, safe beach on Lake Martin. There'll be lots of us going and there's even a ramp to roll wheel chairs into the water." Johnny sat down.

The activities director stood. "Let's give Brother Johnny a big hand."

"I almost forgot!" Johnny slapped his temple with the heel of his hand and stood. He raised his hand for silence. "Don't forget to vote for God's candidate in the upcoming election. Our Christian Brother James Forbe will guarantee that your grandchildren will pray again in the schools, our hallowed halls of learning. When the time comes, we'll have buses to take you to the polls. Any questions?"

"How's your wife doing, Brother Johnny," asked a wrinkled, toothless patriarch rising as he spoke.

"Oh, she's doing fine as always," he responded, but didn't really know. He was divorced. The itinerant nature of his ministry helped him keep his marital status secret.

"Why don't you bring her with you some time?" continued the patriarch.

"She's busy serving the Lord in her church," Johnny lied. "Now why don't we sing, 'God be with you till we meet again.'"

As the singing began, Johnny again strayed barefoot into his rocky field of memories.

"Where are you going, Johnny," asked Miriam. "You haven't

been home a single night this week."

"'I was glad when they said unto me, Let us go into the house of the Lord,' Psalm 122:1. I've got a meeting in the Lord's house, Precious."

"What about your own house?"

"I serve Jesus. Jesus said, 'If any man come to me, and hate not his father, and mother, and wife, and children, and brethren, and sisters, yea—"

"Do you mean that, Johnny? I know you love your children."

"Yes. I love them. I love you. But I got to put God's family first. You know that."

"I know it," said Miriam. "But I can't live with it."

"Sure we can. 'All things work together for good to them that love God—"

"Listen Johnny," she interrupted, "I can't take any more verses right now."

"—to them who are the called according to his purpose,' Romans 8:28."

She sighed deeply. "I'm going to leave you, Johnny. I'm taking the kids with me. When you get your priorities sorted out, we'll talk."

"Brother Johnny, Brother Johnny, are you all right? I thought you were about to fall."

Johnny opened his eyes. Someone gripped his right arm.

"We're always glad to see you, Brother Johnny." The activities director shook his hand as the flock drifted toward the TV that now reverberated from the corner of the day room. "These folks love you and look forward to your weekly visit."

"'Blessed be he that cometh in the name of the Lord,' Psalm, 18:24." Johnny still remembered every verse he had ever learned, over one thousand in all. He knew his Bible. At least, he knew the words in it and how to use them, and God was blessing him richly.

"They seem so relaxed after your visit. I wish you'd come every day. It's good therapy, I think."

"'He which testifieth these things saith, Surely I come quickly,' Revelation 22:20." The verse didn't quite fit but that was no problem. The Holy Spirit would use the word of God. "The dear folks have that wonderful television preaching and Bible study all day long. That'll keep them going till I get back."

"It's not the same thing, Brother Johnny. I saw in *Time* magazine about a study that shows TV evangelists get old folks' blood pressure up. I've seen it happen here. Our folks argue so much that sometimes we turn the set off or switch to another channel. Those TV preachers stir our people up."

"'For my thoughts are not your thoughts, neither are your ways my ways, saith the Lord,' Isaiah 55:8. God has mysterious ways."

"I'm sure that's true. But 'I love Lucy' and 'The Andy Griffith Show' do them a lot more good than those television preachers. You come anytime you want to. The more often the better."

"Have them ready for the baptizing trip next Saturday. Now, I've got to go over to Wal-Mart in Alex City and pick up a paper and some groceries. The prices are a lot better at that Superstore."

As the grinding starter labored to turn the worn-out engine of his '87 Cutlass Ciera, Brother Johnny thought about the encouraging words of the director and said out loud, "God is so good to me. I can hardly wait to see what blessing He has in store for me at Wal-Mart."

4

"Hey, there, Brother Johnny!"

Johnny turned toward the voice. "Darn!" he grunted under his breath, using the strongest expletive in his vocabulary. "God help me!" he prayed, but there was nothing God could do short of striking her dead. She was headed his way.

"Hello, Miss Gaylor. You look very nice today."

A litany fast-forwarded through Johnny's mind. *Not, "Reverend Gaylor," for God calls no woman to be a minister. Not, "Sister Gaylor" for she's a Unitarian, yet she does run that home for abused women.*

"Thank you. I'm on my way to work." Janet Gaylor said. "By the way, I want to thank you for visiting those folks at the retirement centers. They always tell me how much they enjoy your visits."

"I carry them a word from the Lord, Miss Gaylor." Johnny eased back a step.

"Are you all right?" asked Gaylor.

"Yes, just fine, thank you. I was saying that I carry the elderly a word from the Lord."

"Just carrying yourself would be enough," replied Gaylor. "You show them attention and it makes them feel good. What brings you to Wal-Mart at this hour?"

"'Study to shew thyself approved unto God,' Second Timothy 2:15. I came to get some groceries and the *Montgomery Advertiser*. It has complete coverage of the Bonnie Sue Turner death penalty case," he replied.

"You're concerned about that, aren't you?"

"'Father, forgive them; for they know not what they do,' Luke 23:34. What are we gonna do about Bonnie Sue?" he said.

"What can we do? She's been condemned to death for murder," said Gaylor.

Although Brother Johnny seldom spoke to those the Baptists considered godless Unitarians, he was glad she had approached him after all. He needed to talk to her. The Unitarians were against the death penalty.

"Bonnie Sue's accepted Jesus. 'He that believeth on the Son hath everlasting life,' John 3:36. God has given her life eternal. The State of Oklahoma shouldn't execute her."

"The same could happen in Alabama," said Gaylor. "You should have thought about that when you were busing all those old folks here in Alex City, Dadeville, and all over east Alabama to vote for the death penalty."

Johnny said, "I pray it won't happen in Alabama."

"There are convicts on death row in Alabama. What about Jeff Shirley?" Gaylor asked.

"Jeff Shirley murdered his wife in cold blood. 'Vengeance is mine, saith the Lord,' Romans 12:19. He's getting what he deserves. We've got to teach respect for human life."

"I have visited Jeff Shirley several times," said Gaylor. "He has converted to the Muslim faith and prays to God five times a day. That sounds to me a lot like what you call repentance."

"Heavens, Miss Gaylor! When somebody becomes a Muslim, that means he has rejected our loving Savior. 'Jesus said, I am the way, the truth, and the life: no man cometh unto the Father, but by me,' John 14:6."

"Looking at it from a purely biblical angle, why should God favor one over the other? They're both his children. The Bible says, 'God is no respecter of persons,' Acts 10:34."

Johnny thought he caught a twinkle in her eye.

"I just remembered I got to be in Wedowee at 5. It's been nice talking to you."

"It was good to see you, too."

Johnny hastened toward the checkout almost colliding with another man who entered the aisle he was leaving. It was Stanley Hannah. They both stopped and shook hands.

Johnny said, "Reverend Hannah, what are you doing in town?"

"To celebrate my brother-in-law's birthday tomorrow. Good to see you."

"Good to see you again. Give your folks my regards."

"I'll do that. You have a good day." Stanley Hannah said, continuing toward the woman in the aisle ahead of him.

5

As JANET TURNED into the produce section, a man's voice reached her ear. An unmistakable masculine fragrance touched her nostrils.

"Hello, Reverend Gaylor."

She spun around, almost losing her balance.

"Stanley! You'll give me a heart attack!" She was glad she had slipped on her Liz Claiborne slacks and jacket and not the worn-out Levis she normally wore to the market.

"As long as it's not fatal." Stanley hugged her. An elderly shopper started up their aisle then chose another one.

Janet felt him against her and thought of their first meeting just four months ago in Washington.

She gently pushed him back. "I want to look at you." She gazed up into his deep blue eyes. "What are you doing here so early? You on your motorcycle?"

"No, too slow." He stepped back, still holding her hand. "I hopped an early flight and rented a car in Atlanta. My, you look good."

"How did you find me?"

"I called your office. You need some help?"

"I came to pick up some things for this evening. Since you're here, you can decide what to have for dinner."

"Let me take you to the Paella."

"Don't you get tired of eating out? I'll cook dinner tonight."

"Fine with me. I'll push the cart and let you choose, since you're the cook."

Janet laid her hand over his and squeezed. "I've missed you."

"I've missed you, too, Janet. I—"

"Hi, Reverend Gaylor. Hi, Mr. Hannah." The slender pre-adolescent girl in Gap jeans and boat-neck sweater appeared out of nowhere and leaned on the shopping cart which moved. She jumped back. Her dark eyes sparkled. Auburn hair flowed into a ponytail. "I hope I didn't bother you." There was an "I caught you in the cookie jar" expression on her face.

Janet blushed as she released Stanley's hand and smiled at the child she knew from the Unitarian church in Orchard Hill.

"No. Not at all, Emma," she lied. "Good to see you. You're out of school today?"

"Had to go to the dentist. Momma's over there somewhere, and I'm just looking around." She pulled a can of artichokes from a shelf, shrugged, and returned it to another shelf, upside down.

"How are Susie and my sister?" asked Stanley. "I just got in and haven't been by their house yet."

"Susie's fine. Her mom, too. Susie told me you were coming. Got to go now. Mother will be looking for me."

Janet and Stanley watched as she disappeared at a full run around the end of the counter, swerving to miss the elderly lady who, once again, ventured into the aisle where they stood. This time, she stayed.

"Emma's going to be an attractive young woman," said Stanley. "She's a good friend of Susie. They're usually together when I see them."

"She's also quite mischievous," said Janet, "and sometimes a little reckless for her age."

"What do you mean?"

"You won't believe it. She once hid a farting cushion in my pulpit chair at the church. I thought I'd die when I sat on it."

"What *did* you do?"

"Fortunately, I didn't flinch. I looked over at the fellowship president who was about to get up and make some announcements. The whole congregation exploded with laughter. When the noise subsided and the president said, 'I *will* get to the bottom of this,' the congregation again erupted into hysterics."

"How did you know it was Emma?"

"I just knew it. She has a reputation for shenanigans. But she's also intelligent and conscientious. When she outgrows her devilish stage, she's going places."

"I know you'll keep an eye on her," said Stanley.

Janet glanced at her watch. "I've got to hurry. Got a couple of appointments back at the shelter as soon as I finish shopping. Could you be at my place by seven?"

"I'll check my appointment book and see if I have an opening." Stanley pretended to reach for his Day Runner.

"Stanley Hannah!"

Stanley winked. "Right now I'll run on over to Orchard Hill and get settled in with Karen and Zack. See you later."

"Take care." Janet blew him a kiss, then hurried down the aisle toward the meat department.

"Would you like another baked yam?" Janet pushed the bowl toward Stanley.

"I think I've eaten enough yams to last me a year." He pushed his plate back and rubbed his stomach. "By the way, what was that spice in the pork loin?"

"Rosemary. Did you like it?"

"I like everything you do." Stanley reached across the table and took her hands.

"You want dessert?" said Janet. A light flush rose to her olive cheeks.

"It just crossed my mind," said Stanley.

"Then I'd better go get it." She pulled loose, rose, and retrieved a dish from the refrigerator. She set a chocolate cream pie and a spatula on the table and sat back down across from him.

Stanley cut and served himself a slice and savored the first morsel. He pushed the pie across the table to Janet. "You could cook for me every day."

"You mentioned that a couple of times before I left Washington for Orchard Hill," Janet said.

"You're not having any pie?"

"No. I'm watching my figure."

"You're quite successful at it." Stanley smiled. "Have you ever thought about coming back to Washington?"

"Not really," said Janet. "I like it down here—small town, mild winters, good people."

"I miss you," said Stanley, "and I hardly know you."

"I miss you, too," said Janet. "Since the night we met at that Cuba rally on the Mall, we've seen each other so seldom."

"Had it not been for our mutual friend introducing us, I'd never have met you."

"Dan the matchmaker. I would never have chosen to go to a pro-Castro rally," said Janet. "My mother was one of the Cuban boat people."

"It wasn't pro-Castro; it was pro-Cuba, anti-embargo."

"Whatever it was, it wasn't my kind of gathering—all that shouting in Spanish. Weren't most of the demonstrators protesting the rally?"

"Yeah. That Florida-based group was there. They want to keep the pressure on—run Castro out of office."

"And your group wants to let him grow old and retire."

"Perhaps. Weren't you born in Cuba?"

"No. I was born in Madison, Wisconsin, to my Catholic

mother and Unitarian father. They met and married there."

"How did you wind up in Washington, D.C.?" asked Stanley.

"After getting a degree in Social Work at the University of Wisconsin-Madison, I was offered an internship at All Souls Church in Washington. I couldn't turn it down."

"Do you know why your senior minister sent you to the rally?"

"He told me I needed some exposure to social protest."

"He told me he thought you were on the wrong side of the Cuban problem," said Stanley, "that maybe the rally would broaden your social conscience."

"What do you mean 'the wrong side'?" I'm for all Cubans, those in Cuba *and* those in Miami."

"Me, too," Stanley said, gesturing with his hands.

"You too? How many Baptist disaster relief teams have you taken to Florida? Have you ever set up a soup kitchen in Miami?"

Stanley said nothing.

"You think by taking doctors and nurses to Cuba every year—I'm sorry." Janet reached across the table and patted Stanley's hand. "I didn't mean to get so worked up."

"You have a point," said Stanley.

"No. I'm not being fair. You're doing a good job, I'm sure." She smiled. "You going to finish your dessert? If you don't want it, there might be something else."

Stanley cut his eyes at her without raising his head, then finished his pie before speaking again. "Do you know that you're the first person I've dated since my wife's death, over a year ago?"

"I'm flattered," replied Janet. "Have you ever thought about returning to Alabama?"

"I'd like to, but being a liberal Baptist minister—"

"A liberal what?" Janet raised her eyebrows and opened her mouth in mock disbelief.

"A liberal Baptist—"

Janet laughed. "That's an oxymoron."

Stanley smiled and continued, "I feel like the Lone Ranger in this state. Do you know why Tabernacle Baptist Church fired me?"

"I knew you were pastor there but not why you left."

"I told them the creation stories in Genesis were myths."

"What's so bad about that?"

"Baptists trace their genealogy back to Adam and Eve. A week later, the deacons told me my job was a myth."

They sat silent for a few moments.

"You're no ordinary Baptist preacher. I knew that from the night we met."

"How did I give it away?"

"Your Moto Guzzi was a hint. And you didn't try to convince me to become a Baptist."

"My faith is the philosophy I live by, not a product I sell."

Janet said, "I like that," and began to clear the table. "Now back to your story. Tabernacle isn't the only Baptist church in Alabama."

"News spreads quickly." Stanley stood, took the dishes from her, stacked them in the sink, and turned on the hot water.

Janet bumped him aside with her hip and squirted detergent on the dishes. "Let's leave them to soak."

"I'll wash them. It'll only take a minute." He reached for a sponge. "Then maybe you'll invite me to dinner again."

Janet stepped back and watched Stanley wash his hands and rinse the dishes. "Do you have to be a preacher?"

"Well, I majored in political science at Samford."

"Have you ever thought about running for public office?"

"In Alabama?"

"Why not? You're an Alabama native."

"Yep. Born right here in Tallapoosa County—in Orchard Hill to be exact."

"With this fanatic running for governor, Alabama could use some fresh ideas. A Unitarian is running against him."

"Doesn't have the chance of a snowball in hell." Stanley laughed.

"That sums it up," Janet replied.

"I've been thinking about Jimmy Forbe. We were roommates at Samford, you know. That prayer amendment business he's pushing has me puzzled."

"What do you mean?"

"Jimmy doesn't know a Unitarian from a unicorn. In modern jargon, he's theologically challenged. He used to kid me about going to church all the time."

"He's got religion now. In this state, that's a plus—if it's the right religion."

"Still, he was more confortable in bars—oh well, that's enough of politics. Let's talk about you. Are you really happy here in Tallapoosa County?" Stanley dried his hands and turned toward Janet.

She took his hand. They walked to the small living room and sat on the couch.

"I'm making a difference in Alex City," Janet replied. "We saw over two dozen abused women and children last month."

"There are other people who could do that work."

"They need me and I need them. And I'm close to the church in Orchard Hill. Did you know that the last minister they had commuted from Atlanta?"

"Still, it would be nice if we were closer," said Stanley. "I'm beginning to like you."

"What do you like?" She placed her hand on his thigh.

Stanley placed his arm around her. "Well, you're loving,

compassionate, and not bad looking."

Janet pushed him away. "That's not very flattering."

Stanley pulled her back. She responded to his embrace. A tingling rippled through her flowing out to the tips of her fingers. Their lips met. She felt herself melting into his—

A lively rendition of the "William Tell Overture" on his cell phone broke the spell. Janet tensed.

"Oh, hell," said Stanley as he reached for his phone.

Let it ring, Janet thought.

Stanley rolled his eyes as he pressed the keypad and said, "Hello. Stanley Hannah here." He listened.

"It's Susie," Stanley whispered to Janet.

As Stanley began to speak into the receiver, Janet walked into the bathroom, turned on the cold water, and splashed it on her face. She looked into the mirror as the water dripped down, mixing with the angry tears running down her cheeks. She needed to be held—to be loved. So many years since Victor had walked out. She shuddered. Stanley was different. She reached for a towel, patted her face dry, and returned to the living room where Stanley stood waiting. From the look on his face, she knew the evening was over.

"I guess I'd better get back over to Karen's before it gets too late. I missed Susie this afternoon. She was still at soccer practice when I left, and it's about her bedtime now."

"I'm sure that's important," said Janet. She wondered if he detected the sarcasm in her voice.

He took her hand as they walked toward the door. "Will I see you tomorrow?"

"I'm afraid not. I'll be at the shelter all day and then I have to get ready for the church service on Sunday morning. What about Sunday afternoon? We could go see *Smokey Joe's Café* at the Shakespeare Festival in Montgomery."

"My flight leaves for Washington from Atlanta at mid-afternoon."

Stanley kissed her lightly on the lips, hugged her—burying his face in her hair, then turned and walked to his car. As he touched the latch to open it, he stopped, looked back over his shoulder, and called, "Why don't we meet down on the coast some day and work all this out?"

"I'd like that," said Janet,—"with the telephone off."

As Rachmaninoff's "Piano Concerto No. 2 in C Minor" flowed over the National Public Radio station, Stanley accelerated the rented Escort onto Highway 280 for the half-hour drive to Orchard Hill. He blinked his eyes to clear his vision and breathed deeply to ease the tension of opposites tugging at his soul.

6

Susie came running into Emma's back yard and spotted her in the sycamore tree. "Hi, Uncle Stanley's here and today's Daddy's birthday."

Emma, munching on her sausage biscuit from breakfast, looked down at Susie. "That's good news. But I've heard some bad news."

"What?" Susie frowned as she sat on the rope swing.

"You heard about the floods in North Carolina?"

"Yeah. Why?"

"There were over a million deaths."

A mockingbird cycled through its repertoire from the top of the tree.

"No! Couldn't be a million. You mean a hundred . . . or a thousand."

"A million. I saw it on TV."

"That's terrible," said Susie. She looked at the ground. "I didn't know a million people lived in North Carolina."

"I didn't say people. I said deaths. Dead chickens, ha, ha, ha. I fooled you. Your freckles are flashing."

"Emma Wedgwood, I'm not going to speak to you for a whole week!"

"Then, don't speak, but listen. I saw your Uncle Stanley yesterday at Wal-Mart, and guess who he was with—holding hands."

"You didn't see him. You're pulling my leg again."

"Cross my heart and hope to die. I saw him. If I didn't see

him, how would I know he was holding her hand?"

"Whose hand?"

"Reverend Gaylor's." Emma giggled. "He was holding her hand and she pulled loose when she saw me."

"He had supper with Reverend Gaylor but he wouldn't hold her hand. He's a preacher." Susie slid off the swing, jumped, and barely missed Emma's dangling feet.

Emma raised her legs higher. "I'll bet he's holding Reverend Gaylor's hand right now."

"He's not."

"He is."

"He's not. He went birthday shopping with Momma. When he gets back, I'm gonna to ask him if he did what you said." Susie started toward her house at a trot, her red hair waving.

"You better not." Emma jumped to the ground and gave chase.

"Yes, I am."

"You do and I'll tell your mother about Jeremiah."

"You do and I'll squeal about Paco." Susie ran up the steps and lunged for the screen door.

"You wouldn't."

"Yes, I would. Cross my heart . . ."

"Girls," called Zack Holland from the other side of the screen. "Are you fussing again?"

"No, sir," said Emma. "We're playing. We play like this all the time."

"That's right, Daddy. We're playing chase."

7

James Forbe looked up from his donuts and coffee as Dick Little entered the small private office adjacent to the main hall of the Forbe-for-Governor headquarters. Dick wore khaki pants, a solid-blue shirt, and striped tie. He claimed that vertical stripes on his ties made him look taller than his five-feet-five frame.

"Hello, Dick. Is everybody here?" Forbe asked.

Dick dropped onto the worn sofa against the wall in front of the desk.

"Hey, my little friend. You look uptight. You need to get married; settle down; have some kids."

"I've thought about it but the right woman hasn't come along yet."

"You ever thought about changing your last name?" Forbe leaned back and laughed.

"Come on, Jimbo. Get serious. I need to discuss something with you before the strategy session begins."

"Okay, get it off your chest. The session can wait."

"This is not easy to talk about."

"Come on! You got my attention now. Let me have it!"

"A reporter has been asking me questions about an affair in your past."

Forbe jumped to his feet. "What? Shit! What did you tell her?"

"Nothing. I felt that he was just fishing. I told him absolutely nothing."

Forbe detected the change of gender. *So, it wasn't her. Why the hell would she be asking about that anyway?* "You said, 'no comment'?"

"No, I said nothing. I turned my palms out and shrugged." Forbe attempted to lighten the mood. "At least that will be hard to quote."

Dick's expression did not change. "Is there something you need to tell me?"

"No! Of course not! What could there be to tell you?"

"Jimbo, I'm your campaign manager. I'm also an attorney. The lawyer in me says there's something to it. If there is, I need to know it."

"I tell you, dammit, there's nothing. Nothing happened!" Forbe pulled out his handkerchief and wiped his forehead. He sat back down.

Dick looked directly into Forbe's eyes and enunciated each word. "Listen to me. I'm your friend. Tell me exactly what it was that *didn't* happen."

"Dammit, Dick, you're worse than a lawyer." Forbe leaned forward and let his elbows fall on the desk. He rested his forehead on the tips of his fingers and rubbed up and down. He pressed his thumbs into his bulging cheeks and sat silent for a long moment. "It happened when I was still mayor of Birmingham. Barbara Willis covered the mayor's office when she was at the *Post-Herald*."

"I've heard of Barbara," said Dick. "She's a good reporter."

"That's not all she's good at. Barbara Willis is a piece of work."

"And . . ."

Forbe waved his hand. "We'd seen each other sporadically for about six months when she took a job with the *Atlanta Journal-Constitution*."

"I assume you mean you were having sex. Just tell me, is everything under control now?"

Forbe raised his head and looked at Dick. "Hell, it was under control then! I knew what I was doing. There are a lot of women out there—good-looking women, like Barbara—who will trade their ass for a pinch of power."

Dick said, "And politicians who'll trade their power for a pinch of ass."

Forbe tensed. "Don't get sassy, Dick."

"You gotta be careful. If anybody, I mean anybody, breathes a word to the press, we can roll up those banners and go home. Is it over?"

Forbe looked past Dick. "I'd been in my second term less than a year. I began to think about the state house. Hell, Montgomery might even be a springboard to Washington. I knew—"

"We're not in Montgomery yet. If this thing gets out—"

Forbe interrupted with a wave of the hand. "I'm getting to that. I knew that sex and politics didn't mix. When the heat's turned on, sex always breaks the surface. Some reporter sees it and jerks off." He paused, then chopped his hand as he spoke. "The news media is a fucking sex addict."

Dick allowed Forbe to calm down. "So you and Barbara broke up."

"We were looking for a way out. When she left, we simply agreed to end it."

"Jimbo, religion is an important factor in this campaign. What if the religious—"

Forbe again waved his hand. "My religion is public. My affair was private."

"Until it rises to the surface."

"I'll deny it—keep the lid on it." Forbe rose to his feet,

walked to the window and looked out onto the dumpster of Radio Shack.

"Does Betty know?" Dick asked without rising.

"Hell, yes, she knows! I never told her, but she knows. No man can keep that a secret from a woman who loves him."

Dick rose and motioned toward the door. As Forbe started toward the exit, Dick called his name softly, "Jimbo."

Forbe stopped.

Dick moved alongside and placed his arm around Forbe's shoulder. "Be sure you don't do anything to light that fire again or you'll blow the lid right off."

FORBE WALKED AROUND and greeted each person in the room before motioning for all to be seated. Forbe and Brother Johnny Carroll, along with three other men and two women, sat down around two folding banquet tables joined side by side to make a large square.

Dick remained standing and called the meeting to order. He thanked each person who had agreed to serve on the strategy think tank. "Y'all know why we're here. We've got to be prepared for the debate. That bleeding liberal is gonna come at Jimbo with everything he's got. That's why we're here, our missionary to the senior citizens, and the rest of you."

Forbe liked Dick, who preferred to be called Richard. Forbe was amused when Little's name appeared in some alphabetical listings as "Little, Dick." Dick, always calm, was a superb organizer but didn't have a sense of humor. "What we got, Dick?"

"We've got plenty but we've got to get it together. Chuck Lyell has an intellectual think tank researching for him and writing his speeches. Unitarians, the ACLU, and some liberal professors from the religion departments at Auburn and Alabama. Even some Yankees from Boston."

"It's 'damnyankees,' Dick—all one word." Forbe rolled back and laughed as if he had invented the joke.

Little took a deep breath and expelled it through his pursed lips. "Jimbo, there's not much time."

Forbe's chair squeaked as he tilted forward and rested his elbows on the table. "What we got to match them?"

"We've got the Southern Baptists, the Freewill Baptists, the Missionary Baptists, the Independent Baptists, the Primitive Baptists, the Methodists, some Presbyterians, and some Lutherans. We've got the Church of God, the Assembly of God, the Holiness, the Church of the Rapture, and a few big fish in the legislature.."

"That's twelve holy armies and some generals. What more do we need . . .ah . . .ah . . .ah . . ." Forbe turned his head and sneezed. "Dam . . . darn, that felt good."

A chorus of voices chanted, "God bless you."

Dick continued. "We've got a couple of speech writers from the Concerned Cooperating Christians but precious little time to lay out our position on school prayer."

"I thought I did pretty good in that opening rally." Forbe turned to Brother Johnny. "What's the missionary position, Reverend Carroll?"

Johnny's eyes dilated. His mouth flew open. The red started at his neck and rose up both sides of his face to the tips of his ears. "Well, it's . . . a . . . well . . . it's the man on t-t-top . . ."

Forbe roared, as the men and women around the table coughed. Dick Little turned away from the table.

Forbe re-gathered his composure. "This is not a marriage enrichment seminar, Reverend Carroll. What's the missionary position on school prayer? You are a missionary, aren't you?"

"But . . . I thought you were talking about—"

"I know what you thought. You're probably an expert on it. Now give us some good stuff for the campaign. How about some holy wisdom from that book you've memorized."

"'Blessed is the nation whose God is the Lord', Psalm 33:12," said Brother Johnny—his color returning to normal. "The United States of America was founded under Christian beliefs. In God we trust. We had better stand up for God in our schools or it will lead our country on a downward spiral."

"Thank you, Brother Johnny," said Dick. "That's all very eloquent, but we can't limit ourselves to quoting the Bible. We've got to have a broader basis for our position."

When the four-hour strategy meeting ended, James Forbe stood and placed his arm around Brother Johnny's shoulder. "Thank you, my dear Brother Johnny, for agreeing to raise up the armies of God to join us in the battle and save the great state of Alabama. You want to lead us in a word of prayer? We might be the only ones praying for the salvation of our state."

8

"LET US PRAY as Jesus prayed," Reverend Gaylor instructed the Unitarian flock of Orchard Hill as wasps circled overhead under the arching, wainscotted ceiling of the century-old church.

"Our Father, who art in heaven, hallowed be thy name . . ."

Emma listened to the words she had known from memory since she was a toddler. Always the same words. *I wonder what would happen if we changed something? Would it still be a prayer? Susie's church makes up new ones. Do they work?*

The prayer ended and Emma watched as Reverend Gaylor rose and surveyed the few dozen worshipers sprinkled about the capacious building. The lower windows were raised and sunlight filtered through the stained glass above. Emma looked up and watched the wasps, tiny black angels flitting about the holy space.

Janet Gaylor dropped her eyes to the lectern and began to read.

Pancosmos spoke with a voice of thunder
To the minute, slithering amphibian prostrated before her:
"Why trouble my tranquility with your supplication?
Have I not distributed my wisdom throughout creation
In morsels that even you can devour?
Scan the biosphere!
Scrutinize the stratosphere!
Pancosmos is here to illumine and nurture you
That you might transmute into me.

"Those inspired articulations of an eminent Indian sage form the text . . ."

I wish she wouldn't use so many big words. I can't stay awake when she talks like that.

" . . . my commentary this morning. There is a growing dichotomy . . ."

Oh, no! Here she goes.

" . . . an effort on the part of religious conservatives in our country to make the Christian religion the measure of all things . . ."

I wish I weren't too old for children's church. There are some good things about not growing up.

"The centuries-old battle against the scientific discoveries of Charles Darwin . . ."

Susie claims her pastor preached that Charles Darwin tried to destroy the Bible, saying that we came from monkeys and not from Adam and Eve.

"The inspired creativity of countless scientific and literary geniuses of all times and races is relegated to a secondary and suspicious role because the only inspired writing God supposedly had anything to do with was the Bible. No one can utter an authentic word of wisdom . . ."

Emma tried to follow what the reverend was saying but the words were too big or the sentences too long. She wondered what was going on in the Baptist church she could see through the open window. The churches were so close she often recognized the songs that Susie's church was singing.

"There is a growing polarization in our society between those who wear their religion like a crown for all to see and admire, and those who prefer to wear it like an undergarment—adequate to cover their nakedness but not proper for public display."

Emma perked up. *This is getting good,* she thought.

"The former would adorn the school rooms with the Ten Commandments, In God We Trust, and other symbols of their religion. The latter would rather live simple lives of honesty, integrity, and compassion in places . . ."

Not so good, she moaned.

"Our conference has issued a statement endorsing the liberal issues that Mr. Charles Lyell supports. Nonetheless, every member should vote the dictates of his or her own conscience for the person best qualified to lead our state." Gaylor raised her hands above the congregation and chanted, "Go in peace."

And so they did—to the Wedgwood Family Restaurant on the bypass—for a piece of fried chicken. Emma spotted her favorite piece as she stepped into the serving line. In addition to fried chicken, there was potato salad, biscuits, catfish, hush puppies, cole slaw, collards, and iced tea. If she had any appetite left, there was chocolate pie, chocolate cake, coconut cream pie, apple pie, and banana pudding. As she nibbled on a crispy-fried drumstick at her father's restaurant, she scanned the parking lot to watch for Susie. There was very little banana pudding left and that was Susie's favorite. Would she make it in time?

9

Susie thought of the wasps that probably circled at that moment over Emma's head. She struggled to stay awake.

"Let us pray," intoned the Reverend Billy Doster, pastor of Orchard Hill Baptist Church. "Oh, Holy God, Creator of Heaven and Earth, Sustainer of Life, Author of Salvation, Merciful Forgiver of Sins . . ."

Don't God already know who he is and what he does? Susie thought drowsily.

Reverend Doster's voice faded in. " . . . we humbly stand in your presence this morning, trusting in your sublime wisdom to do what is right in this forthcoming election . . ."

Don't God always do what's right?

"You know, oh holy God, that the forces of evil are leading this great nation that you founded down the broad, slippery road to destruction. That fallen angel, Satan, will not rest until America becomes a new Babylon . . ."

That's the name of a rock group.

"Oh holy God, we beseech thee to let the voters of our great state see the handwriting on the wall, 'Mene, Mene, tekel, upharsin' . . ."

Minnie, Minnie, tickled who?

" . . . balances and found wanting. Oh holy God, Father of our Lord Jesus Christ, we will not tell our people who to vote for, for it is not our business to become embroiled in the politics of this world, but we know thou wouldst be happier with thy servants leading our state . . ."

God should be happier with his servants leading everywhere.
Susie gingerly opened the chewing gum Mr. Tom Brandon had
given her in Sunday School. Mr. Brandon had been giving
chewing gum to every kid in Sunday School for as long as she
could remember. He told them it made them leave church with
a good taste in their mouth. She was going to need it today.

" . . .you will put it into the hearts and minds of the voters of
this great state to elect the man who will restore prayer, praise,
and purity to the schools of Alabama. In the name of Jesus of
Nazareth we pray, and not our will but thy will be done, Amen."

"Amen!" echoed the congregation.

"And now the deacons will come forward and take the
morning offering," announced Reverend Doster.

Susie did not have anything to drop in the plate. She always
gave her quarter in Sunday School in the envelope on which she
marked that she had read her Bible every day, studied the Sunday
School lesson, and was staying for preaching. Maybe when she
grew up she could drop a dollar in the offering plate, like the
grown-ups did.

She continued to think about what the preacher had prayed.
It had been a very long prayer. It sounded like a sermon. *Maybe
the real sermon will be short,* she thought.

She was wrong.

"The text for the message God has laid on my heart this
morning is taken from Second Chronicles, the seventh chapter
and fourteenth verse. Open your Bibles and follow the Word as
I read."

Susie brushed her fingers across her tongue and flipped the
pages of her Bible. She found the passage quickly. They had a
sword drill at Church Training every Sunday. She often won
stars for finding Bible verses fast.

"'If my peeeople . . .,'" the preacher read in a tone and

cadence that Susie called his preaching voice. He sounded like the narrator on "Unsolved Mysteries."

"'. . . which are caaaalled by my name, shall huuuumble themselves, and pray.' My dear brothers and sisters, God has given me a sermon on prayer. The Almighty has told me to preach on the subject, 'Vote for Prayer.'

I vote for short prayers, thought Susie.

"Now, I do not intend to tell you who to vote for when you go to the polls on Tuesday. Baptists do not endorse political candidates, but we do endorse righteousness according to God's holy word. The nation that prays together, stays together. Praise the Lord! If we are called by His name, we . . ."

Susie squirmed in her seat as the pastor preached on. Her eyelids were so heavy. A beeper went off. The pastor paused until the beeping stopped, then continued. If the preacher didn't quit soon, the Methodists and the Unitarians would beat them to the Wedgwood Restaurant, the only place to eat out on Sunday unless you drove over to Dadeville or all the way to Alex City. The Unitarians always beat them but with the Methodists it was a close race. *I hope they don't run out of banana pudding.* She finally dozed and later awakened to a watch beeping the hour. She looked around. Her mother bumped her with an elbow. Susie started pushing buttons on her own watch. Fortunately, it was a quiet beep. The preacher was still talking.

" . . . is simply to bring you impartial information so any intelligent, dedicated child of God can know which levers to pull in the booth. Now, let us stand and sing our invitation hymn, as announced in the Order of Service of our bulletin."

As the congregation rose to sing, "Just as I Am," the preacher pled, with outstretched arms, for all the lost souls to come forward and accept Jesus and for all the unchurched Baptists to choose Orchard Hill as their church home.

"And now some important announcements: The doors of our sanctuary will be open beginning at seven o'clock tomorrow evening to pray for the future of our state. We will join churches all over Alabama to lift our hearts . . ."

The preacher just prayed about the election. Ain't God writing it down? Susie looked at her watch, "Twelve fifteen," she said out loud.

"Shhhh!" whispered her momma.

I'll miss eating with Emma. Susie liked to eat.

"Be sure and read the most recent mail-out from the Concerned Cooperating Christians. This non-partisan publication will tell you who are God's candidates in this election. Just read how our elected representatives vote on those things that matter eternally. Now, may the grace of God, the communion and fellowship of the Holy Spirit and the love of Jesus abide with each and everyone now and forevermore. Nevertheless, not our will but thy will be done, in the naaaame of Jeeeesussss, Amen. And the people said . . ."

"Amen!" The congregation responded.

"Why does the preacher always say that thing at the end of his prayers?'" Susie asked as she rode with her family out to the bypass for dinner.

"Amen?" asked her momma.

"No. Why does he say, 'Not thy will but our will be done.' He says the same thing every time he prays."

"You mean, 'not *our* will but *thy* will be done,'" replied her father, Zack, emphasizing the words Susie had inverted. "That's so he'll always have a way out. You're old enough now to figure out that not everything the preacher prays for comes true. When it don't, he can always say that we prayed for the wrong thing or that God decided to say 'no.' The preacher always has a way out."

Susie liked her father's practical way of looking at things.

"And if what he prays for does happen?"

"He'll point it out to you in his next sermon."

"Now, that's enough," said her momma. "Prayer is prayer and it's not for us to try to explain it away. God really does answer prayer."

"Then why don't the preacher pray for things we really need, like stuff at school?"

"You just wait, honey," said her mother. "When Mr. Forbe is elected governor, things are going to change. We may even see some miracles when he gets prayer back in the schools."

"I wouldn't be so sure," said her father. "The only miracle he's concerned about will begin and end on election day."

As she led her parents into the serving line, Susie waved at Emma then looked toward the dessert trays. Her eyes moistened. There was no banana pudding left.

10

"Susie, can you come over tonight and us watch the governor's debate together?" Emma asked as she and Susie stepped off the school bus. "We both got it as homework."

"Sure—if Momma says it's okay. I'll be over right after supper."

"Look at all those people!" Emma, wearing faded jeans and T-shirt, leaned back in a beanbag and munched on snickerdoodles Susie had brought over after supper. "I haven't seen that many people in all my life."

The image on the screen shifted to the road and parking area.

"Look at them church buses!" Susie, dressed in frayed, knee-length shorts and blouse, leaned forward in the other beanbag, a stack of cookies in one hand and an orange soda in the other. "Hey, there's one from the 'Shadow of the Valley Rest Home' in Dadeville." She pointed with the soda can.

"Valley of the Shadow," corrected Emma. "Your eyes must be crossed."

Church buses leaned over to disgorge the faithful on the road. A flood of pickup trucks and SUVs with a sprinkling of cars and station wagons inundated the small parking lot of the Co-Op Community Center and flowed into the Methodist Church grounds nearby.

"There's people everywhere," said Susie.

"Looks like more cars and trucks than people," said Emma.

Above honking horns, the roar of engines, and the din of excited people, came the voice of the announcer. "Small town and rural citizens from across Montgomery County are pouring into the meeting place. Designed to accommodate Saturday night dancing, the Co-op Center this evening will host the Baptists, Methodists, and Pentecostals, and a few Unitarian Universalists, not to square dance, but to jump and shout for their leader. The conservatives call their candidate a crusader against the evil forces that have denied their little children the right to pray at school. The liberals call their leader the champion of secular schools." The scene switched to the interior of the auditorium.

"The governor's debate must be important," said Susie. "Look at that stage with two pulpits."

"Daddy says it's important because of the prayer thing," said Emma.

"Don't sound like a big deal to me," said Susie. "We pray at church and sometimes when me and you play."

"But we don't do it at school," said Emma.

"Might help," said Susie. "Our school is falling apart and . . ."

"Shhh," whispered Emma. "It's starting."

The noise ceased as a middle-aged man, wearing a dark, business suit and red tie, walked to the center of the stage. Polite applause arose from the gathered assembly.

"He looks like Tom Brokaw," said Emma.

"No he don't," replied Susie. "Looks like Peter Jennings."

"Good evening, ladies and gentlemen. I'm Ted Majors, of the Alabama Public Televison Network, chosen by the two major candidates in this election to host this debate. Without further ado, I present to you Mr. James B. Forbe, better known as Jimbo, and Mr. Charles D. Lyell. Some call him Chuck."

"That's a funny nickname," said Emma.

"Which one?" asked Susie.

"Jimbo. I wonder where he got it?"

Amidst roof-rattling applause, two men strolled from the wings onto the stage and stopped behind the lecterns. Majors walked to a small desk and sat facing the adversaries—his back to the audience. Both candidates raised their hands to the crowd and the applause ceased.

Majors addressed the candidates. "The rules for this encounter are simple. Each of you will be allowed a brief opening statement. I will then ask questions either drawn from your remarks, or selected from submissions sent in by churches, school children, and teachers from across . . ."

"Our school sent in some questions." Susie pulled a list out of her notebook. "Let's see if he uses one."

"You have one minute to respond, after which your opponent will give a rebuttal. At the end of the debate, each of you may give a closing statement. You drew straws and Mr. Forbe will begin." Majors nodded toward the candidate who now held a white handkerchief in one hand.

"Mr. Forbe sure is sweating," said Emma. "It must be hot in there with all the people and lights."

"He's scared," said Susie. "He's wondering who's gonna win."

"He won't know until the election. Now quit talking."

James Forbe wiped the sweat from his brow and cleared his throat. He took a deep breath and looked at the audience. "My fellow Alabamians, we face a major crisis in this great nation. Our children have lost respect for parents, guvnahs, and God. Some are turning on fellow students with knives and guns. This all began in 1962 when the Supreme Court of our great nation outlawed prayer and kicked God out of the public schools."

Emma asked, "You going to take notes?"

"We'd better. Hey, let's tape it!" said Susie. "You got a blank tape? Hurry!"

"Why didn't you think of that sooner? Yeah, yeah, I got one . . . Here it is . . . Okay. It's recording. We'd still better take notes," Emma said.

"Okay, I'll take notes but now you shut your trap. We're missing stuff," said Susie.

" . . .crime has increased and family values have decreased among those destined to be the leaders of tomorrow. I, Jimbo Forbe, propose to change that in Alabama. If elected in November, I'll put God back in our schools."

"Can he do that?" asked Susie.

"Do what?"

"Put God in school. Why would God want to go to school?"

"I don't know. They say he goes everywhere."

The TV voice continued. "Prayer will solve our problems when it echoes again down the halls of our hallowed institutions of learning. Blessed is the nation whose God is the Lord." The audience applauded. Forbe nodded toward the moderator and stepped back from his podium.

A smiling face appeared on Emma's TV as the camera panned the crowd and stopped.

"There's Brother Johnny!" said Susie.

"How do you know?" asked Emma.

"He's on TV a lot."

"Take it, Chuck," said Forbe as he wiped his forehead.

"Mr. Lyell's skinny!" said Susie.

"Not skinny; he's tall and slim like me. Mr. Forbe's chubby like you."

"You toothpick, I'm not chubby. Momma says it's baby fat."

"Shhh. Mr. Lyell's fixing to talk. He's a Unitarian like me," said Emma.

Chuck Lyell began. "I was in the Alberta Jones Middle School yesterday in Orchard Hill and . . ."

"Hey! That's our school!" Susie jumped to her feet. "I didn't see him."

"God was still there," said Lyell. "I saw him in the smile of little Angie, the paraplegic, who, in spite of her handicap, pursues her education with a passion. I saw him . . ."

"I know Angie," said Susie.

"I saw him in the soccer coach . . ."

"That's Coach Tidwell he's talking about," Susie spoke again.

"Susie, if you don't stop mumbling, we won't hear a thing he's saying."

" . . . who without adequate equipment for practice, is building a competitive team. There are a lot of things missing from Alabama schools, but God is not one of them. I—"

"Wait a minute!" Forbe interrupted as he wiped his brow. "That's liberal hogwash. What about crime, sex, illegitimate children, and abortion? You seen God there, Mr. Charles D. Lyell?"

"Wow! Mr. Forbe looks mad," said Emma.

"Yes, I've seen God there. I've seen God hugging poor, affection-deprived adolescents, whose parents have to work three and four jobs to make ends meet and are seldom at home."

Emma watched as Forbe raised a hand and opened his mouth but Majors quickly stood and motioned him down. "You may continue, Mr. Lyell."

"That's all I'll say for the moment," replied Lyell. "Let my opponent speak what's on his mind."

Forbe waved his hands back and forth, palms down. "That's all right. That's all right. I'll wait my turn." He wiped his brow.

"It is your turn, Mr. Forbe, to respond to the next question,"

Majors said. "You say there is a correlation between the presence of school violence and the absence of official school prayer. Do you think prayer in the schools will change that, and if so, how?"

Susie observed, "It's a good thing that modifier is there."

"He's not a modifier," laughed Emma. "He's a moderator. He's there to keep them from fighting."

"Whatever," said Susie.

"It's a matter of public record," Forbe began, "that something is frightfully wrong with our education system. Grammar school children are reading dirt, junior high girls are having babies, high school students are hooked on drugs . . ."

Susie said, "Some girl in junior high dropped out of school last year to have a baby. Did you know that?"

"Yes!" exclaimed Emma. "She sat right behind me at the football game. I thought she swallowed a watermelon seed. That's what everybody said."

Forbe's voice faded in. " . . . that was not true thirty-five years ago. Now, I am not so naive to think that a simple school prayer will fix all our problems. But it'll go a long way." A timid applause began, then grew. Forbe raised his hands. "School prayer can make kids think about spiritual things. Your mike, Chuck."

"Do you ever think about spiritual things, Susie?" asked Emma.

"I'm scared of the Holy Ghost. Is that what you mean?"

"No. I mean about prayer and God and sick people. I wonder if God can cure them."

"I don't know about sick people, but I prayed in Sunday School one time to get computers at school, but it didn't do no good," said Susie. "Not one computer."

The voice from the TV again seized their attention. "I do believe prayer changes things and is therefore very important.

Second, let me remind the audience that the constitution does not keep children from praying at school . . ."

"Ain't they gonna answer our questions?" asked Susie.

"Which one?"

"The one about getting our school toilets fixed."

Lyell's voice continued. " . . . and they may pray at the beginning of the day, over their lunch, before tests—and I'd wager there is a lot of that going on . . ."

A ripple of laughter sloshed over the audience.

" . . .violence and intolerance go much deeper than the absence of an officially sanctioned school prayer. Let me—"

"Chuck, you're missing the point," Forbe interrupted. "Since prayer was removed from the schools, crime has increased— immorality has increased—drug abuse has increased—"

"Let me finish!" said Lyell. "I'll respond to your rationale, Mr. Forbe." Lyell paused. "The cock's crowing does not make the sun rise."

Laughter rolled across the auditorium.

"We don't need a state prayer at school," Lyell continued. "We need quality education. Robert Ingersoll wrote, 'The hands that help are better far than lips that pray.' Thank you."

"You quoted an atheist, Mr. Lyell. That's part of the problem. Of course, he don't believe in prayer. Who would he pray to?" Forbe paused. "Maybe you're lacking faith in God."

Amens rose from the audience.

"What's an atheist, Emma?" asked Susie.

"That's someone who doesn't have faith in God. Mr. Lyell's already said he saw God at our school, so he must have faith," said Emma.

"Just what exactly is faith?" asked Susie.

Emma looked at Susie. "That's a hard one. But I think faith is believing something you know's not true."

"I'm thirsty," said Susie.

Emma said, "Me, too. Mother made hot chocolate. I'll go to warm it up. Holler if they ever say anything important."

"Don't worry." Susie leaned back on the beanbag and closed her eyes.

11

"Susie, wake up," said Emma.

Susie shook her head. "I was listening and resting my eyes."

"You were snoring. You didn't take a single note while I was out."

"I gotta good idea." Susie dropped her voice to a whisper. "Let's take the video to school and get the teacher to show it. That way we won't have to make a report."

"We'll try it. But we still better listen in case the teacher has a different idea."

Lyell's voice faded in. ". . .not here to examine each other's religious beliefs, Jimbo. Whether I'm an atheist, an agnostic, or a man of faith has nothing to do with this campaign . . ."

"The hell it . . . oops, ah . . . excuse me . . . doesn't! Of course . . ."

"He cussed, Susie, right there on television. Isn't Mr. Forbe a Baptist?"

"Yeah. Daddy says lots of Baptists cuss when the preacher's not around. Mr. Forbe forgot where he was."

"I heard our minister cuss in church one Sunday. She tripped going up to the pulpit and said, 'Crap!' Everybody heard her."

"Wow!" said Susie. "Maybe Baptists cuss in private and Unitarians in pubic—public." Susie corrected herself and looked at Emma. "I beat you to it."

". . . a true believer would jump at the chance to get our children on their knees again. A true believer—"

Lyell interrupted. "We're not talking about believers and non—"

He stopped in mid-sentence as the moderator stood.

Emma yawned and stretched, "This hot chocolate's making me sleepy. How much longer are they going to fuss?"

"I don't know," replied Susie yawning, too. "Look's like it's going on 'til midnight."

"Ab-so-lute-ly not," said Lyell, accenting every syllable. "The religious right has an interest in making people think that the Supreme Court ended what was a common practice in our schools. But laws requiring school prayer were not nearly as widespread as people presume. Prior to 1900 . . ."

Susie yawned again, "My granddaddy wasn't even born in 1900."

" . . . As for whether the Supreme Court has thrown God out, I do not believe God is bound by the decisions of the United States Supreme Court." Laughter again rippled across the crowd.

"The next question is first to Mr. Forbe," said Majors. "You have said during this campaign that our nation was built on Christian foundations. Does that mean that our founding fathers intended that religion be an integral part of our government and our schools?"

Forbe smiled. "The Declaration of Independence says, 'We hold these truths to be self-evident, that . . .'"

"We had to learn that by heart," said Susie.

"Looks like Mr. Forbe did, too," said Emma.

"Those were our founding fathers talking about God Almighty in one of the basic . . ."

"My Uncle Richard says 'God Almighty' a lot," remarked Susie.

Emma spilled some chocolate and ran to the kitchen for a rag.

"Public schools prayed for nearly two hundred years . . ."

"When did they study?" quipped Emma as she wiped up chocolate.

"That must be the longest prayer ever," said Susie.

" . . . Washington is screaming from his tomb, 'let my people pray!'" Forbe shouted into the microphone. Much of the audience stood and whistled as a storm of applause blew through the room.

Majors waited for the noise to subside and the people to take their seats. "Mr. Lyell, you have one minute to respond."

Lyell took a deep breath. "Our founding fathers came to this country to escape the oppressive hand of religion in government and in public life."

"I had forgotten that's why the penguins came," remarked Susie.

"Not, 'penguins,' Pilgrims," said Emma. "And the Puritans, too."

"Whatever," said Susie.

Lyell's voice continued. ". . . from lands where there was not only a state church, but where the practice of religion was enforced by the strong arm of the law. Attendance at chapel and church was mandatory . . ."

"My chocolate's cold," said Susie.

"Why didn't you drink it while it was hot?"

"It burned my tongue."

"You're impossible, Susie Holland! Now hush up and listen!"

" . . . was founded by men and women who came here to get away from state-sponsored religion. The men who framed our Constitution and Bill of Rights did not intend to reestablish on American soil what they had found intolerable in Europe."

"That's when the penguins . . . uh . . . Pilgrims came," said Susie.

" . . . but this is Alabama. So here are some Alabama ques-

tions for my distinguished Alabama colleague. Would you be
pushing prayer into the schools if our citizens were mostly
Muslim? Would you be pushing prayer if the prayers came from
the Koran?" Lyell stepped back from his podium. Applause
rippled across the room like waves on the shore of a small pond.

"Our minister, Reverend Gaylor, read from the Koran not
long ago," said Emma. "She said it was the same as the Bible for
millions of people."

"Our preacher wouldn't do that," said Susie. "God only
speaks in the Bible."

"Why would God do that?" asked Emma, surprised.

"I don't know," said Susie. "Something to do with perspiration."

Emma looked at Susie with a puzzled expression but did not
respond. She knew it wasn't perspiration but couldn't think of
what it was.

Forbe wiped his brow, motioned for silence, and looked at
Lyell. "I'll answer that. I know there's a handful of Mohammed's
followers in Alabama, and if we can get our children interested in
God again, we'll convert 'em to Jesus. Hallelujah!" Fully two-
thirds of the audience came to its feet.

"One final question," said Majors as the noise abated, "Mr.
Lyell, why do you not think a school prayer amendment would
work? Why would it not be beneficial for our schools and
nation?"

Lyell swept the audience with his eyes from left to right then
back. "In the years before state-supported religion and prayer
were made illegal, religious minorities suffered. Even where non-
Christian children were allowed to remain silent, they were
ostracized by fellow . . ."

"What does 'oysterized' mean?" asked Susie.

"Maybe something like clamming up," answered Emma.

"Oh," said Susie.

Lyell's voice continued, " . . . in many cases they were accused of being atheists or devil worshipers. State-sanctioned religion is divisive. Look at Northern Ireland. Look at Israel. More people have been killed throughout history in the name of religion than for any other cause. In today's America, more division is something we do not need." Lyell nodded to Majors.

Majors motioned to Forbe.

Forbe's voice rose with each word. "We've got to put prayer back where it can mold the tender minds of our children—teach them what to believe. Not only would it be beneficial for Alabama, but in Washington it might even catch on. God knows they need it."

After a full minute of clamorous applause, Majors stood and motioned for the audience to quiet down. "Each of you has a closing statement," he instructed. "Mr. Lyell, you will speak first."

Emma let out a long breath. "Ah, they're about through."

"They wouldn't be about through in my church," said Susie. "When the preacher says he's finished, he talks for another hour."

Lyell looked straight at the audience. "My fellow Alabamians, this election is not about religion or God. We can't ban either nor should we want to. It's about politicians. Some want to blame everything bad on the absence of school prayer. But, let me remind you, a lot of good things have happened since state-sponsored prayer was abolished from the schools."

"Good things?" said Susie. "We don't have computers."

"Shhh! Let's see what it is."

"There has been a leap in civil liberties, environmental awareness, women's rights, science, technology, and medicine. Did those good things happen to America because we banned prayer in school? Of course not. Neither should we blame the court for America's ill—"

"Hold on there a minute, Lyell! Are you saying we're better off now than before 1962? That's preposterous! One day—"

Majors interrupted. "Let Mr. Lyell finish, please, Mr. Forbe."

Lyell motioned with his hand toward Forbe. "My opponent is a frequent quoter of the Christian scriptures. I am not, but I've read them. I submit that Jesus was against school prayer. In the Gospel of Matthew he said: 'But thou, when thou prayest, enter into thy closet, and when thou hast shut thy door, pray to thy Father which is in secret . . .' I rest my case. I ask for your vote in the upcoming election. Thank you. Your turn, Jimbo."

Scattered applause rose from the audience.

Forbe paused, looked upward and raised his hands toward the ceiling, palms up.

"He's going to pray!" said Emma. "That's how they do it in your church, isn't it?"

"When a revival preacher comes," Susie replied.

"I pray God will forgive my adversary for that bit of blasphemy," intoned Forbe. Redirecting his gaze toward Lyell, and slightly expanding his chest, he added, "If Mr. Lyell read the Bible as much as I do, he would not be as prone to misquote it."

"At least it was a short prayer," said Susie.

"So you like short prayers. Me, too," quipped William Wedgwood as he slipped into the room. "I can't believe you young ladies have watched the whole thing."

"We had to, Daddy," said Emma. "It's homework. Look! I think they're about through."

"I'm tired of listening," said Susie. "Mr. Lyell's hard to understand and Mr. Forbe sounds so raspy."

"Like Johnny Cash with bronchitis," said Wedgwood.

"Now, my closing remarks," said Forbe. "Students have a

right to pray out loud, like Jesus did with his apostles . . ."

"I don't want to pray out loud at school," said Emma. "Somebody might hear."

Wedgwood chuckled. "Somebody's supposed to hear, Sweetheart. Hopefully, God—if he's listening."

"When I'm elected, I'll restore freedom of religion to the children of Alabama. A vote for Jimbo Forbe will be a vote for the Father, the Son, and the Holy Ghost. And the people said . . ."

The audience roared, "Amen." Applause and stomping feet shook the building.

As the television switched from the Co-op Community Center to the network studios, Susie said, "I don't care if we pray at school. Maybe we could get some good things going."

"I don't want to," responded Emma, "but what can we do about it?"

Wedgwood smiled. "You can vote for Mr. Lyell."

"You know we can't vote, Mr. Wedgwood," said Susie.

"Why don't you write both men a letter?"

"That's a good idea, Daddy!" said Emma. "Will it make a difference?"

"Probably not," replied Wedgwood, "but at least you can tell them what you think."

"What can we say?" asked Susie.

"You two are never at a loss for words. I'll get the addresses for you."

"Thank you, sir," said Susie. "You're right. Emma and I can do it."

Crumpled paper littered the floor before Emma and Susie handed the letter to Wedgwood. He smiled as he silently read the finished product.

Dear Mr. Forbe and Mr. Lyell:

We like the way ya'll tell us the things that are in the Bible. We remember a lot of good stories from the Bible we learned in Sunday School—like when Eve was bit by a rattle snake and threw an apple at Adam who ate it then got naked, and God saw it and hung a fig leaf on him, and Moses heard about it and broke the ten amendments.

But we don't know if we should pray at school since we already pray at church. But we need a soccer field, more computers, more teachers, and less homework in our school. Whichever one of you becomes governor, will you get all that for us?

Sincerely,

Susie and Emma

P.S. Don't forget the homework. That's real important.

Wedgewood chuckled to himself as he dropped the letter in the mail box. *Who knows?* he thought. *Maybe one of them will listen.*

12

"Congratulations, Governor-elect Forbe! Boxes have been tabulated from most of the voting precincts and you have 78 percent of the votes. You're as good as in," shouted Dick Little above the roar of the crowd in the Forbe campaign headquarters. Forbe had been in prayer with Brother Johnny Carroll and had not seen the announcement on Channel Twelve. Brother Johnny had insisted on spending election night on his knees and Forbe felt he owed his religious consultant the respect of kneeling with him at least once.

"Get me the phone," said Forbe. "I want to call Chuck Lyell to console him."

"Why don't you wait a few minutes, Jimbo?" said Dick. "Lyell should be calling you to concede victory."

At that moment, an aide handed Forbe the phone. "It's Lyell, Jimbo."

"Hello, Chuck. What's on your mind?" Forbe asked, struggling to contain himself.

"Just calling to congratulate you, James. I'm conceding defeat. With only a few boxes still out in the rural areas, I can't possibly wipe out your lead."

Victory! he thought. "Thank you, Chuck. That is magnanimous of you. God has chosen me to lead the people of Alabama. This is His doing. God answers prayer."

"I would rather think it's the doing—or the undoing—of the people of Alabama. Good night."

Forbe slammed the phone to the table forgetting it was a

cordless and the cradle was elsewhere. He reached for his hand-kerchief. "Damn poor loser. They campaigned against me and now they want to rub it in. They are sure as hell going to pay for it. God, I need a drink." After several swipes of his handkerchief across his forehead and as many swallows of bubbly grape juice, Forbe pointed his glass at Dick and asked, "You know why you always take *two* Baptists fishing with you?"

"Naw, Jimbo. Why?"

"Because if you just take one, he'll drink all your beer. Ha, ha, ha, ha."

13

"Jimbo, just two months since your swearing in and we
have the text of the prayer amendment to be introduced this
week in the senate," said Dick Little, Administrative Assistant to
Governor James Forbe. What do you think about this wording?
'This sovereign state recognizes the right of the schools within its
boundaries to celebrate non-sectarian, non-proselytizing, stu-
dent-initiated voluntary prayer—'"

"What a sissy-ass prayer that'll be! Ya'll afraid to say what we
want? I promised prayer and the schools are going to get a
prayer—an unadulterated all-American Christian prayer. Delete
that 'non-sectarian, non-proselytizing' bullshit and give me a
Baptist prayer with balls!"

Dick smiled, looked at Forbe, moved his head from side to
side, then asked, "What about the other education bills, Governor?"

"What do you mean?" asked Forbe.

"With our poor literacy rate—"

"Listen, Dick," Forbe interrupted with a wave of his handkerchief. "In Alabama, literacy ain't everything. Let the liberals
worry about education. Get on with that prayer amendment.
That's what got us elected. And don't forget that other business.
You know what I mean. Get on with it."

"Whatever you say, Governor." Dick turned to leave.

"Hey, one more thing. What you got perking for the Unitarians?"

"Guess they got what they had coming. Backed the wrong
candidate and lost."

"That's not enough. They practically endorsed Lyell. We can't let that go unpunished. Besides, being a religious organization, they can't campaign for political candidates."

"The Baptists did."

"Not officially. Can't we take away their tax-exempt status or something like that?"

"That would be a little complicated. They'd bring in the ACLU and tie us up in court. We don't need a lawsuit this early in your first term."

"I'll be damned if I'll let them off easy. Get on it and get back with me . . . soon! Wait a minute!"

"Yes, Governor?"

"The prayer bill will probably have to offer exemptions for atheists and other non-religious nuts. Is that correct?"

"To keep it out of courts—definitely."

"Are the Unitarians Christians?" Forbe leaned back and stared at the ceiling.

"I don't think all of them are."

"Whatever they are, they aren't going to be happy with my prayer. I read in the *Advertiser* where one of them said they didn't want Baptist prayers rammed down their kids' throats. Fix the amendment so their kids will have to . . ." Forbe paused for effect, "will have to swallow my friggin' prayer."

"What do you mean?"

"Make it mandatory for all school kids except bonafide atheists, Jews, and Mohammedans." Forbe rocked forward in his chair and brought his fist down on the desk. "They can't mess with ole Jimbo Forbe and get away with it."

"I think they're called Muslims," said Dick.

"Take that politically correct bullshit to the other camp. It doesn't wash here."

"Anything else?"

"Naw, that's all. Now get out of here and go to work!"

Forbe leaned back in his chair and swiveled toward the window. *Finally, things are going my way. The new governor of Alabama. I like that.* He sneezed, let out a deep sigh, and closed his eyes.

"GOVERNOR, MRS. Forbe is on line two," came Judy's voice over the intercom.

"Yes. Thank you, Judy. Hello, Betty, dear. What's going on?"

"Jimmy. There's something I've been needing to tell you." She paused.

"Well, go on," said Forbe. "I'm busy. What is it?"

"I hate to mention it over the phone."

"Hold it till I get home this evening."

"No. Listen. Several weeks ago, I felt a lump in my breast— something suspicious. I had Doctor Carver check it out. The results are back from the biopsy—"

"A lump, biopsy? What's wrong?" Forbe sat up straight in his chair. "Speak up!"

"That's what I'm trying to do. I have a malignancy in my breast and—"

"Why haven't you mentioned it before? I can't believe you didn't tell me sooner."

"I didn't want to worry you . . . getting your cabinet up and running and all. Besides, I didn't know for sure it would be anything—"

"I'll be right home." Forbe reached for his handkerchief.

"No. Don't worry about it right now. Dr. Carver said it's very small—probably in its earliest stage—and can be removed and followed up with radiation and chemotherapy. I have a good chance for a total—"

"Remove your breast?" Forbe almost shouted into the phone.

"No, dear. Just the malignancy. It's quite small."

"Why not get a second opinion?"

"Come on, Jimmy! Just because Carver's black doesn't mean she doesn't know what she's talking about. She did a biopsy."

"I'm not worried about that. I still think you ought to get a second opinion."

"Jimmy! Sharika Carver graduated *summa cum laude* from Duke Medical School. She's one of the best OB-GYNs in Montgomery. I trust her completely."

"Are you sure?"

"Yes, I'm sure. I wouldn't have called you at this hour but I knew Dr. Carver was on that healthcare task force meeting at the capitol."

"Oh, yes. She'll be here this afternoon."

"Don't you worry about anything," said Betty. "Sharika Carver is a darned good doctor. I'll see you this evening."

"I'll be home early." Forbe pressed the disconnect button and stuffed his handkerchief back into his pocket. He sat for a long time with his elbows on the desk, face cupped in his sweating hands. Thoughts of Birmingham invaded his mind.

"Jimbo, are you really going to run for governor?" Barbara asked.

"I'm not only going to run. You're looking at the next governor of Alabama."

"I can't believe it. I'll be stretched out one night beside the most powerful man in the state."

"That's what I'm counting on—becoming a powerful man."

"Oh, Jimbo, you've got me so excited!"

"I wish I could say the same."

"Come on. You're just a little uptight."

"I think I'm over-relaxed right now."

"You just need little ole Barbara's han—"

"Don't, Barbara." Forbe turned away. "I can't tonight."

Both fell silent. Then Barbara whispered, "Is it Betty?"

Forbe sat up in bed. "Hell, I don't know. Shit, Barbara, you're quite a woman."

Barbara raised up and said, "I know it's Betty. I'm so sorry."

"You don't have to be sorry. God, it's not your fault. It's just that . . . well . . . I've been thinking. Yes, I've been thinking about Betty. Do you mind if we get dressed and talk about it?"

Barbara placed her hand on his thigh and inched it upward. She whispered in his ear, "I'd like to talk, but not about Betty. I'd like to talk about us."

As her smooth hand moved upward, Forbe found that he was not as relaxed as he had been a moment ago.

14

A SMILING DICK LITTLE burst into Forbe's office. "Less than a hundred days and we've got it!"

"Yeah. Good. No problem with the Democrats on that bill?" asked Forbe.

Forbe laughed to himself as Dick handed him the text of the bill. Dick was a kid with a new toy. He'd been hesitant at first to get the ball rolling but now he stood there fidgeting like an adolescent—his first legislative success.

"Had the first reading three weeks ago," Dick said. "The K-12 Education Committee reported it back to the House three days later. Passed there with a comfortable margin although the Senate changed it slightly."

"Changed it! We had a good bill. What changes?"

"Well, that phrase, 'bless the Baptists, Methodists, Pentecostals, and all other true Christians,' was a little too sectarian, I believe they said."

"I thought it was great. What was the final wording?"

"Here it is ready for your signature. Read it."

Forbe read the amendment. "A hell of a prayer. It will be mandatory?"

"We had a hard fight but we kept that in the bill. By the way, we changed the labels atheists, Jews, and Mohammedans to unbelievers, children of the Jewish faith, and Muslims."

Forbe frowned. "I didn't want it watered down."

"We didn't water it; we oiled it so it would slide through without scraping."

"How soon can we expect it to take effect?"

"As soon as it is ratified in a referendum thirty days from now. Shortly, all the school kids will be praying again."

"You foresee any problem with the referendum?"

"None whatsoever. Not with Alabama's religious makeup. The referendum is a formality. The new school term will be opened with prayer."

"Fantastic!" Forbe smiled a big smile. "I'll count that as my second victory. Now, there's my John Hancock," he said, signing the bill into law. "Ought to make all the religious nuts happy. The schools will tick like clockwork. Now, let's get down to the business of running this state like it ought to be run."

15

"BYE, MOMMA!" SUSIE, new Reeboks bouncing, ran to catch the bus to Alberta Jones Middle School, her long hair flying. The bus had already stopped before Emma, loaded with books, came tearing out of her door—Keds pumping. Emma was late for everything.

Thirty minutes later, the bus belched forty restless pre-adolescents onto the steps of the once-white stucco building. Susie stopped to look at the moldy stuff dripping from the roof like chocolate syrup on a white cake and said to Emma, "Ain't they ever going to paint our school?"

The cracked glass rattled as Susie hit the bar on the front door and both girls bounded into the crowded hallway on the way to their fifth-grade trailer out back.

Susie saw Mrs. Haley signing in at the office. Mrs. Haley never wore a dress—always pants. Although Susie had been in Mrs. Haley's fifth grade only a few weeks, she knew her routine. First she signed in at the office, as all teachers have to do. Then she stopped at the water fountain for a drink and as she straightened up pushed her gold-framed glasses back up her nose. Next, a trip to the bathroom. She arrived at the locked trailer door in about three minutes, opened it, turned on the lights and let everyone in. Then she put her lunch and jacket in the closet.

Susie liked Mrs. Haley but not the amount of homework she gave, especially in math and history. Susie took her seat in the center of the classroom and watched Emma go to the back of the class. Mrs. Haley seated everyone alphabetically.

Although Susie struggled with math and history, she breezed through the exploratory foreign language class—FLEX, it was called. It was her favorite because Mrs. Haley did not give tests or homework in that class, only exercises. It had been fun learning how to say "hello" and "goodbye" and "how are you?" in Latin. They were learning Spanish words now—*hola, adios, como estas*—and she was sure German, French, and Italian would also be fun. Everybody who did the exercises got a good grade.

Fifteen minutes after Susie arrived, the bell rang and Mrs. Haley clapped her hands and called above the noise, "Everybody quiet! Time for roll call. I see empty chairs. Let's see who's missing. Yes, Gary, what is it? Why are you standing?"

"Can I go to the bathroom?"

"Why didn't you go before the bell?"

"I didn't have to."

"Why can't you wait till I finish calling the roll?"

"I don't know if I can."

"Tell me, Gary, why is your bladder synchronized to this narrow window?"

Gary frowned and wrinkled his brow. He looked at the windows, looked back at his teacher, shrugged, then sat down. Mrs. Haley returned to the roll call.

"Candice?"

"Here."

"Ashley . . . Ashley?"

"She's eating breakfast."

"Drew."

"He's at breakfast."

"Looks like half—"

The door opened and the odor of bacon preceded the tardy students into the room. The roll call soon ended and Mrs. Haley walked back to the blackboard behind her desk and raised the map to uncover three Spanish questions written on the board.

Susie reached for her *Voces y Vistas* textbook. As she lifted it to the desk, half of it to fell to the floor.

"Susie," said Mrs. Haley. "Be careful with your textbook!"

"I try, Mrs. Haley. It came apart by itself."

Mrs. Haley addressed the class. "Everybody pass your homework to the front and prepare for today's exercise. The copier's broken again, so look at the questions on the board and fill in the exercises on a blank sheet of paper."

The copier's broke, thought Susie. *The windows are broke. Something is always broke. The classroom computer don't work. The Coke machine don't work.*

" . . . you asleep, Susie?" was all she heard as she returned from daydreaming. "Susie, you're not going to finish your exercise if you don't start writing."

Pulled back from her dream world, Susie rushed to finish the questions and laid her work on the teacher's ancient desk. "Mrs. Haley, why don't things work at our school?"

"What do you mean, Susie?"

"I mean, the copier don't work—"

"Doesn't work," said Mrs. Haley.

"Yes, ma'am. Half the computers doesn't work right—"

"Don't work," said Mrs. Haley.

"Which is it, Ma'am? Don't or doesn't."

"It's, ah, go ahead, Susie. What were you telling me?"

"Our textbooks are falling apart. We don't have enough computers. Now we got to go to school the year 'round—all year long. Are all schools this bad?"

"I hope it'll get better. Mr. Forbe promised changes in the schools."

"What kind of changes, Mrs. Haley?"

"I'm not sure, honey. The only thing he's mentioned so far is prayer."

"But we need money to fix things."

"I don't know. Now you run back to your seat and leave those things to the grownups. We'll have new books and equipment one of these days."

Susie was not so sure. This was her fifth year in school, and she had rarely seen a new textbook. *I wish we could do something about it*, she thought. *I wonder what Emma's thinking.*

EMMA GAZED ABSENT-MINDEDLY out the window at the puffy clouds floating by. She thought about the starving children in Africa and people dying of cancer and AIDS. She twisted in her seat and rubbed her hair between her fingers. Then, she began to cluck. The sad thoughts went away.

Emma learned to cluck when her baby brother was small. Her mother made a clucking sound to entertain the baby. Emma could imitate it when she sucked her tongue against the roof of her closed mouth and pulled it away. The sound escaped through her nose. There was no external movement of the lips. She could cluck without making any motion whatsoever. When bored, she clucked. When sad, she clucked. She stopped if the teacher came close. Sometimes, the teacher threatened to make the whole class stay after school but no one had ever caught her.

Emma listened. She stopped clucking. Silence filled the classroom like a morning fog. No rustle of papers, no coughs, no clearing of throats, no whispers. She pivoted her eyes to the left without moving her head, then to the right. All students stared straight ahead. She looked at Mrs. Haley's empty desk. She did not have to look behind her.

"Emma, go to the principal's office!" were the most dreadful words she had ever heard at school. She had never been to the principal's office.

"Why? What have I done?"

"To the principal's office, Emma Wedgwood. And don't try to look so innocent. I finally caught you."

Emma shuffled out of the room. Just barely into the fifth grade and she was in trouble.

At the principal's office she was told to take a seat outside the door and wait. She began to daydream. She had first gotten into serious trouble at home the year she was supposed to start to school. She touched the scar over her right eye, and drifted back in time.

"Emma! It's time for supper. Come on in!" Her mother's voice penetrated the dusk a second before the freight-train whistle blared its warning.

"Just a minute. I'll be there in a minute," Emma shouted back. She was six years old and not afraid of the dark. She headed for the sycamore tree. It was so much fun to climb the sycamore—lots of limbs and a view of all of Orchard Hill. From the top she would see the freight train in the twilight as it lumbered through the middle of town.

"Emma! Come in for supper!" she heard above the rumble of the train.

"I'll be right there." She jumped for the lowest limb and swung her leg over the branch. Up she went—limb to limb. She saw her mother set steaming dishes on the table then turn toward the window.

"Emma Wedgwood, you come in right this minute! It's supper time and besides, you shouldn't be out after dark. Emma, are you in that tree again? You come right down!"

She reached for a small branch near the top of the trees as the north-bound train whistled goodbye. The branch snapped and

Emma plunged south-headfirst. Striking limbs on the way down, each breaking her fall but none stopping her, she hit the lowest limb, where the swing was attached, reached for the rope and missed it. The red, east-Alabama clay approached in slow motion before everything went black.

The coma lasted three months and preempted her first year in school. Everything turned out okay because although she was a year older than Susie, she and Susie had started school at the same time. The only bad thing—boredom.

"Emma Wedgwood . . . Emma, you are Emma Wedgwood, aren't you?"

Emma's head jerked up. Trembling, she stared into the face of the Albert Jones Middle School's maximum authority. "Yes, yes ma'am. I'm Emma."

"Come into my office, Miss Wedgwood. Let's take a look at that note from Mrs. Haley."

"Yes ma'am."

"Hmmm . . ." the principal said looking at the teacher's note. "School prayer starts tomorrow. Maybe it'll help calm you kids down. Now, tell me about this clucking noise your teacher mentioned in the note. You want to demonstrate it for me?"

16

"ALMIGHTY GOD AND Father of our Lord Jesus Christ, we acknowledge our dependence upon Thee. Thou art the supplier of all our needs. We beg thy blessings upon us, our parents, our teachers, our schools, our nation, and all our churches. May thy holy will be done! In the name of Jesus we pray, Amen."

Emma looked at the prayer on the blackboard. *That sounds so funny—begging God. What kind of blessings? What needs is he supplying? Why do we have to pray at school? I thought we came here to learn other things—not what we learn at church.*

"All right, boys and girls, all together now," said Mrs. Haley. "Let's read the Alabama Prayer from the blackboard. When everybody has learned it by heart, we'll close our eyes and recite it like we do the Lord's Prayer in church."

A dozen voices began. "Almighty God and Father—"

Mrs. Haley interrupted, "Now young people, let's all do it together—everybody."

"One, two, three—Almighty God and Father of our Lord . . ." The fifth graders read the prayer without enthusiasm.

Emma saw Susie looking back at her making a face.

Emma mouthed, "You and I wouldn't do a prayer like that."

For days to come, she thought again about the "blessings" word and the "needs" word. Every time she recited the prayer, the two words flashed on and off in her mind—pulsating commercials telling her something important.

17

"Tom, you left a jumbo pack of gum in your pocket again," said Mary. "It went through the wash."

"Yeah," said Tom. "I forgot to take it out after church. I'll have to get some more for the kids next Sunday."

"Those kids appreciate what you do. I'd hate to see you miss Sunday School."

"What are you talking about?"

"I'm talking about your health. You ought to see a doctor. You know you've been having that heartburn and stomach pain too long and too often."

"Naw. I don't need to see no doctor and pay him to tell me I got acid indigestion. I take Tums and it goes away. Ain't you never had heartburn? You know how it feels."

"Yeah. But six months . . . and you have it every day. I'm gonna make you an appointment."

"Naw, Mary. I'll be all right. Just don't worry about it."

"I can't help but worry. It ain't like you to have stomach trouble. And it ain't like you to have blood on your underwear."

"What are you talking about, woman?"

"Tom Brandon, you know what I'm talking about. You're bleeding on your underwear and you think I don't know it? Tom, you got to see the doctor."

"I ain't been to a doctor since that huntin' accident twenty years ago."

"That's even more reason you're going to one now."

"Naw, I ain't going."

"Then I'm going to put you on the prayer list at church and everybody'll be asking you what's wrong—"

"All right, all right. You win. But you'll see; ain't nothing wrong. Probably piles."

"Could be; but just the same, it won't hurt to check. And we'll get him to check your heart while he's at it. Maybe even your head." Mary smiled.

18

IRENE HALEY STOOD and snapped her fingers at her buzzing fifth-grade class. The noise level dropped. "Now, open your books to the chapter on Mr. Charles Darwin. Today, boys and girls, we will study one of the great men of science. Before we begin, I must tell you that our state government has put a disclaimer at the beginning of your book. You can read it. It says that there are many unanswered questions about the origins of life which are not mentioned in this text. Now children, you may study about other origins of life at church or at home. However, here at school, we are going to study about the *scientific* origin of life. Those of you who have done your homework know what the lesson on Mr. Darwin is about. Ronnie, tell us what you've learned."

Ronnie almost fell from his seat as he swirled around to face the teacher. "I'm sorry, Mrs. Haley. Could you say that again?"

"Who is Charles Darwin?"

"I'm not sure, Mrs. Haley. Does he play for the Braves?"

Students laughed.

Mrs. Haley snapped her fingers again. "Evolution, Ronnie, evolution. What is evolution?"

"Oh, yes, ma'am. Isn't that about . . . I mean . . . where we all came from monkeys?"

"It's evident you haven't studied the assignment. Susie, what is evolution?"

Susie was prepared. She and Emma had studied together. She looked at the teacher, smiled, and stated with clarity and conviction: "Evolution is where all living things on earth change because of natural erection."

Mrs. Haley pivoted toward the blackboard—putting her back to the class. Snickers erupted here and there in the classroom.

Susie looked back toward Emma and mouthed, "What'd I say? Ain't that right?"

Emma kept silent—hands over her mouth.

Mrs. Haley turned her still slightly red face back toward the class. "Hush!" She walked back until she stood by Susie's desk. "It's election—I mean, selection. . . . Susie, it's natural selection. Now, go on."

"Yes, ma'am. The ones that are the weakest live and the strongest die," said Susie, glad that for once she had done her homework. She shot a glance at Emma who still had both hands over her mouth.

"Thank you, Susie, but I think you mean, 'the strongest live and the weakest die.'"

"Yes, ma'am. Ain't that what I said?"

"I'm sure it's what you meant. Now, Ronnie, I think the monkeys might have some objection to being linked to us human beings, although, according to Mr. Darwin, we do have a common ancestor. If we and the monkeys go back far enough, millions of years, we all jump into the common skin of a mammal. Can any of you . . . yes, Susie, what is it?"

"We learned at church that the Bible says that God created Adam and Eve not too long ago. Is that the same thing?"

"Not exactly," replied Mrs. Haley. "But we're not studying about religion. We are studying what scientists say about the beginning of life and its development. According to science, Susie, evolution is true."

"Do I have to believe it's true?" asked Susie.

"Until after the test," replied Mrs. Haley with a smile. "After the test, you can believe whatever you wish. Is that fair enough?"

"I think so."

"How about the rest of you?"

"You're the teacher, Mrs. Haley," said Jeremiah.

"Whatever you say," said another.

"Very well, then, let's look at the work of Mr. Darwin."

EMMA LIKED THE class about Mr. Darwin and evolution. Her last name was the same as Mrs. Darwin's maiden name. She wondered if she might be a direct descendent of Mrs. Darwin's parents. *That would make her—*

"Emma, are you daydreaming again?"

"No ma'am. I was thinking about Mr. Darwin's wife. We have the same last name."

"That's all well and good," said Mrs. Haley. "But that will not be a question on the next exam, so you need to sit up and pay attention."

Shortly, the bell called the evolving scholars to the lunchroom where Emma and Susie sat munching hotdogs and french fries.

Between bites Susie said, "Uncle Stanley's in town again. I wonder what he thinks about evolution."

"Why don't you ask him? By the way, I saw him and Reverend Gaylor together again." Emma paused for effect. "Holding hands."

"I ain't surprised no more," said Susie. "Uncle Stanley couldn't even come to supper last night. Said he had important business to attend to."

"Monkey business," said Emma. "If they're holding hands where everybody can see them, no telling what they're doing when they get by themselves."

"Yeah," said Susie, eyes open wide. "They might even be kissing."

Emma looked up and motioned with her head. "There's Marie. She doesn't look too happy."

"Marie," said Susie. "Come sit with us."

"Hi." Marie placed her tray on the table across from Emma and Susie and sat down. She began to pick at her food.

Susie and Emma looked at each other, then back at Marie.

Emma asked, "Have you been crying?"

"No, not really . . . yes," she stammered.

"What's wrong?" asked Susie.

"Daddy's in the hospital at Alex City and I'm scared. I'm scared to death."

"So that's why we didn't get chewing gum at Sunday School last Sunday," said Susie. "Your daddy wasn't—"

Emma punched Susie in the side with her elbow. "I was in the hospital at Alex City once and got well," said Emma. "They got good doctors over there."

"Daddy might not ever come home," Marie said.

"What's wrong with him?" asked Susie.

"Daddy was having a lot of heartburn and stomach trouble and when he went to the doctor, they told him he has colon cancer," Marie said. "He's got to have an operation."

"That's terrible!" said Susie. "Is he going to—"

Emma again punched Susie in the side. "Oh, I'm sorry, Marie. Is there something we can do?"

"Momma says we should pray—pray and trust God that everything will turn out okay. But I'm still scared. I don't remember Daddy ever being sick before."

"Why don't we pray for him?" asked Emma.

"Yeah. We pray for sick people all the time at church. The ones that don't die get well." Susie threw her hand to her mouth and dodged Emma's elbow.

"We can pray for him right here in school," said Emma.

"I don't want to bother anybody at school," said Marie.

"We pray the Governor's Prayer every morning," said Emma. "Maybe we could pray for something important for a change. Would that be okay?"

"Yeah, sure. Anything."

"You want to help me write it, Susie?"

"Yeah. I know a lot about prayers."

THE FOLLOWING MORNING after roll call, Emma raised her hand as the teacher snapped her fingers to call the class to order. "Mrs. Haley, could I say something before we recite the Governor's Prayer?"

"Sure, Emma. But it's called the 'Alabama Prayer.' What would you like to say?"

Emma hesitated. She had put the frog in the teacher's desk drawer the first week of school, and was afraid Mrs. Haley knew who did it. Then, there was that thing about the clucking a couple of weeks ago. "Would it . . . uh . . . would it be possible to add something to the . . . uh . . . prayer?"

"That depends, Emma. What do you want to add?"

"Well, Marie's daddy is in the hospital sick, and her mother said that they had to pray for him to get well. I wonder if we might add a little bit to the Governor's . . . I mean, the Alabama Prayer. It wouldn't hurt, would it?"

"What could it hurt?"

"I wouldn't want our school to get in trouble," said Emma.

"The governor won't even know about it," Mrs. Haley said. "It's a sweet thing to do, Emma. Have you thought about what you want to say?"

"Yes, ma'am. I've written it down. Susie helped me last night.

She's a Baptist. They make up prayers so she's had some experience." She handed the paper to the teacher.

Irene Haley looked at the petition and smiled. She wrote the request, in its entirety, on the blackboard beneath the Alabama Prayer.

Moments later, the children recited the Alabama Prayer with renewed enthusiasm then read the postscript, "Dear God, don't let the governor get mad at us for adding something to his prayer. Please help Mr. Tom Brandon get well. Not thy will but our will be done. In your name we pray, Amen." If anyone noticed the reversal of words in the closing sentence of the prayer, no one mentioned it.

A few days later, the doctors operating on Tom Brandon informed his wife that the surgery was a complete success and from what they had observed, the cancer had not spread. Marie told Emma and Susie who told the classmates about the miracle.

That evening, Emma reported to her father about how God healed Mr. Brandon—an answer to prayer.

"God may have played a part but don't you think some credit should go to the doctors and nurses who did the actual work?" he said.

"Well, I guess so. I hadn't thought of that." Emma decided that church stuff was getting more complicated as she grew older.

19

Late Thursday afternoon, Coach Tidwell encouraged Susie. "Susie, you're the best goalie we ever had. It's not your fault the Lightning Bolts beat us yesterday. Our forward defense broke down. When there are twenty-three goal attempts, some are bound to get through. You stopped ten of them. You were great!"

Everyone loved Coach Tidwell. In his tenth year at Alberta Jones Middle School, he coached football, soccer, basketball, and track. He loved his boys and girls. He made them feel like plants that had been watered. Coach Tidwell could turn a disappointing loss into a moral victory.

"Thank you, Coach," said Susie, beaming. "We'll do better next time."

"It'll be our last game, Susie, and you're right; you will do better. This is our greatest team ever."

"I'm going out for track next week, Coach. I'm a little heavy, but I know I can run."

"Sure you can, Susie, but I won't be here to train you."

"What do you mean?"

"Have to have the old ticker attended to—may need a transplant. After fifty-five years, the old pump has started missing a beat every now and then. Must be in my genes. But I'll be back before the end of the year. You'll do well with Coach Jarmon. He once ran in the Olympics."

"Wow! That's cool," said Susie. "But I'll miss you, Coach. Is there anything we can do for you?"

"Run like a gazelle and remember me in your bedtime

prayers. I'll be back before you know it."

"Got to go, Coach. Here's my bus." Susie looked back and frowned as the bus pulled away. Coach was getting old but she knew men older than him whose hearts were fine. Surely, he would get well . . . but a heart transplant? *Uncle William had a heart operation a couple of years ago and died. A heart transplant sounds bad. I gotta talk to Emma.*

20

SINCE BECOMING GOVERNOR, Forbe rarely shared a weekday lunch at home with his wife. He felt strangely drawn to this slender, chemo-balding woman seated across the table. Adversity drew him close to her—as close as his secrets permitted.

"Has it been three weeks already since your surgery?"

"To the day," replied Betty.

"Any way of knowing how the therapy is going?" Forbe asked as he took another sip of Chardonnay.

"Not yet," Betty said. "I still feel nauseated after the treatments. Sharika says it's too early to know if they're successful. She wants to give it a little more time."

"Then what?"

"If radiation and chemotherapy don't work, I'll go to the Baptist Cancer Center for more surgery."

"You could still lose your breast?"

"Not necessarily, Jimmy. But even if it comes to that, it's not the end of the world," Betty comforted him. "I've got a good oncologist. And the church is praying."

"You really believe in that, don't you?"

"It won't hurt. I've been on their prayer list for almost a month now."

"Don't you get discouraged?"

"Jimmy!" Betty shook her head at him. "You ought to be happy the Baptists are praying for me."

"Why's that?"

"Look what they've done for you. You rode into office on the Baptist vote."

"Like Jesus rode the ass into Jerusalem?" Forbe recoiled from Betty's frown. "I'm sorry, Sweet. I just couldn't pass that one up."

"We have a good church . . . wonderful people . . . their prayers are important."

"Certainly," said Forbe. He looked at her lean white face, and thinning hair. "Let them pray."

Betty rose from the table. "I've got to go. Don't want to be late for my radiation."

Forbe rose. "I'll take you."

As his vehicle pulled into the street, Forbe saw the state troopers poised to follow. "Those troopers are like chiggers," he said to Betty. "I've always got a couple on my ass."

"Or some other unmentionable place." Betty laughed.

"Check out that motorcycle!" Forbe exclaimed as a motorcyclist slowed to allow Forbe's retinue to fall in behind him.

Betty said with mock annoyance, "Check out the motorcycle or that female passenger with the painted-on riding suit?" Both cyclist and companion wore red helmets and black clothing.

"Come on, Betty. The motorcycle is a Guzzi. I saw the decal on the tank. Aren't many of those around."

"I didn't know you had that much interest in motorcycles."

"I don't. But my college roommate, Stanley, had Guzzi posters all over the room. That's about all he talked about—where was he going to go when he got his first Moto Guzzi."

ON THE GUZZI, Stanley turned and shouted to Janet, "Did you see that car back there, the Crown Victoria with the state troopers behind it?"

"Yes, what about it?"

"I think that was the governor. Haven't seen him since college."

"Who was the woman?"

"Must be his wife, Betty."

"She gave me a going over. I'm thirsty."

"Hang on. We'll be at the park in no time."

Minutes later, Stanley turned off Woodmere Boulevard into Blount Cultural Park in east Montgomery. As the park road veered right toward the theaters, Janet said, "Stop! I see our table down there by that sculpture of children climbing a tree."

Stanley stopped. "There it is, all by its lonesome." A small copse of trees draped with Spanish moss spread from the road to the small lake. Swans, geese, and ducks rippled the water searching for handouts.

Stanley eased down to a parking area among the trees. He retrieved drinks and sandwiches from one of the saddle bags while Janet extracted a table cloth, napkins, and potato chips from the other. "It is a perfect summer day for motorcycling and picnicking," Stanley said. "Overcast, low humidity, and what a beautiful site."

They surveyed the acres and acres of manicured lawn, gardens, and bronze sculptures—one of which consisted of five running children, who appeared to be suspended in mid-air. The Alabama Shakespeare Festival anchored the park on one side and the Montgomery Museum of Fine Arts on the other.

As they spread their picnic, Janet said, "It's so nice to be here alone with you, Stanley." She caught him by the hand and pulled him close.

After a long, passionate kiss, Stanley said, "I thought you were thirsty."

Janet faked a memory lapse. "Oh, yes. I'd forgotten. Open me a Heineken."

As they sat sipping their drinks and munching ham and cheese sandwiches and chips, Janet said, "Why are you so different from Baptist ministers I have known?"

"My taste in refreshments?"

"Not just that. Important things. We fall on the same side of some liberal causes—the death penalty, abortion, gay rights, the Palestinian question, appreciation and respect for other religions. You are not a typical Baptist."

"I came by it honestly after a slow start. Have I ever told you that my grandfather once led the church you now serve?"

"What? Your grandfather was a Unitarian Universalist minister?"

"You heard it right. Back in the thirties he was minister of the Orchard Hill Universalist Church—had a congregation of over five hundred—the largest Christian church in the area."

Janet frowned. "We seldom have over fifty now, even on a good Sunday. What happened?"

"The persuasive power of Baptist camp meetings and the tendency of human beings to want something for nothing. In the camp meetings, the wind-sucking revivalists worked the congregation into a sweat at the gates of a burning Hell then offered them Heaven for free—'Jesus paid it all.'"

"The Unitarian Universalists don't believe in Hell," said Janet.

"Right, but the ticket to Heaven was not free."

"Baptists have told me that their churches got big because God wanted them to grow."

"Cow dung," said Stanley, "Pardon my Greek. Baptists got big when they learned how to market their faith."

"Stanley, you're hard on your church."

"The Southern Baptist Convention has slipped its moorings. My Baptist Alliance for Progress is a thorn in the Convention's flesh. By the way," Stanley changed the subject. "I've got some news for you."

"You're moving back to Alabama."

"Not exactly. I'm going to Cuba."

"You're what?"

"I'm going to Cuba in a few days."

"One of your humanitarian trips?"

"Yes and no. I'll be taking a shipment of medicines, but the purpose of the trip will be political. I'm to be briefed by my associates when I get back to Washington. I'm not sure who I'll be meeting in Cuba but it won't be the Baptists this time."

"Sounds mysterious."

"That's what I thought, too. All I know is that something is brewing in Cuban politics and a high-level official in Havana has asked to meet with me."

"I'm impressed."

"I'll fill you in when I return."

Janet reached for the cold pack. "You want another beer?"

"No, I'm driving. I'll have coffee."

Janet pried off the cap of another Heineken, then said, "Now, I want to change the subject and ask you a question that might make you uncomfortable."

"Don't worry about that. Shoot." Stanley poured a steaming cup of coffee from the thermos.

"Okay. We've been going out for many months now. We've been alone together several times at my apartment, yet you've barely touched me in the right places."

About to sip his coffee, Stanley set it down. He tried to dodge the question. "We've had some distractions."

"You've allowed some distractions. Is something wrong with me?"

"No! There's nothing wrong with you." Stanley moved

around the table and placed his arms around her. "It's not you. It's me."

"Are you gay?"

Stanley laughed. "No! You should know that."

Janet smiled. "I've noticed an awakening on occasion but no action. Am I unattractive to you in some way?"

"Janet, please, please. You're a beautiful person. It has nothing to do with you. It's something I have to work through. Give me some time."

"Are you still dealing with the loss of your wife?"

"Not that either. It's not all that complicated—has to do with my religion. Please be patient. I'll work through it, soon. I promise. You are sexually very appealing."

"I'll try to be patient, but you're sexually appealing, too."

"I'll be careful—"

"You don't have to be careful!" Janet sprang to her feet, walked to the edge of the lake, and gazed at the black swans swimming toward her.

Stanley watched but did not speak.

After a few moments, she returned to the table and sat beside him but facing out. Stanley embraced her and their lips met. Finally, Janet pulled away and said, "I'll wait. I think you're worth waiting for."

"You ready to pick up our theater tickets for tomorrow and head back toward Dadeville?" asked Stanley.

"Sure. Refresh my memory. What are we going to see?"

"*As You Like It.*"

"I'm glad it's not *Much Ado About Nothing.*" They both laughed. "I'll get the tickets," she said. "I need to walk a bit."

Stanley carried their bags back to the motorcycle where Janet met him after picking up the tickets.

Stanley threw his leg over the motorcycle, pulled it upright and kicked back the stand. He turned the key and touched the starter button. The 1000cc v-twin roared to life. He handed Janet her helmet, pulled his on and buckled it. Janet pulled her helmet on, stepped on the footpeg, and swung her leg over. She settled down behind him and placed her hands on his waist. Stanley engaged the gears and moved past the theater, out of the park onto Woodmere again, toward the Eastern Bypass and the Interstate. As he wheeled onto the acceleration ramp of I-85 North, Janet locked her arms around his waist. As he accelerated, he felt Janet's curves mold into his back and her hands caress the region below his belt. Soon the Moto Guzzi California flew northward and Stanley's left hand crawled southward along Janet's firm and compliant thigh.

21

FORBE SAT WITH elbows on his desk, hands clasped, and chin rested on extended thumbs.

Dick entered Forbe's office. "Morning, Jimbo. You look troubled. What's eating you?"

"It's Betty. She looks like death warmed over."

"Keep your chin up, Governor. These things take time. Cancer comes on slowly and sometimes it goes out that way."

"Thanks, Dick. I'm trying but it's not easy. Let's get down to business. Maybe it'll stop me from worrying about something I've got no control over." He sat up straight and stretched. "How's that legislation coming on the authorization for golf courses in state parks?"

Dick took a deep breath. "We're having a little trouble there. Some opposition from—"

"Dammit, Dick! I don't care who we got opposition from. We received fifty thousand dollars in campaign contributions from the Golf Development Association. We both know what that was about. Push the ball . . . I mean, bill!"

"Yes, Governor. But we may have to take it out of the education budget."

"That's fine. Education's got enough money if they would just get their priorities right and cut out waste."

"I don't know about that. Alabama is way below national averages on educational spending and teacher salaries."

"Yeah, but we're ahead of Arkansas. That's good enough for me. Alabama's at the top of almost every list I see."

"Yes, you're right. On most lists, Alabama comes right before Alaska. Now, about the education budget, we'll have to give them something."

"Not while I'm guvnah. I've given the religious nuts prayer for the schools. That's all they asked for and that's all they're gonna to get. They weren't the only ones that voted for me. We've got to look out for other interests, and . . . my second term."

"We can look out for both—the other interests and the schools," said Dick. "The schools have some serious needs. If our administration could make some strides in education, you'd be a strong candidate for a repeat term."

Forbe knew that Dick was considering a run for Lieutenant Governor next term, but he decided not bring it up at this point. *Maybe that's why he was pushing the education agenda*, he thought.

"Educators didn't contribute much money to my campaign. You got to have money to run. I go where the money is." Forbe held both hands in the air and rubbed his thumbs and index fingers together.

"If we don't help the schools, where are they going to turn?" asked Dick.

"In God we trust. They've got those plaques up. They've got prayer. Let 'em use it. Besides, I've given money to higher education from the estate I inherited. Now, let's move on to something else."

Dick's shoulders slumped "Okay," he said. "It's one of those *other interests*—the casino lobby. They've been rather insistent lately."

"Everybody knows I'm officially against casinos and lotteries," said Forbe. "I can't afford to alienate my Baptist constituency."

"Unless we are willing to give in a little, we will undercut our ability to tap into gambling money for the next election," said Dick.

"Put it off awhile!"

"Governor, we can't put everything off. We have promises to keep or there won't be any money for a second campaign."

"Let's get with it then."

"Do you recall your pledge to the Alabama Casino Gambling Association during that meeting last summer?"

"Refresh my memory."

"You promised, off the record, that you would support offshore casinos—"

"Yes, I remember that," said Forbe.

"On Wilson Lake, Guntersville Lake, Smith Lake, Lake Martin, Lake Hardin, and Lake Eufaula."

"They didn't mention any damn lakes," said Forbe. "I thought they were talking about the Gulf Coast!"

"I believe the specifics came out after you left the meeting. You told me to stay and work out the details."

"Weren't they talking about the Gulf Coast?"

"They weren't. And they're expecting your support."

"Off-shore gambling casinos on Alabama ponds?"

"I'm afraid so."

Forbe rose, walked to the window, and looked down at Dexter Avenue which ended like a rolled-out carpet at the capital steps. "Are the legislators from the lake districts aware of the proposal?"

"They're aware, but they aren't talking about it. Like you, they depend on the conservative Christian vote, but many of them got campaign funds from the Gambling Association."

Opposition on both sides, Forbe thought. *Closing in. Everyone wants something, and there ain't enough to go around. Compromise*, he thought. *Think.* Forbe turned to Dick. "Set up a meeting with the legislators from the districts surrounding the lakes. We'll see what we can do without coming out openly in favor of casino gambling. Anything else?"

"I have several more things." Little opened another folder. "There's a problem with the name of the new student center at the junior college you attended before going on to Samford. Everyone is pleased with the small building your foundation donated, but the name you suggested lends itself to . . . well, let me say, certain unbecoming sounds."

"What's wrong with "Forbe University Center for Under-graduates?""

"It's not the name, Jimbo. It's the initials. Regardless of how you feel about the education lobby, it's not the message you want to send."

"F.U.C.U. I'll be damned!" Forbe threw his hands to his forehead and blew his breath out through pursed lips. He looked at the stack of folders Dick cradled in his hands. "What else?"

"More campaign promises, Jimbo. A pretty diverse group."

"Just read me the tabs."

Dick looked at the folder labels and smiled. "There are the Baptists, of course. And the Casino Gambling Association, the Golfers Association, the Save the Parks Coalition, the Lard Bucket Lobby, and the Low-Fat Diet Fellowship. And there's—"

"We'll figure something out. This is what politics is about. Work up some proposals. Maybe I can handle some of it with executive decrees."

Dick turned to leave, then stopped and turned back toward Forbe. "Just one more thing, Jimbo—something to think about. There have been some problems with the school prayer."

"What do you mean, *problems?*"

"There are reports of harassment of non-Christian students in some of the schools."

22

"JEREMIAH GINSBERG, WHAT'S wrong with your eye?" shouted Esther at her son, more startled than angry. "Have you been fighting? What's that on your forehead? . . . Jeremiah, it's a cross!"

"I'm sorry, Mother. Is it something bad? Don't get upset, Mother." Jeremiah let his books drop to the floor. "Some boys at school put it there."

"Son, I'm . . . forgive me. I didn't mean to shout at you. It just shocked me. You know you shouldn't be fighting. Let's go wash your face while you tell me what happened." Esther's surprise abated and apprehension took over. Even before her ten-year-old son began to recount the day's activities, she had a good idea of what had happened.

Her family had warned her about moving to a small town in Alabama. The current governor had won election on a promise to put prayer in the schools and in a state where most church members were Baptist or Methodist, no one expected it to be a Jewish prayer. In fact, one national Baptist leader had said that God did not hear a Jew's prayer.

"I don't want to leave Boston. I was born here," she had said to her husband.

"My job has migrated south. We've got to follow it."

"How far south?"

"Uncle Jacob says there's a sporting goods plant in Dadeville, Alabama."

Housing was cheaper in Orchard Hill so they had settled

here—just ten miles from Jonathan's new job. What the uncle had not told them was that in their new city religious bigotry was a force to be dealt with.

"Jeremiah, what did they put this on with? I can't get it off."

He looked embarrassed. "I think it was a permanent marker. They said it was as black as my soul. You know what I mean?"

"You poor thing. Let's go get dinner ready for your father. Maybe he'll know something that will get it off."

As they later sat around the supper table, Jonathan looked at his son. "Jeremiah, it looks like you also have a black eye. You need to tell us everything that has been going on at school."

Between bites, Jeremiah began to relate a series of recent happenings at Alberta Jones School that they had not heard before.

"You remember, Father, when you let me wear my yarmulke during Hanukkah? I thought it would be okay, since the other students wore crosses and stuff."

"And it wasn't? What happened?" asked Jonathan.

"The class bully grabbed it from my head and wouldn't give it back. Then he tried to flush it down the toilet."

"Tried?" asked Esther.

"Yes. A yarmulke won't flush. Stopped up the toilet and flooded the restroom. When he blamed it on me, the teacher knew he was lying and made him stay after school."

"What else?"

"You remember when I told you I needed to carry a Christmas present for Jesus to school and you told me not to worry about it?"

"Yes."

"Well, the teacher didn't say anything, but some of the boys told me I was going to hell for not accepting Jesus."

"And what did you tell them?"

"I asked them if Jesus would accept *me*."

"Has the new school prayer had anything to do with this?"

"Well, when everyone stands to recite the Governor's Prayer, the teacher tells me I can stand in the bathroom and pray my own prayer until the rest of the children have finished."

"Has the teacher been unkind to you?" asked his father.

Esther interrupted. "I've talked to Mrs. Haley and she is very supportive."

"Yes. She's very nice and tells me not to worry about what the bullies say. She says it's kid stuff."

"Are all your classmates unkind?" Esther asked.

"No. Just three or four. Most are okay, especially Susie, Paco, Emma, and Katasha. They're real nice. Some of the boys make fun of me for talking to Susie or Emma."

"Son, painting a cross on your face with indelible ink is not kid stuff," his father said. "Has anything else happened that you would like to tell us about?"

"Just one thing. Some of the boys said their pastor was going to witness to me. They said he would catch me some day after school and show me the way to Jesus."

"Has the pastor *witnessed* to you yet?"

"Yes, sir. He said I was a sinner and that if I didn't accept Jesus I would go to the bad world when I die."

"And what did you tell him?" asked Esther.

"I told him I was Jewish and that I went to the synagogue in Auburn every Friday. He said that going to the synagogue wouldn't get me into heaven. He said that the Jews had killed Jesus, but that if I would invite him to come into my heart, Jesus would forgive me."

"And what did you do?" asked Jonathan.

"I told him I didn't understand what he was saying and that I wanted to talk to you first."

"And?"

"That was the day I asked you if I needed to accept Jesus to go to heaven. You said I didn't, so the next time he met me after school, I told him no. I didn't want to accept Jesus. He said that was too bad and that he would pray for me until I did."

Esther looked at her husband, then her son. "Has anything else happened?"

"Well, after school today, the same boys told me that Jesus was going to punish me for not going to church."

"And what did you tell them?" Jonathan asked.

"I told them that I didn't think he would, 'cause Jesus was a Jew like me. That's when the big one hit me in the eye and dragged me to the bathroom where they painted the mark on my head. They said calling Jesus a Jew was worse than cussing. Is that right, Father?"

23

"Emma, have you heard about Coach Tidwell?" asked Susie, long-faced, as they alighted from the bus. Although they were in the same class, they had hardly spoken to each other all day.

"I heard he was taking a few weeks off."

"He is. He's got to have a heart transplant."

"That's pretty serious."

"That explains why he told me to pray for him," said Susie.

"Why don't we add on another prayer during home room tomorrow?" said Emma as they walked toward the sycamore tree. The resident mockingbird sang from the top of the tree. A katydid fiddled backup.

"I . . . don't know."

"Are you afraid it'll make the governor mad?" asked Emma.

"I don't want to get our school in trouble," said Susie.

"We prayed for Mr. Brandon and nothing bad happened," Emma said. "Besides, I heard Mrs. Haley tell Mrs. Jones that the governor doesn't know what's going on in the schools anyway."

"Okay. You want to write this one?"

"You write it. You're good at writing prayers." Emma climbed onto the lowest limb of the tree and sat with her back against the trunk.

"Dear God," said Susie out loud as she wrote. "Make the coach well . . . Naw . . . don't sound right. We ought to give God a good reason to make him well."

"Come on, Susie. Just do it."

"God's real busy. We've got to give him a good excuse to

work on our stuff and not somebody else's. Give me an idea."

"Okay, let's see . . . uh . . ." mumbled Emma from her perch in the tree. "When Daddy's car breaks down, he doesn't go buy a new one. He fixes the old one. It seems to me that it would be easier for God to fix the coach's old heart than to have to get him a new one. Besides, somebody's got to die before there's a heart for a transplant. I saw it on television. You writing?"

"Yeah."

Emma continued. "Hey, why don't we include the governor's wife? She's got cancer. I saw that on television, too."

"We don't want to give God too much to do," said Susie. "He'll have his hands full with Coach Tidwell. Fixing a heart's a pretty big order."

"God can do anything, can't he? Let's include the governor's wife. When God gets through fixing the coach, he can fix her. Since they both live in Alabama, God can do both things while he's passing through."

"Okay. Give me a minute. You could come down out of that tree and help."

"I'm already helping. I got you started, didn't I? And, I told you about the governor's wife."

"All right. Here's what I got." Susie read the prayer to Emma who made several corrections.

"How did we end that last one?" asked Susie. "We ought to be sure we get that part right. In church they always put it close to the end of every prayer. Daddy says it's important."

"Look at the last prayer. Don't you have a copy of in your notebook?"

The following morning, Emma again asked the teacher to let them add something to the Alabama Prayer. Again, Mrs. Haley had no objections but smiled as she read the petition before writing it on the board. The children hurried through the now memorized Alabama Prayer.

They slowed down as they read the words from the black-board:

Dear God, instead of letting people die and then having to make new ones, why don't you keep the ones you got—like Coach Tidwell and the governor's wife? First, we want you to fix Coach Tidwell's heart, then help the governor's wife get well from cancer. You could save yourself a lot of trouble. Not thy will but our will be done. In your name we pray, Amen.

24

TIDWELL WALKED OUT to where the track team gathered. "My, my, it's good to see y'all this sunny Friday afternoon." Everyone stared, mouths open.

"Coach, you're already back?" Susie exclaimed.

"Yep. Y'all ready to get down to business?"

Emma spoke. "But we thought you'd be gone for months and you're back in less than a week."

"Aren't you glad to see me?"

"YES!" everyone shouted in unison.

"Your substitute ran us to death," said Susie.

"Then y'all ought to be in shape." Tidwell laughed. "You ready to hit the track and show me?"

No one moved.

"Come on! Let's go!"

Everyone continued to stare. Emma spoke again. "Aren't you going to tell us what happened, Coach? Nobody can have a heart-transplant and be walking around like you are right now."

"Okay." Tidwell rubbed his hands together. "They didn't have to operate. The cardiologist put me on a new medication and I'm fine. Now let's go."

The young athletes rose and followed their coach toward the track.

"Jeremiah." Tidwell addressed the tan-skinned athlete holding Susie's hand.

"Yes, Coach?" Jeremiah turned Susie loose.

"They say you ran track in Boston. That right?"

"Yes, sir. I ran in the Boston Marathon for Kids. How'd you know that?"

"I have my little birdies flying around listening." Tidwell caught Susie's eye and winked.

She blushed. "We thought you were gone for good, Coach."

Emma said. "We prayed for you at school."

"Well, I'm glad you did. God works in mysterious ways. The doctor called it a spontaneous normalization of my heart rhythm, but I know better. And I feel great, and so will all of you after about twenty laps. Move out!"

Emma did feel good—down deep. She always felt good when somebody got well—like she did after her fall from the sycamore tree. *Maybe the prayer cured the coach and maybe the medicine did. Who knows how these things happen?* As she ran the warm-up laps around the track she thought, *I wonder how the governor's wife is doing. I've got to get home in time for the news on TV.*

EMMA WALKED IN the door of her house on Sycamore Street, dropped her books on the coffee table, and collapsed on the couch. She pressed the remote and the TV sprang to life. The WSFA reporter, standing outside the governor's mansion, spoke into a microphone. "...breaking news. First Lady, Betty Forbe, who has been in treatment for a malignancy, is at home and doing well. Mrs. Forbe told reporters earlier this afternoon that the cancer seems to have gone away. The First Lady's personal physician, Dr. Sharika Carver, said that the remission was nothing short of miraculous."

"Wow!" Emma said aloud. "I wonder if Susie heard that!"

25

"EMMA, EMMA, where have you been?" shouted Susie as she spotted Emma in the sycamore tree. "I ain't seen you since school let out on Friday."

"Quiet, Susie! You're going to scare the mockingbird. Ahhh. You made him stop."

Susie lowered her voice. "Where have you been?"

"Where have you been?" Emma countered.

"Trying to see Uncle Stanley. He's been riding Reverend Gaylor everywhere on his motorcycle—Alex City, Dadeville, everywhere. Did you see it?"

"I saw him go by the restaurant. Did he ride you?"

"One time. I called for you but you didn't come out."

"I've been at Daddy's office down at the restaurant. He's got a new computer and he let me go play with it."

"A new computer, that's cool! Can I see it sometime?"

"Sure. It's got some games on it and some other good stuff. It's even got some programs to help me with my homework, and it's connected to the Internet."

"I wish we had computers at school."

"Me, too!" Emma jumped to the ground. "Let's go watch cartoons."

"Your house or mine?"

"Mine," said Emma. "I'll beat you to the door."

Emma bounded onto the porch a jump ahead of Susie. "No fair! You had a head start."

"No, I didn't. You go to the den while I get some Cokes."

"Have you heard about Mrs. Forbe?" asked Emma as she entered the den with an orange soda for Susie and a Coke for herself.

"No. What happened?"

"Mrs. Forbe got well."

"Wow!" said Susie. "And Coach Tidwell, too. You think our school prayer had anything to do with it?"

"I don't know. We're just kids." Emma recalled her conversation with her father a few weeks earlier. "Maybe it was the doctors and nurses."

"Yeah, but our class has prayed for three people and all three got well," Susie said. "Maybe God helped the doctors and nurses."

"Yes. That could be."

Susie sipped her soda and wiped her mouth on her sleeve. "I've got a good feeling about the prayers we wrote. I think we ought to write one about our school."

"You want to pray that Mrs. Haley won't give us so much homework?"

"I don't want to pray about people. I want to pray for computers." Susie sat her soda down hard on the coffee table.

"Computers? Are you crazy? You think prayer will get us computers?"

"It won't hurt to try. The governor sure didn't do nothing. Get me some paper!"

Emma said, "If we pray for computers and don't get them, everybody's going to laugh."

"That's why Daddy told me the last part of the prayer's important—the 'my will, thy will' words. When we put that in our prayers, we're covered," said Susie. "It's like insurance."

"I don't know if Mrs. Haley will let us ask for computers."

"I think she will. She said that when we got prayer in the

schools, some good things would happen. What could be better than new computers?"

"Okay, but while we're at it, why don't we ask for computers for all the schools in Alabama," said Emma.

"That might be too many," said Susie.

"You're right. Let me think . . . hummm . . . I got it. We'll tell him to start with our school and keep going till he runs out."

"Good idea!" Susie began to write.

The following morning after the roll call period, Mrs. Haley's class read from the blackboard an addition to the Alabama Prayer:

> Dear God, please send some computers to our school and then to all the other schools that need them. We've never asked you for any real stuff before. You can look it up. Not thy will but our will be done. In your name we pray, Amen.

26

"How did this damn bill get on the floor?" shouted Forbe to Dick Little.

"My brother, Patrick, authored the bill," said Dick, pushing his palms toward Forbe to calm him down. "He—"

"Don't you have any control over your damn brother?" Forbe interrupted.

"Patrick is a Democrat and has a mind of his own," said Dick. "I told you that when I became your campaign manager. My brother and I are close but we don't argue politics—ever."

"Why is the bill already on the floor?"

"That's what I'm getting at. The bill was introduced by Patrick, referred to the Finance Committee by the Senate President, and reported back the next day."

"That's too damn fast. Besides, we control the committees."

"Governor, this one bounced out of the Finance Committee like a basketball. It passed the Senate and more than likely will pass the House, too. Are you going to sign it or not?"

"You know damned well I'm not. Has anyone figured out where the frigging money's coming from? They're talking about millions of dollars."

"I'm afraid they're planning to re-allocate the funds earmarked for the golf course construction and maybe even dip into the windfall expected from the lake casinos, whenever that goes through."

"The hell they will! I'll veto it. I'm getting on the phone with our party leaders to see what's going on." *How the hell did this happen?* he thought. *It makes no sense, taking money from important projects, and putting it in education. It's ridiculous.*

"Calm down, Jimbo! You might as well prepare to sign the bill. The Senate passed it without one dissenting vote and the House will come close. A veto would be futile."

"BILL, WHAT THE hell is going on?" inquired Forbe of William Hargrave, senator from Eufaula and chairman of the Finance Committee. "Overriding my veto like that is going to weaken the governor's office."

"You should have signed that bill, Governor. Common sense told you that."

"I can't sign bills that will bankrupt the state. Where's the money coming from? You voted against the golf course bill and the lake gambling casinos in the Senate."

"I know, Governor. Those bills would have benefited my district—a new golf course in Point Park and a casino on Lake Eufaula."

Forbe spoke, enunciating every word. "Why did you let it happen?"

"I don't know, Jimbo. I just don't know. By the way, we're all happy about Betty's good news."

"Yes, Bill, we are both delighted about that. But I'm unhappy about that bill. A computer for every ten public school students? Again, I ask you, where's the damn money coming from?"

"We killed the golf course appropriations."

"That won't be near enough."

"We tabled the casino gambling bill."

"That doesn't make sense. We could get some of the money there," said Forbe. *What's wrong with him? He's not talking sense.*

"Listen," said Hargrave. "The Senate voted to float a bond issue to fund educational expenditures pending the outcome of a referendum on a lottery. If the lottery passes, the bond issue will be liquidated and, in its place, lottery revenue will go directly to education. Then we'll bring casino gambling back on the floor."

"You still haven't answered my question. Why? Why? Why?"

"I don't know, Jimbo. I don't know what came over us. We knew Patrick Little would propose big spending on education."

"Those liberal Democrats want to throw money at everything. We're supposed to be reasonable and stop them."

"I know that, Jimbo. But we didn't count on bipartisan support for his bill. Heck, we didn't even expect he would get significant support from his own party. This bill not only carried all of the Democrats, but most of the Republicans, too."

"What the hell do Republicans mean voting for that kind of legislation? I mean, what kind of Republican—"

"I've talked with some of the senators and representatives," Hargrave interrupted. "They all tell the same story."

"What?"

"They all said, 'I don't know what came over me. I felt moved to hit the yes button.'"

"Sounds like a holiness camp meeting," Forbe raised both hands and looked up in a gesture of mock praise.

"It's weird, I'll have to admit," Hargrave replied. "You ought to sit in on one of those sessions."

"When I want to feel the spirits, I'll get me a scotch-and-soda. I could sure as hell use one now."

"It's strange, but you need to experience—"

"Dammit, Bill!" Forbe jumped to his feet. "This is the Alabama Legislature—not some kind of touchy-feely, spirit-filled Pentecostal revival."

Hargrave stepped back.

Forbe smiled and sat back down. "I'm sorry."

"Don't worry about it. You've been under a lot of strain."

"Can you call for a reconsideration? Is there time for a reversal?"

"I'm sorry, Jimbo. Not during this session. Nobody will touch it, for sure."

"Hell, this whole state's bent out of shape. I'm fed up. I'm going to get in a round of golf before that rain moves in. You want to go?"

Before Hargrave could speak, Forbe grabbed his cap and walked toward the door. As he turned the knob, he looked back at Hargrave standing with his mouth open. "Listen, Bill. There's not enough money for that many computers. It'd take a miracle to pull that asinine bit of legislation off." He turned and hurried toward the elevator.

"COMPUTERS! SUSIE, NOT A MONTH HAS PASSED SINCE WE PRAYED AND WE'VE GOT computers all over the school, looks like in every classroom!" Emma almost ran into Susie before skidding to a stop.

"I know." said Susie. "I just came from the west wing. All the rooms over there's got 'em. It's like they rained down from heaven!"

27

"Emma, did you hear about the fight after school today?" asked Susie from the rope swing in Emma's yard.

"Yeah. Paco told me. But it wasn't exactly a fight. Some bullies jumped on Jeremiah again," said Emma sitting in the tree.

"I wish Uncle Stanley was still here. He'd go over and straighten things out."

"Get Jeremiah to become a Baptist?" Emma asked.

"No! Uncle Stanley wouldn't do that. He'd straighten out those other boys," said Susie.

"Why don't they like Jeremiah?"

"'Cause he don't recite the Governor's Prayer. I cried when I heard it. He's real cute."

"He's your sweetheart," Emma said as she threw a small twig at Susie.

Susie dodged. "Yeah. He has the biggest brown eyes, the darkest hair, and the nicest tan you ever saw—"

Emma interrupted. "He's older than you."

"Just a few months. I think he likes me, too."

"Do you think anybody else likes him?"

"Yeah. Some other girls, but they stay away because those boys make fun of him all the time."

"Emma, I've got an idea. I've been thinking a lot since our school got computers. Maybe the school prayers are working. Let's write a prayer about Jews and see what happens."

"You really think it's the prayers?"

"Think about it," said Susie. "Before the computers, there

was Mr. Brandon, then Coach Tidwell, and the governor's wife."

Emma said, "It's probably a coincidence. Daddy says it's when two things happen about the same time but don't have anything to do with each other. What in the world are we going to ask for?"

"I thought about doing the prayer. You think about something to go in it," said Susie.

"Why not try to get some more Jewish people into Orchard Hill," said Emma.

"Yeah," said Susie. "Then the Ginsbergs wouldn't be so lonely, and Jeremiah would have some classmates to stand in the bathroom with him during the Governor's Prayer."

When the girls finished admiring their work, Susie left the prayer with Emma who agreed to present it to Mrs. Haley. The following morning, Susie and Emma's home room class added another postscript to the Governor's Prayer.

> Dear God: You must know how it feels to be lonely, since you lived by yourself before you made us to keep you company. The Ginsbergs are lonely, too. If you would bring some more Jews into our town, maybe those boys wouldn't make fun of Jeremiah. Don't bring too many—it might start a war. Not thy will but our will be done. In your name we pray, Amen.

28

"THE SANCTION OF homosexuality is the last step in the decline of Christian America," boomed Dr. Henry Stanton, the pastor of Montgomery's Tabernacle Baptist Church, to his weekly television audience. "Some call them *gay*, but the Bible calls them homosexuals. The great Roman Empire that ruled the world during the time of Jesus embraced homosexuality and a few centuries later it met its fate . . ."

Emma started to switch to cartoons but wondered what the preacher was talking about. She had heard Reverend Gaylor use the "gay" word in sermons. She listened on.

" . . . so will be the destiny of our great nation if it does not turn from its wicked ways. God condemns the sin of homosexuality and punishes its practitioners. God gives men AIDS to castigate them for their . . ."

"God gives people AIDS?" moaned Emma under her breath. *That's terrible*, she thought.

" . . . who engage in this unholy and unnatural act will be cast into the fires of a literal hell where the worm dieth not and the fire is not quenched . . ."

"On top of AIDS?" Emma spoke out loud.

"Did you say something, Emma?" called her mother from the bedroom.

"No, Mother. I'm just talking back to the television."

"You'd better start talking to the shower and get ready for church. Your brother's out of the bathroom now."

" . . . to all homosexuals under the sound of my voice, I tell you to repent from your wicked ways and believe the gospel. If you repent . . . if you change your wicked ways, you'll find a church home here at Tabernacle Baptist."

Emma did not fully understand what the sin of homosexuality was. It didn't sound the same as what Reverend Gaylor said about it at her church. At their church, everybody was welcome—gays, Lebaneses, and trans . . . something. If the Baptists knew more about gays, they would welcome them, too. Maybe that's what the Baptist preacher on television meant when he told all homosexuals under the sound of his voice that they had a church home at Tabernacle Baptist. *Susie and I have another prayer to write for school,* she thought as she went into the bathroom.

29

"MAUDE, DO YOU see that?" whispered Luke motioning with his thumb back toward the entrance of the sanctuary at the Tabernacle Baptist Church in Montgomery.

Maude looked back. "Yeah. Two men. What about it?"

"They're wearing earrings."

"And?"

"They're holding hands."

"Maybe they're brothers."

"They're grown men, Maude. Grown men don't hold hands, not here at Tabernacle Baptist."

"Turn around and quit staring. Maybe they're Russians. I've seen Russian men kissing on TV. Maybe they hold hands, too."

"These ain't Russians. They're too neat."

"I said, quit staring!"

"I've seen these freaks on television, Maude. They live together. They sleep in the same bed. They do ungodly things. What in tarnation are they doing here?"

"Watch your language, Luke! You're in church. Maybe they're coming to repent," Maude whispered.

"Repent, heck! They should've done that at the door and turned loose. They're coming here to stir up trouble like those—" Luke stopped for a moment, than leaned closer to Maude, "Like those Yankee niggers used to. Asking for more rights, demanding things. Aw hell, Maude, there's more. There's a whole harem. And women. Some of the women look more like men."

THE CHURCH ORGAN was located directly behind and slightly above the pulpit. Aunt Bessie, the organist, sat with her back to the congregation and in her rearview mirror followed the Minister of Music as he directed the singing. She had played at Tabernacle Baptist for forty-three years and never missed a note. In her mirror, she caught sight of the strangers walking down the aisle as she began the fourth movement of an organ prelude arrangement of "Oh, How I Love Jesus." At first glance, she saw only their heads, and thought it unusual that so many strange men and women would walk in at the same time. When she saw their hands splicing them into couples—men to men, women to women, both her hands slipped a half octave on the keyboard and her left toe snagged on low A as her right heel wedged between high F and G. The resultant discord woke the sleep-deprived, who had already drifted off to their Sunday morning repose, and jolted the rest of the congregation to erect posture.

All eyes turned first toward Aunt Bessie, then as if on cue, to the strangers leading each other down the center aisle to the empty pews at the front of the church. An audible respiratory sucking lowered the air pressure in the auditorium a full millibar with a sound not unlike the bellows on a blacksmith's furnace drawing in air before blowing it across the coals of the fire. Then everyone swallowed and barely breathed out enough air to make a candle flicker.

Aunt Bessie pulled her feet from both shoes and with her fingers simultaneously depressed six harmonic notes corresponding to A flat ending the hymn in the same key it had started.

THE TWENTY STRANGERS filed into the second two pews on the left side of the sanctuary. Three deacons already seated on one of the pews slid to the end. The preacher looked at the Minister of Music who was already looking at him and gestured toward the pulpit. Brother Roger jumped to his feet and announced, "Let us all stand and sing hymn number nine, 'All Creatures of Our God and King.'"

The pages rustled, the organist played the introduction, and Brother Roger moved his hand in a downward chop. Five hundred voices intoned the first line which mimicked the title. In the split second between "creatures" and "of", five hundred Baptists again turned their attention to the new creatures who were still thumbing pages searching for the hymn.

Following the pastor's sermon, which lacked some of its customary bluster, Dr. Henry Stanton omitted his habitual altar call to the lost and abruptly announced, "We will now stand and sing our invitation—sorry, I mean to say, our closing hymn. Brother Roger, what's the number?"

"Let us turn over to page 181," said Brother Roger. Then he looked at Stanton, arched his eyebrows, and shrugged before saying, "And stand as we sing all the verses of, 'Who At My Door is Standing?'"

Tabernacle Baptist Church would never be the same again.

30

"Emma, did you hear about all the conversions at Tabernacle Baptist Church in Montgomery?" Susie inquired as they awaited the Monday morning school bus. The bus was late.

"What is a conversion?" Emma asked. "I don't think we have those at our church."

"A conversion is when somebody comes to Jesus," replied Susie, "and then joins the church. Everybody gets happy when people walk the aisle."

"What does 'walk the aisle' mean?"

"That's when people walk down the middle aisle in the church and take the preacher's hand."

"You mean shake it?"

"Yeah, I guess. Sometimes they hug the preacher. When somebody does, we call it a conversion. Then they're baptized. When Brother Johnny preaches in our church, lots of people do it, especially children and old people."

"Did you?" asked Emma.

"Yeah, but I can't hardly remember. I did it before I started to school."

"Was yours a conversion?" asked Emma, puzzled. Susie was a good girl like her.

"They said it was. Said I confessed I was a sinner and asked Jesus to come into my heart. The next week I was baptized. Momma said they had to put a stool in the baptismal pool for me to stand on. Have you been baptized, Emma?"

"Not yet. Didn't know I was that bad. I don't remember ever

hearing much about conversions. I think anybody who comes to our church two Sundays in a row is considered a member. Anyway, what's so special about conversions in Montgomery?"

"They were all homosexuals," replied Susie. "Twenty of them."

"Homosexuals? And they joined a Baptist church?"

"I guess they did. Hey, you know what I'm thinking?"

"I can't read your mind, but if I could, it wouldn't take long," Emma laughed.

"Do you remember what we prayed about in school a few days ago?"

"Yes, about getting some homosexuals into the Baptist church . . . that's the church! The church I saw on TV that didn't have any!"

"I'll bet our prayer had something to do with it," said Susie.

"I'm still not sure," said Emma. Again, the conversation with her daddy flashed through her mind. "Could be a coincidence, but the prayer and the conversions did come pretty close together, didn't they?"

"They sure did. We better be careful what we pray about. I believe some of it's coming true."

"I'm beginning to wonder, too," said Emma. "But we shouldn't make up our minds too quickly."

"Something crazy has also happened at our church here in Orchard Hill," said Susie.

"Did you have some conversions, too?"

"No, it was the other way around. We lost some members."

"Lost some? How?"

"The chairman of the deacons and his wife and family left the church," said Susie.

"What about? Was there an argument?"

"I don't think so. The night they left, they told our church that the Lord was leading them to change over to the Jewish faith and go to church with the Ginsbergs."

"You mean the synagogue?"

"Whatever!" Susie turned her palms up at shoulder height and arched her eyebrows. "How did you learn the big words I always get wrong?"

"I'm older than you are," said Emma.

"Just a year."

"A year and a half older," said Emma. "That's time to learn a lot."

"But we're in the same grade," said Susie.

"That's because I fell out of the tree and got started late."

"I thought that bump on the head would have made you dumb."

"I guess it jarred a lot of big words loose," said Emma. "Now listen to this . . . about the Ginsbergs. We lost a family, too! They told Reverend Gaylor they were leaving our church to go to church with the Ginsbergs."

"To the sinnergogue in Auburn?"

"Yes. To the *syn-a-gogue*." Emma stressed each syllable.

"We prayed about Jeremiah," said Susie. "Remember?"

"Yes, we did. But we didn't pray for Baptists and Unitarians to turn into Jews," responded Emma.

"Maybe God ain't got enough Jews to go around," said Susie. "Had to make some new ones."

"I'm mixed up," said Emma. "Maybe it's not coincidence."

"You're beginning to see what I see."

"Yes," said Emma. "It does look like some of it's coming true."

"I'm glad you finally see it. You'll—"

The sharp blare of the school bus horn severed the sentence.

"Are you two going to stand there all day or are you going to school?" the driver shouted through the open door.

"I'VE BEEN THINKING about what we talked about this morning," said Emma, from her perch on the first limb of the sycamore tree, to Susie in the rope swing.

"About what?" Susie shoved off.

"About some of our prayers coming true," replied Emma.

"So?"

"I'm thinking about Paco?"

"You think about him a lot, don't you?" Susie smiled.

"I do not!"

"He's Spanish."

"He's not Spanish. He's Cuban."

"Ain't that the same thing?" asked Susie.

"No. Spanish people are from Spain and Cubans from Cuba. It's two different countries on opposite sides of the world. Don't you pay attention in geography?"

"Yeah, but . . ."

"Paco's having problems."

"And you want to write another prayer," said Susie.

"I think it's time we prayed for something big." Emma extended her arms out in opposite directions and bent her fingers forward. "Something real big . . . oops!" She grabbed the limb above her and continued. "If we pray for something big, then we'll know if it's coming true. Paco left Cuba with his family three years ago. They first went to Spain, then came to Orchard Hill. A relative in Alex City had something to do with getting them over here."

"What's the problem? People come to this country all the time," said Susie.

"That's what I'm getting at. Your Uncle Stanley told us last summer that the United States has been trying to change the

Cuban government for a long time without much luck. He said that because of the embargo, or something like that, it's hard for Cuban people to get medicines and food."

"My Uncle Stanley talked about that? How do you remember all that stuff?"

"I already knew Paco so I listened to what your uncle said about Cuba."

"So what do you want to pray about?"

"I'm getting to that. Paco is a Catholic and says what we've been adding to the Governor's Prayer don't sound like prayers, but he wants us to pray for his country anyway."

"We've got to be careful about big things," said Susie. "We could mess stuff up big time."

"They're already messed up," said Emma. "That's what your Uncle Stanley said. Maybe we can straighten them out."

"What does 'barco' mean? You sure you know what Uncle Stanley was talking about?"

"He said our government had put an embargo or a barco . . . now you got me mixed up. Whatever it is, he said it was on Cuba and needed to be lifted. Maybe God can figure it out."

The next day, Emma and Susie's Alberta Jones Middle School home room class recited the following prayer:

Dear God: You probably know about the trouble between the United States and Cuba. We don't want to tell you what to do, but you might lift the "barco" or whatever it is, if it's not too heavy. Other than that, whatever you come up with, we'll back you 100 percent. Not thy will but our will be done. In your name we pray, Amen.

31

"*SEÑORES Y CABALLEROS*," came the melodious female voice over the intercom, "*dentro de diez minutes, aterrizaremos en el aeropuerto de Holguín. Por favor . . .*"

Stanley Hannah looked at his watch and then pushed the button on the armrest that brought the seat upright. He checked to make sure his seatbelt was fastened and reached under his seat for his briefcase.

"*. . . Gracias por volar con Cubano de Aviación.*"

He was always thankful when flying with *Cubano de Aviacion* —after landing.

Stanley looked out the window at the landscape sliding past. The lush vegetation of the Cuban keys had dissolved into a faded canvas of pale green patches punctuated with palm trees. An occasional highway distinguished itself by being practically free of any motorized vehicles. Even from the low altitude to which the aircraft had descended on its long approach to the airport, Cuba appeared to be uninhabited. Only the dry, cultivated fields scrolling beneath him and a sporadic farm house gave evidence of human activity.

I wish Janet could be here to see this.

As an asphalt scar materialized in the midst of the farmlands, Stanley could make out, some distance beyond it, a wooded area that had to be Holguin, the province capital. Scattered white structures timidly lifted their heads above the trees which became greener and thicker as the Russian-built Ilyushin IL-62 approached the single runway. The aircraft bumped over columns of hot air radiating upward from the parched fields. Stanley gripped the armrests. A hundred thousand frequent flyer miles had not inoculated him from the stomach flutters produced by turbulence at low altitudes. He hoped the Russian economic crisis had not affected the safety of the planes they built.

This was Stanley's first visit to the eastern provinces of the 750-mile long island. Since the collapse of the Russian/Cuban partnership, the pro-Cuban Baptist Alliance for Progress, of which he was the Executive Secretary, had established a regular schedule for delivering humanitarian goods, especially medical supplies, to churches, schools, and hospitals in the west. The hold of this aircraft cradled a half-ton of over-the-counter drugs.

The enactment by Congress of the Helms-Burton Act in 1995, had initially caused difficulties in his operations. Were it not for the behind-the-scenes pro-Cuban policies of certain high-level administrators in Washington, his work would be at worst impossible and at best legally inadvisable. Even with the good graces of the Department of Treasury that authorized the trips, everything had to be done in a surreptitious, convoluted manner to keep from irritating Congress and attracting the attention of the press and the anti-Castro Cuban exiles of southern Florida. Red tape and more red tape. But he was here. As the plane bounced onto the runway, Stanley thought, *God and Congress work in mysterious ways.*

His Baptist Alliance for Progress, a liberal spin-off from the Southern Baptist Convention, had contact with Cuban Baptists in Havana—on the western end of the island. This was his first visit to Holguin, near the Sierra Nevada mountains where Castro had begun his successful uprising in 1959—and not far from Guantanamo, the anachronistic American naval base occupying Cuban soil. Although he succeeded in taking advantage of the trip to bring needed medical supplies, he was apprehensive. This time he did not expect to see familiar Cuban Baptist faces. A cryptic letter from a Señor Roberto Paz portended a different kind of encounter.

Stanley relaxed his grip on the armrest as the Ilyushin braked and taxied toward the terminal. Inside, long lines formed and stagnated at passport control.

"*Señor Ahnah, Señor Estahnlee Ahnah.*" Recognizing the labored Spanish pronunciation of his name, Stanley looked in the direction of the voice and waved his passport. A green-fatigued official motioned for him to come to the front of the queues.

"*Bienvenido a Cuba, Señor Ahnah,*" said the official. Then in heavily accented English he said, "Velcome to Cooba. Ve ah deelighted to áve you een ouwer beeutiful cointry."

Stanley reached for an extended hand. "*Gracias Señor ah . . .*"

"Paz, Roberto Paz, *Delegado Provincial del Instituto Cubano de Amistad con los Pueblos.* Welcome to Cuba."

"*Mucho gusto,*" Stanley continued.

"The pleasure is mine," responded Paz in Spanish. "Your personal luggage has been expedited through customs. Your shipment of medical and humanitarian supplies will be delivered this afternoon to our provincial headquarters. Please follow me. Someone is anxious to see you." A Russian-built Skoda with driver waited at the curb outside the terminal.

The Institute of Cuban Friendship with the Nations was a two-story stucco home located in what was once a plush residential neighborhood of well-to-do citizens of Holguin. It was still a residential neighborhood of citizens but no longer plush and no longer well-to-do. The revolution had redistributed the wealth, Stanley observed silently, but in the redistribution there had not been enough to go around.

Armed guards stood at the door of the *Instituto* as Stanley and

Paz arrived. But nothing prepared Stanley for the presence of the imposing bearded figure in military fatigues standing before him as he entered the entrance hall of the house.

32

"I GOT SOMETHING to tell you, Susie!" said Emma as they walked toward the playground swings.

"What's up?" said Susie.

"Katasha, Paco, and Jeremiah want to help with the prayers. They said anything to you?" Emma sat on a swing.

Susie took an adjacent swing and pushed off. "Yeah. Jeremiah asked me where we got the prayers. He's so cute!"

"Did you tell him?" Emma watched Susie swing higher and higher.

"Of course, I didn't! You ever told a boy he's cute?"

"Not that. I meant did you tell him we write them down?"

"Yeah," shouted Susie.

"And . . ."

"He didn't believe me. So I said he could help write the next one. That okay?"

"Cool!" responded Emma. "I'll tell them. When do you want to meet?"

"It don't matter to me," said Susie. "Anytime after school."

"What about tomorrow?"

"Where?" Susie's excitement blossomed.

Emma jumped and grabbed the chain as Susie's swing passed her on the forward arc. The swing stopped and Susie sailed onto the grass barely maintaining her equilibrium.

"Emma Wedgwood! You thought you had me, didn't you. I'm fast since I been running track."

"You surprised me. Let's meet at Daddy's restaurant. The bus can drop us off there and Daddy can take everybody home later."

"Whatever. Now, leave my swing alone." Susie sat and pushed off again.

At that moment the bell rang and both girls joined the rush back to class.

FIVE BRIGHT-EYED fifth-graders elbowed and shuffled to create space around a table in the back corner of the Wedgwood Restaurant. An aura of intrigue and excitement energized the quintet. Besides Emma and Susie, there was Paco, the Cuban student, Jeremiah, the Jewish boy, and Katasha, whose Aunt Sharika was an OB-GYN in Montgomery. Susie squirmed in next to Jeremiah while Emma squeezed in between Paco and Katasha.

"*Vaya!*" Paco exclaimed. "This seem to me like planning a *golpe de estado.*"

"What's a 'gulpy distayo'?" asked Susie.

"It means to turn over the government," said Paco, not certain he said it right.

"You mean overthrow the government," said Emma, remembering something she had studied in Civics class.

"I don't speak Spanish yet," said Susie. "If I write the prayers, you'll have to speak English."

"I'll try," said Paco. "I think in Spanish, and it come out funny in English."

"If you want to speak in foreign languages," said Jeremiah, "I'll throw in a little Yiddish."

"And I'll add some kiddish," said Emma. "Now, let's get on with the meeting. You know what we are trying to do?"

"*Sí,*" replied Paco. "We're trying to stir up things."

"Right on," exclaimed Jeremiah. " We're going to call down fire from heaven on the gentiles."

"Who are the gentiles?" asked Emma.

"That's everybody who's not a Jew," replied Jeremiah.

"That's us," said Susie.

"Oops," said Jeremiah, then added, "We're going after the bad gentiles. You understand?"

"Not exactly," said Emma. "You tell them, Susie."

"We don't go after people in the prayers," said Susie. "We help people. Now, I've been thinking that—"

"You're dangerous when you think," said Emma.

"Cut it out, Emma! I've been thinking we ought to do a prayer about more things at school. Paint's flaking off the walls so bad that every time a train goes by, it snows on our desks."

"Our toilet stinks,"said Jeremiah holding his nose. "Smells worse than the food in the cafeteria."

"The septic tanks are running over," added Susie. "The stinking mess runs like a creek under the fifth-grade trailers."

Suddenly, conversation ceased.

"Oh, Daddy," said Emma as Mr. Wedgwood set a tray of sodas on the table. "You're the sweetest daddy in the whole world."

"Thought you might get thirsty with all that talking," he replied. "What are you folks talking about?"

"Just kid stuff," said Emma.

"Yeah. Just kid stuff," said Susie.

When her father returned to the kitchen and everyone grabbed a soda, Emma said, "I thought the school board took care of those things. Somebody could get sick, real sick."

"Momma said the PTO sent a letter directly to Governor Forbe," said Susie. "He wrote back that God will provide."

"Maybe God *will* provide," said Emma.

"Some strange things have been happening since we started adding on to the Governor's Prayer," said Susie.

"Let's get to work," said Emma. "Go ahead, Susie. You know how to write the prayers."

"Nah. I been writing all the prayers. Let somebody else do it now."

Katasha spoke for the first time. "I'll do it." She reached for the pen and paper as Susie slid them across the table.

The ad hoc committee offered suggestions as Katasha wrote.

"There's the flaky paint."

"And the smelly bathrooms."

"*Y las cloacas desbordadas.*"

"What did you say?" Eight eyeballs turned toward Paco.

"*Lo siento*—I mean, me sorry. The sewage over runs."

"That's better," said Susie.

"Don't forget the shaky trailers," said Emma. "We always have to go into the main building when there's a storm coming."

Katasha read the list back to the others.

"We're forgetting something," said Emma. "There's stuff more important than painting the school and fixing toilets."

"And what could that be?" asked Jeremiah.

"*Si, ¿qué?*" asked Paco.

"The teachers," said Emma.

"What about the teachers?" asked Susie.

"The teachers don't get paid much," said Emma.

"How do you know?" asked Paco.

"Look at Mrs. Haley's car," said Emma. "It's an old green bent-up car—must be fifty years old."

"Maybe she likes old cars," said Jeremiah. "Lotsa people like old, antique cars. You see what I mean?"

"Who ever heard of an antique Toyota," said Emma. "She drives an old car 'cause she can't afford a new—"

"That's enough about old cars," said Susie. "It might be hard to get money for teachers."

"Why?" said Jeremiah.

"Cause Governor Forbe said on television last week that teacher pay was frozen."

"Oh he did, did he?" said Emma with a mischievous gleam in her eye. "Let's put it in a prayer. Maybe we can unfreeze it."

"Where they going to get the money for these things?" inquired Jeremiah.

"Who cares?" said Susie.

"They get it from taxes," said Katasha as she looked up from the paper on which she had been furiously writing. "The money the government spends comes from taxes."

"And where come from the taxes?" asked Paco.

"From the taxpayers," replied Katasha. "And the payers are our mothers and daddies."

"How do you know so much about taxes?" asked Susie.

"Because my daddy is a county commissioner. He talks about it all the time," replied Katasha.

"Wait a minute," said Emma. "If they raise taxes, it could make a lot of people mad."

"They don't have to raise taxes," said Jeremiah.

"Then were's the money going to come from?" asked Katasha.

"Why should they raise taxes?" continued Jeremiah. "The government already collects lots of money. You see what I mean?"

"They collect it and they spend it," said Emma.

Jeremiah continued. "They spend it on stuff . . . you know, new roads, and stuff and to pay government salaries."

"What are you trying to say, Jeremiah? We know all that," said Katasha.

"If the senators lowered their own pay, they could raise the teacher pay. You see what I mean? That way they wouldn't have to raise taxes."

"What make you think they do that?" asked Paco in his best English.

"We can fix it up good in the prayer," said Susie.

"Senator pay cuts could make a lot of people mad," cautioned Katasha.

"Yeah," replied Jeremiah. "But not as many as when you raise taxes. You know what I mean?"

"That's right," said Emma. "When we write the prayer, let's make sure God understands what we mean when we say, 'No more taxes'."

"Let's get with it," said Susie.

"Not yet," said Emma. "Let's talk about some other stuff."

"Like what?" asked Jeremiah.

"New desks?" asked Susie.

"No," replied Emma. "Let's talk about world stuff. We mostly been praying about Alabama and Orchard Hill. You think that's all there is?"

"There was Cuba prayer but nothing happen," said Paco.

"You're right," said Jeremiah. "Maybe we should stick with small stuff."

"Naw!" Susie disagreed. "We been studying about Asia. There's lots of problems over there."

"Yeah, I agree," said Jeremiah. "And the Middle East? Us and the Arabs been fighting for years. Maybe we could stop it."

"I've seen on the news that there's fighting in Asia and Africa and somewhere I can't even pronounce," said Emma. "Why don't we put those places in our prayer?"

"What about *inocentes* in prison?" asked Paco. "There are *inocentes* in prison in Cuba."

"What's that?" asked Susie.

"You know. *Ino* . . . Innocent . . . innocent people," he stammered, "like in Cuba."

"There are innocent people in prison in Israel," said Jeremiah. "Jews and Arabs."

"There are innocent men and women in prison in Alabama," exclaimed Emma. "I saw on TV that they are running tests and finding some prisoners aren't guilty."

"It not just Alabama, or Cuba, or Israel. It all over world," said Paco. "If we write prayer about prisoners, why we not include whole world?"

Emma raised both hands. "There's one more big problem. It's AIDS. Y'all remember Henry—Henry Carmichael?"

"Yes, that was terrible," said Katasha.

"He's a Homo sapien and got AIDS from blood confusion," said Susie.

"He's no Homo sapien. He's a hemophiliac," said Emma. "Henry was a hemophiliac and that's why he needed the confusions . . .Susie! You got me mixed up. He caught AIDS from a *transfusion* and died."

"There's no cure for AIDS," said Katasha.

"We can put it in a prayer, anyway," said Emma. "Now, what else?"

"If we think of anything else, I'll have to get some more paper," said Katasha.

"We've got more than we can chew," added Jeremiah.

"We may have more than God can chew," said Emma. "It'll be suppertime soon. We'd better get it all together."

"I've got a lot here." Katasha looked up from her notebook. "I've been taking notes like I do in school."

"Read it to us," said Susie. "Just the main points."

Katasha looked at her notes. "The main things are, school problems in Alabama, peace in the world, free innocent prisoners, and the AIDS problem."

"Good, Katasha!" said Emma. "You wrote down everything

we said. No wonder you make such good grades."

"Can God handle all that stuff in one prayer or should we give it to him a little at the time?" asked Jeremiah.

"We'd better write more than one prayer and spread it out. God might get upset if we send all this stuff in at once," said Susie.

Thirty minutes later, Mr. Wedgwood again walked up. "Girls and boys, I think it's about time I took you home."

"Just five more minutes," said Emma, "and we'll be through."

"Fine. Five more minutes. I don't want any of you to miss supper."

FOR THE NEXT several mornings at the Alberta Jones school, Mrs. Haley raised her eyebrows and sighed as the students recited the following prayers:

> Dear God: You probably haven't been near our school lately or you would have noticed the stink. Would you please get the governor to fix the toilets and septic tanks, paint the school, build some permanent classrooms, and raise the teacher pay? And while you're at it, why not do it for all the schools in Alabama, without raising taxes—that's important. Not thy will but our will be done. In your name we pray, Amen.

> Dear God: Please get them to quit fighting in Asia, Africa, and other places. It seems that all the money spent killing other people could be spent helping everybody live better. While you're at it, why not stop wars everywhere . . .

> Dear God: If people have to die, let it be from eating too much ice cream or banana pudding—not from AIDS. Why don't you try to fix AIDS? You did a good job with polio and smallpox. While you're at it, why don't you make everybody that's sick get well . . .

Dear God: We heard our preacher read in your Book where you set the prisoners free. Now we don't want prisoners turned loose that might hurt somebody, but if you can figure out who the innocent prisoners are, why don't you turn them loose. While you're at it, straighten out the bad ones and send them home, too. Not thy will but our will be done. In your name we pray, Amen.

33

THE COOL OFFICE air did not keep Forbe from swabbing the sweat from his forehead. "There is no way another school spending bill will get through the House, Dick, much less the Senate."

Dick replied. "An altruistic virus has infected the lawmakers of this state. I've never seen senators and representatives, Democrat or Republican, argue like this. They aren't arguing for and against the bill. They're all for it."

"For it? How can any damn Republican worth his PAC check be for it?" Forbe shouted.

"Calm down, Jimbo! Get control of yourself!"

"I am in control." Forbe lowered his voice a few decibels. "It's the damn politicians that are out of control. You haven't answered my question."

"They're for it because the Alabama voters are for it. Letters, e-mails, phone calls, and faxes applaud it. Everybody wants the schools brought up to national standards in sanitation, safety, aesthetics, academics, and they want teacher salaries raised. The lawmakers are afraid that if they don't support it, there'll be a taxpayer revolt like in California."

"Has this thing hit the national media yet?" Forbe asked.

"Not yet, but when it does, we're going to look like idiots again."

"Like when that simian we had for a governor danced around the stage like a monkey to poke fun at evolution?" Forbe scratched his ribs with his elbows in the air.

"Yeah. Fob James back in '95 at that school board meeting."

Forbe warmed up. "And when that governor wannabe peed in that jug on the Senate floor?"

Little shook his head in disgust. "Yep. Lt. Governor Windom trying to hang on to his powers couldn't hold his kidneys and wouldn't give up the gavel."

"The state house was a zoo til I took over."

Little opened his mouth, then shut it without speaking.

"Were you gonna say something?" asked Forbe.

Dick shook his head. "No. Not right now."

"Barbara Willis must have found a scandal elsewhere," Forbe muttered. "What's the price tag?"

"You don't want to know."

"I guess your brother, Patrick, introduced the bill."

"I'm afraid so. But if he hadn't, someone else would have. This issue is on a roll."

"If they're all for it, what the hell are they arguing about? The damn debate is in its third day."

"Until this morning, they were debating whether to finance the school budget by floating a new bond issue or cutting unnecessary state expenditures."

"Unnecessary expenditures? That's a good one!" Forbe leaned back and laughed. He shifted his eyes toward Little without turning his head. "What expenditures?"

"Among other things, state lawmaker and administrator salaries, including the governor's," replied Dick.

"They can't cut salaries. They're locked in."

"Not any longer. This morning, by a two-thirds majority, the senate set them free. Both houses favor funding the budget by reducing waste and cutting salaries."

"They can't do that, dammit!" Forbe said as he stood up and walked to the window. *This is impossible. Cutting wages, putting the whole budget into the schools.*

"Well, Jimbo, they did, and that's not all. The Finance Sub-Committee reports that the bill will not generate enough funds to get the job done. So the lawmakers have suggested volunteer work crews among state employees to do some of the work at the schools."

Forbe stared at his assistant. "That is the most preposterous thing I've ever heard. What fool would enlist in some nitwit Alabama Peace Corps?"

"That's the name that's being tossed around, Jimbo, except for the 'nitwit.' Some have even suggested that the Alabama Peace Corps would get a colossal send off if you were the first volunteer."

"Oh my God. I'm the goddamn governor, Dick! I don't dig ditches or repair parks. It'll be a cold day in hell before I put on a workshirt and paint some run-down school. Don't let the door hit your ass on your way out. I've got some work to do."

Dick did not move. "That Fort Rucker committee is still in the lobby. They say they won't leave until they speak with you again."

"Hold them off. I won't meet with another damn soul today. I'm exhausted." Forbe returned to his desk and sank into his chair.

"I'm doing the best I can, but the Rucker delegation is persistent. I don't know what to do with them. I know you met with them this morning about the base closing but they say they're not leaving until they get an answer."

"I can't believe they're still here. It's 4 o'clock. I've got nothing more to say to them."

Dick still didn't leave. "It's a sit-in," he said.

"I told them I'd do what I could to ease the impact of the closing. What more do they want?"

"They want the specifics," said Dick. "They know it has to close. They want to know whether you will back the projects they are proposing."

"Tell'em to go home and I'll back anything they say."

"Converting Rucker to a state park, bringing in Six Flags over Alabama, and building the golf courses?"

"Not those damn golf courses. The golf course money went for school computers. Have you already forgot?"

"They said they're not leaving until you agree to talk with them again."

"Tell them I'll meet with them in Enterprise next week. Tell them anything to get them out of my thinning hair. You'd think they owned this place."

"In a way they do, Governor. They're taxpayers. I'll do what I can." Dick turned and walked out the door, leaving Forbe alone.

So this is being governor, he thought as he swiveled his chair. *Headaches, hassles, never enough money, a potential scandal around every corner. Why do we do it? What's the point?* He glanced around his office, at the rug and drapes and mahogany desk, and leaned all the way back in his chair, exhaling a deep breath.

"Why did peace break out during my term?" He said into the silence. *With the base closings, former civilian employees are looking for jobs, and our arms and munitions plants are losing their markets. Those Arabs, Jews, and Africans have been fighting for centuries. Why the hell did they have to quit before the next election?* Forbe picked up his briefcase and left his office by the back door. A state trooper escorted him to the pull-through where the chauffeur had his car waiting.

"Home, Willy," said Forbe to his driver. "Thank God, it's Friday."

34

"HI THERE, BARBARA!"

Barbara Willis looked around and spotted a thirtyish, bespectacled school teacher type waving at her from a textbook exhibit at the World Congress Center in downtown Atlanta.

"I haven't seen you for ages," said Irene.

Recognition flooded in. "Irene, I almost didn't place you. Your hair's shorter. You're looking good." *And older,* Barbara thought. *And we're the same age.*

"Your hair's longer and as blonde as ever," responded Irene. "You look—" she paused, "more mature. You still with the *Post-Herald?*"

"No. I'm here in Atlanta now, with the *Atlanta Journal-Constitution.* You still teaching in Auburn?"

"No. I'm in Orchard Hill," replied Irene, then added, "in Tallapoosa County."

Barbara looked at her watch. "If you've got a moment, let's walk over to the snack bar and do some catching up."

"I was going to suggest the same thing," said Irene.

"I haven't seen you since graduation," said Barbara as they paid for drinks and sat at a nearby table.

"It's been ten years," said Irene. "I love your pants suit."

"Tell me more about yourself, your work. My, it's good to see you. What about Daniel Haley. Did you marry him?"

"Yes, I did. Daniel runs the Paella Restaurant in Alex City."

"I like Mexican food," said Barbara.

"It's not Mexican. It's Spanish-Mediterranean cuisine. Daniel fell in love with Spanish cooking when he was an exchange student at the University of Salamanca in Spain."

"Do the people in Alex City go for it?" asked Barbara.

"All but the Mexicans." Irene smiled.

"I'll have to try it sometime when I'm in the neighborhood. I haven't been in Alabama since the election."

"You married?" asked Irene.

"No. I don't have time for a husband. The paper keeps me too busy." Barbara dropped her head slightly and took a deep breath. She decided to keep the conversation focused on Irene. "Children?"

"None of my own, but I have thirty plus at school."

"Anything going on?" asked Barbara. "I've been so busy on other assignments, I lost track of James Forbe. How's that prayer thing going?"

"I haven't heard of anything outside of Orchard Hill. But, in my classroom, the kids recite cutely worded prayers that they make up."

"How's that?"

"As you may know, the state gave us an official prayer, but one morning, a fifth-grader brought a short prayer to me and asked me if I'd write it on the blackboard so the class could recite it. She told me that she and a fellow classmate wrote it. It was obvious they had."

"Any law against it?"

"Not that I know of—and I liked the prayer. I put it on the board and after reciting the official prayer, the class read the add-on petitions. Since then, the kids have brought several more."

"The opponents of school prayer in Georgia claim that nothing good can come from mixing school with religion," said Barbara.

"That was my exact sentiment before the governor pushed

his bill through," said Irene. "Now, I'm having second thoughts about it."

"You think school prayer *is* a good thing?"

"No, I haven't changed my mind about that. The Alabama prayer is sectarian and in Orchard Hill bullies have harassed some non-Christian children because of it. But the add-on petitions are something else."

"What do you mean?" Barbara asked, her journalistic hormones kicking in. She pulled a writing pad and pen from her satchel.

"I can't be sure, but I think some of them—now don't take me for a religious nut—I'm almost certain some of the prayers are being answered."

"Go on. What makes you think they're being answered?"

"I can't be sure. I hadn't thought much about them, other than to smile at their innocence and simplicity, until I talked with Susie a few weeks ago. The child was utterly convinced that the prayers are being answered."

"Sounds like kid stuff. Did she cite examples?"

Irene paused, the said, "She told me of several people, mostly from the community, who recovered from illnesses soon after being prayed for at school. They even prayed for the governor's wife and are convinced that's why she got well."

Barbara shrugged. "Religious people claim that all the time."

Irene continued. "I know. I wasn't inclined to believe it at first, although I didn't tell Susie so. Then, a few weeks ago, she handed me a prayer asking for computers for Alabama schools. I told her that I didn't think the prayer was—what did I say—realistic. I didn't want the children to pray about something so tangible and measurable that they would be disappointed when it didn't happen."

"But you put the prayer on the blackboard anyway?"

"Yes. I couldn't bring myself to pour cold logic onto the flame of unpretentious, innocent faith."

"What happened?" Barbara asked, leaning forward.

"We now have new state-of-the-art computers in our classrooms in Orchard Hill and, as far as I know, in every public school in Alabama." Irene paused, then continued. "The funding was appropriated by the conservative-Democratic legislature over the Republican governor's veto."

"Wow!" Barbara scribbled on her writing pad. "That's something. To connect the computers with prayer sounds a little far out, yet . . ."

"I don't understand the workings of Alabama politics. I don't think anybody does. Maybe, we would've gotten computers anyway. All the same . . ." Irene again trailed off ending with a slight inflection.

"You have copies of the prayers?"

"Yes. I started to throw them away, then for some reason stuck them in a desk drawer. Since the computer prayer, there have been several more."

"On what themes?"

"The children have escalated their petitions."

"Escalated?"

"They have recently prayed for AIDS victims, homosexuals, world peace, broken toilets, teacher salaries, and prisoners— surprising subjects for children."

"Big time." Barbara continued to scribble on her notepad. "They sound like angels."

"More children are becoming involved in producing the prayers," said Irene.

"Would you give me a copy of them? I'd like to do a little investigating."

"I'll be glad to. Do you agree there might be a connection?"

"I'm a reporter, Irene. Whether there's a connection or not, I smell a story."

"You're not going to use names, are you?"

"Certainly not, at least not without permission. Give me your phone number so I can be in touch. And could you give me the names of some people you think might have an angle on the subject?"

"Let me have your phone number," said Irene. "I'll check with some people and get back with you."

"Here's my card. I'll look forward to hearing from you soon." Barbara looked at her watch. "Darn! I have an appointment at CNN in ten minutes. I've got to run."

"It's been good seeing you. I hope our paths cross again soon," said Irene. "Here's my card."

Barbara took the card. "I have a feeling they will. Bye, bye." Barbara hurried toward the exit and the CNN studios down the street.

As she left the CNN building an hour later she returned to her office and accessed the *AJC* archives on her computer. After a few minutes, she closed the file, and jotted down the name, "Brother Johnny Carroll," and the note, "Forbe's religious adviser during the campaign." Then she checked the on-line white pages, and after making a phone call, said out loud, "Alabama, here I come."

35

"Emma, Emma, have you heard?" Susie shouted as she ran out of her house toward the sycamore tree next door where Emma sat doing her homework. "Come on down! I've got stuff to tell you."

"Can't you see I'm studying?"

"Come down! You won't believe it. I saw it on TV."

Emma pitched her books down and swung to the ground. "Okay, what's up."

"Our school's gonna be fixed, the teachers get a pay raise, and we're going to get a new middle school building in place of the trailers. It's on the news. Come on! Hurry before it goes off."

"We repeat our top story," said the anchor of the WSFA Six o'clock Report, "The legislature approved a multimillion dollar package for Alabama schools."

"It's not just for our school. It's everywhere. I can't hardly believe it," cried Susie.

The news anchor continued. "This has been an unprecedented year for Alabama public schools. The comprehensive package of expenditures, which includes capital improvements and teacher pay increases, comes on the heels of a million-dollar computer funding bill approved a short while ago. Attempts to speak with Governor Forbe have been . . ."

"Our school is going to be fixed," said Emma.

"Yeah, and I bet Mrs. Haley will be happy," said Susie.

"Did they say when they're going to start?"

"I don't know. The TV said the governor's going to send out

work teams to help fix the schools and he's going to go with one of the teams."

"Wouldn't it be fun if the governor came to Orchard Hill," said Emma.

Susie made a face and pinched her nose. "Yeah, and fixed those smelly toilets."

36

THE LONG SERVICE ended and the preacher began the rounds of his gathered flock. Most stood up but a few remained in wheelchairs as Brother Johnny circulated among them shaking hands and giving words of encouragement. An attractive blonde approached him.

"Hello, sir, you must be the good Brother Johnny Carroll." Barbara Willis reached for the hand of the bowed man standing before her. She thought she saw in his eyes a glimmer of recognition.

"'Why callest thou me good? There is none good but one, that is, God,' Mark 10:18. I am but one of His humble servants." Johnny looked up, pointed heavenward with his index finger, and added, "Praise the Lord."

The sermon had been a medley of scripture quotations and religious words. Barbara tried to mimic the jargon. "Do you serve these senior citizens?"

"'Thou shalt worship the Lord thy God, and Him only shalt thou serve.' Luke 4:8." Johnny again pointed up. "I only serve Jesus and try to walk in his paths."

Barbara tried to see over the wall of scripture. There seemed to be someone behind it. "These people appear to love you."

"'He that loveth not knoweth not God; for God is love,' First John 4:8," Johnny added another brick to the rising barrier of sacred words.

"I've heard about your work," Barbara tried again. "God is using you to help these folks."

"God helps those who help—who am I speaking to?"

"I'm sorry. Pardon me for not introducing myself sooner. I'm Barbara Willis, with the *Atlanta Journal-Constitution*."

"It's good to meet you, Mrs. Willis." Johnny gave her a vigorous handshake. "What brings you to Dadeville?"

"It's Miss Willis, or you may call me 'Barbara' if you like. I'd like to discuss with you the subject of prayer. Is there somewhere we can talk?"

"'Let no corrupt communication proceed out of your mouth,' Ephesians 4:29. When I take leave of these dear ones, we can meet in the lobby."

Barbara watched as Brother Johnny continued to shake the hand or pat the shoulder of every person in the day-room chapel before returning to where she stood. She could tell by the expressions on the faces around her that these people truly loved him.

"I don't have an office, but I'm sure we can find a quiet corner in the lobby." He guided her out of the activities room. "Will this be okay?"

"Yes, thank you." Barbara sat on a worn couch, careful to pull her skirt over her knees. She preferred to wear slacks or jeans but had been warned by a friend in Montgomery that Brother Johnny did not take well to women who wore men's clothing.

"The disciples said to Jesus, 'Lord, teach us to pray,' Luke 11:1," said Brother Johnny as he sat down opposite her.

He's certainly consistent, she thought.

As he sat, she saw his eyes shift toward her knees, then quickly to her eyes as she stared directly into his. He briefly closed his and took a deep breath. *There is a human being behind the holy wall,* thought Barbara. "What do you think of the prayer amendment?"

"The Lord will tell me what to say."

Barbara attempted to peep over the wall again. "I had hoped you could share *your* feelings."

"My feelings aren't worth much, but if that's what you want, I'll do the best I can."

Barbara repeated, "What do *you* think of the Prayer Amendment? You."

"It let God back in the schools. Praise the Lord for great men like James Forbe."

"Have you noticed any changes in the schools?"

"What do you mean?"

"I mean, since God returned, have the children changed? Have the schools changed?"

"I'm sure God is working quietly like the yeast that leavens the dough," said Brother Johnny.

"Are you familiar with the content of the school prayer?" asked Barbara.

"I saw it in the paper when it was passed. It's a weak prayer but the governor had to be careful not to offend the ACLU."

"Offend the American Civil Liberties Union?"

"Yes. The godless ACLU is coiled like a Satanic serpent ready to strike at any attempt to spread God's word," Johnny said, frowning.

Barbara thought it best not to pursue that angle any further. "Did you know that the children are adding their own prayers to the official prayer?"

"'Out of the mouth of babes and sucklings thou hast perfected praise,' Matthew 21:16. Children can do righteous things."

"Do you think God might answer some of their prayers?"

"God answers *all* of their prayers! There is no prayer God does not answer."

"You mean, God gives them everything they ask for?"

"I didn't say that, Miss Willis. You're putting words in my

mouth. I said that God answers. Sometimes he says, 'No!' to our petitions."

"Why would God ever say, 'No!'"

"If he gave us everything we asked for, we would be in serious trouble. God says, 'Ye ask, and receive not, because ye ask amiss, that ye may consume it upon your lusts,' James 4:3.'"

"These children are ten, eleven, twelve-year-olds," said Willis.

"At that age they are more likely to ask amiss. They do not yet understand the ways of Almighty God."

"Yet, you indicated earlier that they could conceivably ask for something good. What if they ask God to heal someone who is ill?"

"That is no guarantee their prayer would be answered. 'My thoughts are not your thoughts, neither are your ways my ways, saith the Lord.' Isaiah 55:8. We only see part of the picture. God sees it all. Only He knows what is best, and it may not be what we ask."

Barbara stood. "It's been good talking with you, Brother Johnny. I appreciate the light you have shed on my investigation." *Now I know why Baptist preachers spend three years in theological training. They're memorizing the Bible.*

"I'm glad to be of assistance. 'Thy word is a lamp unto my feet and a light unto my path,' Psalm 119:105." Johnny rose.

Barbara shook his hand, then walked toward the door of the lobby. Before she opened it, she glanced back at where she had left Brother Johnny standing, but she only saw a wall.

37

"THERE HE IS, Jeremiah. There's the governor. Let's go talk to him," said Susie.

"You sure he's the governor?"

"Sure, I'm sure. See how he keeps wiping his forehead? I saw him on TV."

"Think it'll be okay to talk to him?"

"Sure, come on. Don't be a fraidy-cat!"

Jeremiah hesitated, but then followed her toward the steps where the governor and some other men were seated in the shade. Susie's courage faltered as she neared the men. She almost turned away until she sensed Jeremiah near her. The governor looked hot and tired. "Hhhello . . . uh . . . Governor Forbe. I'm Susie and this is Jeremiah."

"Hello, Susie and Jeremiah. That's a nice tan you have there, young man."

"It's not a tan, Mr. Governor. It's the color of my skin," said Jeremiah.

"Oh, I see. Just the same, it's a nice color," said Forbe.

"Yours, too, Mr. Governor," replied Jeremiah.

"My what?"

"Your white skin. It's a nice color."

"Thank you," responded Forbe.

Susie screwed up her courage and waded in. "We're glad you came to Orchard Hill, Governor. Are you having a good time?"

"Out of this world," said Forbe. "I know of nowhere I'd rather be."

"That's good," said Susie, not sure if the governor was sincere. He didn't look too happy. "We knew you'd do it."

"How's that, young lady?"

"We knew you would do it. We prayed in our class that you'd fix the toil . . . the plumbing. But we didn't mean you had to do it yourself."

"Well, here I am." Forbe gestured with open palms.

"I guess God wanted you to see how bad it really was," said Susie.

"I'm glad you've been praying in your school," said Forbe. "That's a good prayer, isn't it?"

"Well, . . . sir . . . uh . . . Mr. Governor, we added our own prayer." Susie feared she had goofed by spilling their secret.

"Your own prayer? And how's that, my little one? My prayer wasn't good enough?"

"Oh, your prayer was fine, Governor Forbe. But it didn't say nothing about . . . you know . . . real stuff. It was too genital."

"It was what?"

"Too, general, Mr. Governor. Too general," said Jeremiah.

"Tell him what happened to you, Jeremiah," said Susie.

Jeremiah darted his eyes at Susie and waved his hand in short strokes.

"Go ahead, Jeremiah. I won't bite you," said Forbe. "With the smell of that sewer in my nose, I don't have an appetite yet."

Susie watched as the governor cut his eyes toward an attractive blonde lady who eased up within hearing distance. She thought she saw him flinch.

"I was beat up by some boys because I didn't pray the prayer, Mr. Governor."

Forbe looked up at Jeremiah. "I'm sorry to hear that. You okay now?"

"Yes, sir. I'm all right, now that the kids in my class prayed about it. You see what I mean?"

'Not exactly. What do you mean when you say you prayed about it?"

"Jeremiah's a Jew," said Susie. "He was the only Jewish kid in the school. And the prayer wasn't Jewish so he couldn't pray—"

"Wait a minute, just a minute," Forbe interrupted. "You kids made up a Jewish prayer for your school?"

"No, sir. We said a prayer to get more Jews and we got them," answered Susie.

"You got what?"

"We got more Jews in the school and now the bullies don't gang up on Jeremiah," said Susie.

"Well, that's just jim dandy." Forbe said as he pulled out his handkerchief and wiped his forehead again. "Don't you think you ought to head back toward your class?"

"Yes, sir. It's about time for the bell." Susie saw Forbe again look sideways but the blonde lady was no longer there.

As Susie and Jeremiah walked toward the row of temporary class rooms, the lady who had been standing nearby stood in front of them. Susie had never seen her before today.

"I couldn't help but overhear you talking with the governor. I'm Barbara Willis, a reporter with the *Atlanta Journal-Constitution* and a friend of Mrs. Haley."

"Pleased to meet you. I'm Susie and this is Jeremiah."

"Hello, Jeremiah. I believe the governor was getting a little nervous."

"I was getting nervous, too."

"Susie, do you think your parents would mind if we met after school and chatted awhile?" asked Barbara.

"What about?"

"About what you were discussing with the governor—the school prayers."

"You want to talk about the school prayers? Which ones?"

"Your prayers. Your teacher told me a little about them. I'd like to learn more."

"I guess it would be okay. Could my friend, Emma, meet with us? We write the prayers together."

"Why, certainly. I would prefer to talk with you both. Where can we meet?"

"We can meet under the sycamore tree in Emma's yard next door if it's okay with our parents."

"I'll have Mrs. Haley clear it with your parents. How can I find the sycamore tree?"

"Oh! There's only one in town and it's on Sycamore Street. You're not from here, are you?"

"No. I live in Atlanta."

Susie said, "My address is number twelve, Sycamore. It's the house with the white columns around the porch."

Barbara wrote it down. "I'll see you this afternoon."

"There's the bell. End of recess. Got to go in. Bye."

"Bye, bye. See you later." Barbara watched as Susie grabbed Jeremiah's hand and pulled him up the steps into one of the classroom trailers.

38

BARBARA HAD ONE more call to make before meeting with the children. The Reverend Janet Gaylor had not been easy to track down. Like many Unitarian ministers in the South, she did not live in the community where her church was located, but rather in Alex City where she directed an abused women and children's shelter.

A single secretary-receptionist occupied the spartan office of AWAKE located in an old downtown furniture store across from Court Square. In smaller letters, the sign on the outside spelled out the acronym: *Abused Women and Kids Endeavor.*

"I have an appointment with the Reverend Janet Gaylor."

Barbara could not drag her eyes away from the scar that pulled the woman's left eye toward the base of her ear on a once attractive face. Several other women, some with children, filled the reception area.

"You must be Ms. Willis from the paper. Janet is expecting you. Right through that door."

Barbara did not move.

"Battle scars," said the receptionist.

"Oh, I'm sorry, I'm terribly sorry. How insensitive of me to—"

"Not to worry," the receptionist interrupted. "I'm used to it. By the way, my name is June, June Gaylor."

"Are you related to Reverend Gaylor?"

"Janet is my sister. I'm the reason she started this agency— me and Siegfried, the Hun. There she is."

"Hi, I'm Janet," said a pretty brunette in a business suit standing in the door of the inner office. "I see you've met my sister."

"Yes, I have, Reverend Gaylor."

"Call me, Janet. And you are Ms. Willis from the *Journal-Constitution.*"

"Yes. I'm so pleased that you took time to see me. But shouldn't I wait my turn?"

"No problem. Most of these ladies have appointments with our counselors. Come on in."

Barbara stepped into a rather large office. Instead of a desk, the room had a small sitting area. Behind it a computer work station occupied the wall. The opposite side of the room held a crib, and toys littered the floor.

"Please be seated, Ms. Willis."

"Please call me Barbara. Are you sure you have time to see me?"

"Yes, I'm sure. I'm curious about the subject you mentioned on the phone."

"You are familiar with the school prayers?"

"Yes. Emma—she's one of the children who goes to my church—recently talked with me about them. She's a bright young lady. Likes to think she might be descended from Charles Darwin's family. Maybe she is."

"I haven't met her yet. I have an interview scheduled with her and Susie Holland this afternoon. I met Susie at the school."

"Handle them with care. They're live embers."

"What do you think about the Prayer Amendment, Reverend Gay . . . er . . . Janet?"

"I'll get straight to the point, although, as a Unitarian minister, that's not my strong suit. The Alabama Prayer Amendment was a populist mechanism used by James Forbe to get elected."

"I gather you are not pleased with the action."

"'Not pleased' puts it mildly. I am appalled. Prayer is a very private spiritual exercise. It's not a religious vitamin to be crammed down children's throats. We certainly don't want the *state* to indoctrinate our children."

"But you do believe in prayer, don't you?"

"We believe in individual freedom, reason, and responsibility. We believe in the basic goodness of human nature. We challenge people to realize their fullest potential as loving, caring, noble persons."

"Do you pray or not?" Barbara said, flatly.

Janet paused for a moment then spoke. "Prayer is an attitude, a frame of mind. It is a recognition that we are not alone in this universe to which we are intrinsically linked."

Barbara paused then decided not to give up. *This minister sounds like Brother Johnny in reverse*, she thought. "Do you think prayer makes a difference?"

"Yes and no. Let me give you the 'no' first. Most of those who enter the doors of this agency are religious people. They pray to a God who they believe raises the dead, defends the oppressed, and lifts up the downtrodden. Yet, they were constantly battered and abused, some by Bible-thumping husbands." Janet paused.

"And the 'yes'?"

"When a battered woman or child walks through that door and says to June, 'I'm Mary or Catherine or Shirley. Can you help me?' that is a prayer. When we mobilize the resources of this shelter, the legal system, and the community to restore dignity and protection to that woman or child, the prayer has been answered."

"So when God hears a prayer, that's the way he works?"

"That is the only way *she* works." Janet smiled. "Would you like something to drink?"

"No, I'm fine, thank you. What about the prayers of these school children?"

"Emma and Susie? I've seen some of their prayers. They are the prayers of innocent, well-nurtured children."

"There are people who believe some of these children's prayers have come true. How do you respond to their claims?"

"Sometimes prayer appears to come true. But it's not some supernatural, cause-effect process. God—if there is a god—cannot be manipulated by our whims. A lot of answered prayer is coincidence."

"Some unusual events have taken place following the prayers of the children in the Alberta Jones Middle School." Barbara thought about her research.

"Certainly. And it made the children feel good. But some important things have not taken place."

"What do you mean?" asked Barbara.

"Look at both sides. When the things religious people pray about go their way, they attribute the results to God. When things don't go their way, they either rationalize or turn away from God."

"In other words, prayer doesn't make much difference in what happens," said Barbara.

"Not in the traditional, orthodox religious sense. But it does make a difference when we deliver our prayers to the right address."

"Like to the *Abused Women and Kids Endeavor?*"

"Precisely, or wherever people are in the business of meeting human need."

"But there are some amazing coinci—"

The phone on Janet's desk interrupted the conversation. Janet answered it. Then she placed her hand over the mouthpiece and said to Barbara, "Excuse me a moment."

"Shall I wait outside?"

"No, no. I'll only be a moment, I'm sure." Janet spoke again over the phone. "Okay, June, put him through. Hello, Stanley. So good to hear your voice . . . Sure, I'll be in town tonight . . . Dinner at seven. Fine . . . La Paella in Alex City. Sure . . . Yes, I've thought about Gulf Shores. Yes, definitely, yes . . . Sure, we can make plans tonight . . . Yes, yes, me, too, but I have to go now, bye." Janet replaced the phone on the cradle, turned to Barbara, and smiled. "Now that was an answer to prayer."

39

Barbara parked on Sycamore Street and walked around toward the sycamore. Susie and Emma met her.

"I'm pleased to meet you, Emma." Barbara took the extended hand of the the dark-eyed, dark-complectioned girl. "I'm told your father owns the best restaurant in town."

"It's the only restaurant in town." Emma laughed.

"Good to see you again, Susie. This is a lovely setting."

"Me and Emma spend a lot of time here," said Susie.

"Susie said you are Miss Willis from the newspaper."

"Yes, that's right. I'd like to talk with both of you. Mrs. Haley called your mothers and they said it would be all right."

"May we sit down?" asked Barbara.

"Sure," replied Susie as she sat in the swing.

Emma climbed to her favorite perch and Barbara pulled up a lawn chair.

"You're from the *Constitution-Journal*, aren't you?" inquired Susie.

"*Journal-Constitution*," said Barbara. "I'm told you two are good friends."

"Yes, ma'am," replied Emma.

"We've been playing together since before we started to school," added Susie.

"Did you and Mrs. Haley go to school together?" asked Emma.

"Yes," replied Barbara. "We were good friends at Auburn

University but lost contact when I moved to Birmingham and later to Atlanta."

"She's my favorite teacher," said Susie.

"Mine, too," said Emma.

"Why is she your favorite?"

"Because she likes people," said Emma. "She doesn't like to see people hurting."

Barbara looked at Susie. Susie appeared to be looking into space. "Why is she your favorite, Susie?"

"It's hard to say. I think it's because she loves our school. She's helped us get lots of the things we needed. She's a good teacher, too."

"Is there anything unusual about her? Is she different from your other teachers?"

Susie spoke. "She's different . . . I mean . . . most of my teachers are good, but Mrs. Haley helps us get things done."

"She's an angel," said Emma.

"I didn't know you believed in angels," said Susie.

"Sure, I do. An angel is someone who loves you."

"You don't mean an angel with wings," said Susie.

"An angel gives me wings," replied Emma.

Barbara smiled as she listened to the interchange. "That's a sweet thing to say about a teacher. Is there some special way your teacher . . . uh. . . . gives you wings?"

"Lots of ways. She lets us add things to the Governor's Prayer."

"That's what I want to talk with you about," said Barbara. "That's why I'm in Orchard Hill. How did you come up with the prayer thing?"

"You tell her, Susie."

"No, it was your idea."

"No, yours."

"We did it together," said Susie.

"What gave you the idea?" Barbara asked again.

"When we saw the Governor's Prayer the first time, it didn't make sense," said Susie. "I saw the governor today at school and told him so."

"Yes, I saw you," said Barbara. "He didn't look too happy about it."

"The Governor's prayer was just a lot of church words," said Emma. "Not about real stuff. Then, when Marie's daddy got sick and she was crying, we decided to see if we could add something to make her feel better."

"And she got to feeling better when her daddy got well," said Susie.

"What are some of the other things you prayed for?"

"We prayed for other people to get well, and they got well, too," said Emma.

"We prayed for computers, and schools everywhere got new computers," said Susie.

"And you believe what happened was the result of your prayers?" asked Barbara.

"I think so," replied Susie.

"At first, I didn't think so," said Emma.

"Where did the prayers come from?" asked Barbara.

"We made them up," replied Emma.

"Then I wrote them down," added Susie.

"In Susie's church they make up their prayers, so it was easy for her."

"But they don't write them down," said Susie. "They say them out loud in church as fast as they can come up with them. Then they forget them."

"I've noticed that you end all your prayers the same way."

"You've seen the prayers?" asked Emma.

"Yes," replied Barbara. "Irene . . . Mrs. Haley gave me copies of the prayers. They all end with the words, 'Not *thy* will but *our* will be done'. Is there anything special about the ending?"

"That's the way people pray," said Emma.

"That's the way we do it in church," said Susie.

"The Lord's prayer sort of ends that way," said Emma. "Is something wrong with it?"

"No, no," replied Barbara, smiling. "It's fine. You've been praying about some important things lately."

"We think they're pretty important," said Emma.

"Are you aware that some of the things you have prayed for are causing some prob . . . uh . . . changes in the state government?"

"No, ma'am," said Susie. "But a lot of good things have happened in our school."

Emma said, "We think the governor must be very happy. After all, the school prayer was his idea."

"Well, yes, it was his idea, wasn't it? I'll be talking with the governor soon I hope. I'll remind him."

"Please do," said Susie. "We would like for him to know how much we like having prayer in the school. Our prayers especially."

"Tell him we'll pray for him, if he needs it," said Emma.

"I'll tell him that." Barbara smiled. "Is there anything else about your prayers you'd like to tell me?"

"Yes ma'am," replied Susie. "We only pray for things that we really need. We try not to be selfish."

"And we only pray for people who really need help," added Emma.

"Do you remember the last thing you prayed for?"

"Yes, ma'am," answered Emma. "We prayed for the prisoners to go free—the ones who are innocent."

"That's an unusual prayer."

"It will be answered, Miss Willis. I know it will," said Emma.

"I believe you prayed for the governor's wife," said Barbara.

"You heard about that, too?" said Susie. "Does the governor know?"

"If he doesn't, he will," said Barbara. "I promise."

Barbara spent another half-hour with the excited pair of children, then picked up a hamburger at McDonald's, and headed for her hotel room in Alex City. She hoped to have her story written by 10 and downloaded, via the Internet, to make the morning paper.

40

THE WSFA "BREAKING news" was confusing. Their omnipresent "man-on-the-scene" at Mount Meigs, near Montgomery, communicated by phone that there had been a massive prison break. Dominating the screen, above a caption reading, "Kilby Correctional Facility," a razor-wire encrusted chain-link fence punctuated with guard towers surrounded massive concrete buildings. A white water tank, which looked like a giant bicycle horn, rose from the center of the enclosure.

Emma listened to the report with growing concern. *We didn't mean for dangerous criminals to get out. Surely God understood that.* As she watched, the "man-on-the-scene" signed off and the news anchor said he had someone else on the phone. The scene switched to a picture of the director of the Department of Corrections.

"There has not been a prison break," said the director.

The anchor said, "Normally reliable sources say there are inmates everywhere—walking, hitchhiking, begging dollars to buy a beer."

"That may be ti .," replied the director. "But these prisoners did not escape. I released them."

"Would you care to elaborate?"

"I issued a directive to release all prison inmates who were innocent."

"How do you know who is innocent?" asked the anchor.

"A few weeks ago, I instructed all wardens to review the files of any inmate who maintained his or her innocence. A review commission opened numerous cases. The commission studied heretofore undisclosed evidence in some cases and DNA testing in others. Scores of inmates have been released."

"Wasn't that unusual?"

"That scores of convicts went free?"

"No. That you ordered them released under those circumstances."

"I had to do it," confessed the director. "I felt compelled to make sure that innocent men and women regained their freedom."

"Can we expect other similar actions?"

"I've also ordered the wardens at all our corrections facilities to intensify their rehabilitation programs and to implement liberal early release procedures if we can get the Parole Board off their . . .uh . . . more actively involved. My goal is to cut our prison population in half by the end of the current year."

"Is that a good thing to do?"

"I'm not certain," replied the director, "but I have been assured by the majority leaders of both the House and the Senate that I have their full backing."

"Are the courts cooperating . . . I mean, are they giving priority to these cases?" asked the anchor.

"The Attorney General pressured—that's probably not the best word—urged the judges to expedite all the reopened cases that come before them for review."

"And the governor?"

"The last thing I heard, the governor was fixing toilets in Orchard Hill."

"He's back in Montgomery," said the WSFA anchorman.

"Then why don't you ask him," said the director. "I'll take no more questions."

"Wow!" said Emma aloud. "I wonder if Susie saw that."

41

BARBARA WILLIS WATCHED the flat, marshy landscape slide by as she rolled down I-85 toward the Alabama state capital. She had mixed feelings about an encounter with Jimmy Forbe. It seemed like ages had passed since the affair. It had ended—if one could call it that—on friendly terms. She wondered how it had ever begun. Forbe was not especially handsome, yet she had been drawn to him. Was it power? Would she be drawn to him again—not to Forbe, the mayor, but to Forbe, the governor? After seeing the WSFA newscast, she had a growing list of questions for Governor James Forbe. She was certain she could conduct a professional interview. Her gray, loose-fitting pants suit might help.

"GOOD MORNING, GOVERNOR Forbe. I'm Barbara Willis of the *Atlanta Journal-Constitution.*" Barbara smiled as she extended her hand.

"I think we've met. It's good to see you again, Barbara." Forbe shook her hand then motioned her to a chair across the desk from him.

"It looks like being governor agrees with you," said Barbara, uncertain how to maneuver through the minefield of their past.

"You look great," Forbe replied.

Barbara changed the subject. "You were unkind to me in that rally interview."

"You still sore about that? I was speaking to the cameras, not to you. You should know that. Is that why you snubbed me at that school in Orchard Hill?"

"I wasn't ready to talk to you yet. Now I am."

"I hope it's not about Orchard Hill. I've already talked with a dozen reporters about that damn work project."

"I would like to talk with you about Orchard Hill but not about the work project."

"Then I'll be delighted to answer the questions. Shoot."

"I would like to ask you some questions about the Prayer Amendment."

Forbe stiffened. "The Prayer Amendment? Come on, Barbara. That matter concluded shortly after my election."

"What do you mean by *concluded*?"

"Finished, terminated, accomplished. I promised school prayer and, by God, the legislature fulfilled my promise."

"What did school prayer mean to you?" she asked as she watched Forbe reach for his handkerchief. *Why did you pass it?* she thought. *Tell the truth.*

"It meant that I would be elected guvnah of Alabama. That's what political campaigns are about, whether it's a prayer amendment or teaching creationism in the schools or posting the Ten Commandments in the courtroom. It's about getting elected in the Bible Belt." Forbe wiped his brow.

"Is it possible that school prayer might be more than you intended?"

"What are you talking about?"

"Do you read the newspapers, Jimbo?"

"Those that are worth reading. Has the *AJC* printed something noteworthy lately?"

"I thought you might be interested in my article in this morning's paper." She handed him a copy of the paper open to her report.

"'School Prayer Backfires in Alabama: Part I.' What the hell is this?"

"Read on."

Forbe scanned the article occasionally glancing at Barbara. "This is preposterous! These kids' prayers have no effect on my government. Writing fairy tales like this, it's a wonder you have a job." Forbe wiped the perspiration from his forehead. "Where'd you get this damn stuff anyway?"

"Got to protect my sources. But they are credible."

"Get off my back, Barbara. You expect me to believe this? There's no way the prayers of a handful of school kids can effect the outcome of legislation in this state. You think I'm crazy?"

"Not crazy, but you do need to open your eyes. Those kids in Orchard Hill may be playing with your state government."

"You're talking nonsense. There are other explanations for what's going on in my state. Don't bring religion into it."

"You brought religion in when you campaigned on the prayer issue."

"I told you I'm a politician. What I did was good politics. I got elected, fulfilled my promise, and the issue died as far as I'm concerned."

"Some issues are bad politics, Jimbo. This one has risen up to haunt you. I predicted it."

"I have nothing more to say about it. We can talk about something else if you like, but not about school prayer." Forbe rose from his chair and walked around the desk.

Barbara stood and spoke giving emphasis to every word. "Pay close attention to what's happening to your government. Some innocent kids are changing it."

"I'm through talking about this subject," said Forbe.

"There's another prayer I didn't mention in my article. Did you know the kids prayed for Betty?"

Forbe wiped his forehead and tried to loosen his tie. "Lots of people prayed for Betty."

"You think their prayers were answered?" asked Barbara.

"How should I know? The important thing is that Betty got well."

"Jimbo, if you aren't careful, something terrible could happen."

"Welcome to Deep South politics. It's like that every day."

Barbara put her hand on his arm. "Jimbo, please." He stopped and listened. "If you don't watch it, this whole business could tear your state apart, and you with it." She gripped his other arm and pulled him to her. Forbe extended his hands around her waist. Their kiss was long and passionate.

42

Dick walked into Forbe's office for the Monday morning briefing. "Jimbo, there is a national trend developing that could have an impact on our state economy."

"Let's get through this quickly, Dick. I've got other stuff to do."

"That may have to wait, Governor. We need to give some time to this."

"In a nutshell, Dick. In a nutshell."

"It could be worse than the cessation of armed conflicts in the Middle East, Africa, the Balkans, and elsewhere."

Forbe said, "Those damn peace initiatives brought disarmament, deactivation of armed personnel, and a slowdown in the arms industries in the state. What could be worse than that? Hell! Get on with it. What's up?"

"Jimbo, you're going to think I'm crazy when I tell you."

"I think you're crazy when you don't say a damn thing," said Forbe as he sat down. "Whatever you have to say will be good news compared to what else I have on my mind. Out with it."

"Hospital admissions are down."

"Does that mean our state employees have quit calling in sick?"

"It means we could face large layoffs of healthcare workers."

"That sounds like good news to me. Why don't you give me the bad?"

"That is the bad. Resulting unemployment could overload the heavily burdened welfare department. Do you know how

188 THE PRAYER AMENDMENT

many people work in the health care industry?" asked Dick.

"No, I don't. Do you?"

"It has to be in the hundreds of thousands."

"Does this situation only affect Alabama?"

"CNN reports that it's spreading beyond our state."

"At last we're leading the way in something." Forbe laughed.

"Governor, this is serious."

"What do the experts say?"

Dick thumbed through some notes. "There are reports that the influenza virus did not arrive this year and that the new common cold vaccine is producing surprising results. All this, along with medical breakthroughs in some other areas, has produced an unprecedented drop in hospital admissions."

"That still sounds like good news to me—certainly over the long haul."

"Yes," said Little. "But it's coming at a bad time with all the peace initiatives and such."

"I'll name a committee to handle it."

"Or mishandle it. We may need some quick action—gubernatorial decrees or a special session of the legislature."

"You think it's gone that far?"

"Not yet, at least, I don't think so," said Dick. "But the potential is there. The Unemployment Compensation Fund isn't designed to handle a lot of claims at one time. When people don't get their checks, they'll get hungry and angry. You remember the uproar last year when people didn't get their state income tax returns until Thanksgiving."

"They got them just in time for Christmas," Forbe smiled. "What do you suggest we do, Dick?"

"Put the State Troopers on alert—maybe even the Guard."

"You're crazy! We don't activate the Guard when people fail to get their refunds on time."

"The Guard might be a little much but at least advise the Troopers to keep their eyes open."

Forbe waved Little toward the door. "Go home and close *your* eyes for a few hours. Get some sleep."

"Jimbo, you asked me for suggestions and I'm giving them. I'm nervous about the repercussions of massive unemployment. We've got to do something . . .soon."

"You'll feel better tomorrow. Now out of here."

"No. I'm staying here tonight to put together some proposals for the legislature. I'll run it past you tomorrow."

"Do as you like, but I'm going home." Forbe rose and walked by Little. "Call me if you hit a snag."

43

FORBE KISSED HIS WIFE before settling his head onto the pillow. He turned off the reading light, and closed his eyes. As he rolled onto his side, he drew his knees into a fetal position. A fitful sleep lifted him into the shadowy world of dreams.

The phone rang. "Forbe here." His eyes quivered beneath closed lids.

"Jimbo, it's an emergency. Get down here!" Dick shouted into the phone.

"Calm down. I just left."

"There are new developments."

"Is there a war somewhere? That would solve a lot of problems."

"Worse than that. I can't talk about it on the phone, Governor. Get down here! Fast!" Dick spat out the words.

"I'm on my way." Forbe pulled at his khaki pants which wouldn't rise up his naked legs. He kicked them down and pushed the buzzer to call his driver. He bent to kiss Betty; she faded into nothingness. Forbe shook his head, turned and hurried from the room.

Moments later, clad in his short, knit pajamas, Forbe stepped into the mansion's pull-through as a bolt of lightning lit a stormy sky.

"Where's Willy?" Forbe asked a slender blonde standing by the open rear door of his black Ford Crown Victoria.

Braless, wearing a white, thin-knit tank top that did not quite reach the waist of her short black skirt, she replied, "He went home. Said something about his wife losing her job at the hospital."

Forbe's memory flickered as he settled into the spacious back seat. "You from Tutwiler?"

"Yes sir. Doing time for sex—"

Forbe cut her off. "I don't care what you're doing time for. Glad to have you on my team. Get me to the office as fast as you can. Where's that escort?"

"In the street, sir." The driver pulled out behind a Humvee that was already moving.

"What the hell! Where are the troopers? I don't move from my house without my bodyguards."

"In the Humvee," replied the driver. "The National Guard loaned it to your state troopers."

"Damn! What's going on? Who are you?"

"There's a riot alert, sir. The state troopers thought it best to play it safe."

Forbe raised his voice. "I asked you who you were?"

"And I told you, sir."

"I don't believe you."

"You're perceptive, Governor."

"That's how I survive. Now tell me who you are or I'll call the troopers."

"I'll level with you, Governor. I'm not an inmate from Tutwiler."

"Then, who the hell are you?"

"If you knew me, you'd be a happier governor."

"Then make me happy! Tell me who you are!"

"That's not exactly what I meant."

"Cut the bullshit! What's your name?"

"My name's Barbie. I'm a reporter."

"Where's Willy?"

"I told you, sir. He had a family emergency."

"Willy is a convict and sleeps at Kilby Prison!" Forbe shouted.

"Not any more. He's free at last."

"Stop the damn car! I'll ride in the Humvee." Forbe could see his driver smiling at him in the rearview mirror. *Damn! She looks familiar.*

"You need me, Governor Forbe. I'm from that big, ole important Atlanta newspaper, the *Journal.* Could we talk about something on the way to your office?"

"You're the reporter who was in my office. You're Barbara." Forbe calmed down. "What do you want to talk about?"

"I'm Barbie, and I want to talk about Orchard Hill and the condition of the State of Alabama."

"Go ahead and talk, dammit, but keep it moving. Get me to my office on the double." He grabbed for a handgrip as the heavy Crown Victoria gathered speed down Gilmer Avenue tailgating the Humvee escort. Stately homes slept fitfully in Forbe's pre-dawn darkness. Lightning flashed and thunder rumbled over-head.

Barbie began to sing, "Sweet hour of prayer, sweet hour of—"

"Cut that out!" Forbe tightened his grip as the sedan swerved onto South McDonough and sped toward Dexter Avenue. Rain fell in sheets. Soldiers stood with weapons ready at every intersection. *The damn Guard was everywhere.*

Barbie stopped singing. "Governor, I'd like to ask you some questions."

"Get on with it!"

Barbie turned her head around, winked, and asked, "Do you believe in prayer?"

"Watch where you're going, dammit!"

She continued to look at Forbe. The Crown Victoria flew down South McDonough, as if on automatic pilot, shadowing the Humvee. It did not slow down; it did not stop for red lights.

"Governor, I really need to know, do you believe in prayer?"

Forbe began to pray, "Our Father, who are in heaven, hallo—"

His head banged on the window as his vehicle skidded sideways to avoid flying debris at the I-85 underpass. "Shiiiit!" Forbe shouted as he watched the Humvee crash through another barricade sending shattered lumber like spinning missiles in all directions. The Ford corrected and Forbe sailed across the seat.

"My cute, little governor, are you all right?"

"Yeah, yeah, sure, but watch the damn road."

Barbie continued to watch Forbe.

Without signaling, the Humvee veered sharply to the left and disappeared around the side of the Montgomery County Jail. Forbe's vehicle, accelerating once again, sped across Adams Avenue and dropped toward the river.

"Hold tight," shouted Barbie. Two blocks later, the auto braked and began a wide right turn. Without warning, it stopped.

"Where are we?" Forbe straightened and peered from side to side.

"Trying to turn onto Dexter. There's trouble up toward the capitol."

He squinted through the rain streaming down the windows and tried to focus on the blinking lights reflecting off the wet street. Three tanks placed end to end blocked Dexter Avenue from curb to curb. Soldiers ran in all directions and gunshots reverberated from the direction of the capitol. Muzzles flashed from windows in the RSA Tower off to his left.

Poncho-covered military types, plodding like Trappist monks

with submachine guns, approached his vehicle. One motioned for him to roll down the window.

"What the hell do you want? What's going on here?" demanded Forbe through the glass.

"We'll ask the questions, Mr. Forbe," asserted the taller who appeared to be an officer. "Where are you going?"

"I'm going to my office. Where the hell do you think I'm going? Now let me pass."

"You have no office here, Mr. Forbe. You're under arrest."

"What do you mean, *under arrest*? I'm the guvnah of this state! I can arrest you!"

"Not any longer, Mr. Forbe. You have been stripped of your authority. We have orders to take you to General Richard Little. Now, get out!"

Forbe screamed to Barbie. "Turn this car around! Let's get out of here!"

"Governor, I can't do that," Barbie cooed. "I've got to ask you some very personal questions."

"Turn this damn vehicle around and move!"

"Jimmy, who do you love best, me or Betty? I got the best boobs."

Barbie raised up on her knees, turned, and leaned over. She pulled up her tank top. Her ample breasts drooped onto the leather seat back. "Governor, can I crawl over in your lap? You look cold and I can warm you up."

"I've got to go!" shouted Forbe. "I've got to go! I've got to go!"

"Get up and go," said Betty, shaking his shoulder. "Get up and go."

Forbe opened his eyes and looked around the room. The clock on the dresser read 3 a.m. He looked at Betty and blinked to clear his eyes. Suddenly, he snatched back the covers and bolted from the bed, holding his crotch.

As he finished, he inhaled deeply to sneeze. It wouldn't blow. As he focused on the outdoor security light through the bathroom window, a forceful ejaculation of air laced with moisture rattled the windowpanes. "That's better than—" Forbe interrupted himself.

Betty called out, "God bless you!"

44

"DICK, COME IN here," said Forbe over the intercom.

Moments later Little entered. "What's on your mind?"

"I'm not sure. Have you read the *Atlanta Journal-Constitution*?"

"What do you mean, Governor? I read it from time to time."

"Have you read the Willis article?"

"Not yet."

"She writes about miraculous healings, international peace initiatives, base closings, prisoner releases—and heaven knows what else. And she's linking it to school prayers in Orchard Hill."

"People talk like that all the time. Your pastor at Tabernacle Baptist and Brother Johnny Carroll, the Bible quoter, are always preaching about how God answers prayer."

"Brother Johnny doesn't write for the *Journal*. Barbara Willis is writing these articles. She's not a preacher. She's straight. I know her quite well as you are aware. Has a good reputation. Doesn't write nonsense."

"You can't believe everything you read in the paper, Governor. The *Journal* prints whatever will sell newspapers. Besides, Barbara Willis isn't infallible."

"Maybe not, but she's close. She's documenting prayers and current events. It looks like prophesy and fulfillment."

"What do you mean?"

"You remember that school repair bill that passed the legislature?"

"How could I forget it?"

"She wrote that kids prayed about it at school a few weeks before it happened."

"Coincidence. Just coincidence," said Dick.

"Did you know that they prayed that *I* would fix the toilets in Orchard Hill? A couple of the kids told me that when I was there working on the septic system."

"Coincidence—"

"Coincidence, hell!" Forbe interrupted. "There were dozens of repairs to do on schools all over Alabama and I got stuck with the damn toilets in Orchard Hill!" Forbe's voice rose in volume. "I spent four hot, humid days in a crossroads school fixing smelly commodes!"

"You could have done something else—painting or carpentry."

"I could have but I didn't. Don't you understand? I felt compelled to do what I did, yet I hated every minute of it."

"Well, it's over now. That was an unfortunate combination of events. You can get on with the state's business."

"What state business? The state business is in shambles. Something is screwing up our programs. Barbara says those kids are doing it."

"You don't really believe that do you, Jimbo? A handful of kids can't screw up the government of the State of Alabama."

"Lawyers with less brains have done it in the past," said Forbe. "No offense intended."

Dick laughed. "These kids are in Orchard Hill. What could they do?"

"I don't know. It may be those damn liberals trying to get even. Who knows what they're doing? You saw how crafty Lyell was in the debate. What's he doing now?"

"Running his radio station. He heads up the APR programming for the University of Alabama at Huntsville. Don't worry about him."

"Dick, I've got an idea. Let's stop those add-on prayers. If the kids stuck to the official prayer, they wouldn't be sticking their noses where they don't belong."

"You're overplaying the importance of prayer, Jimbo. Get real. There's no proof prayer does any harm or any good. There has to be another reason for what's going on in the legislature."

"Maybe so. I don't know. I need to talk to Barbara again."

45

"Uncle Stanley's back," said Susie, "but we don't see him much."

"I really like his red motorcycle," said Emma. "Think he'd take me for a ride?"

"If you can catch him when Reverend Gaylor's not on it."

"He sure comes down a lot. You'd think his boss wouldn't like it."

"He's his own boss," said Susie. "He can come whenever he wants to. But he never came this much just to see us."

"Things must be getting serious."

"He leaves his motorcycle in our garage so he can fly back and forth."

"You sure he'll remember our meeting tomorrow morning?" asked Emma.

"He said he'd be here, but I'll remind him just in case."

"What a delicious meal," said Stanley as they left the Paella Restaurant. "That *gambas al ajillo* appetizer was superb."

"*Shrimp scampi*," said Janet. "Nobody does that dish like Roberto, their chef from Barcelona."

"How did you like the *cordero asado?*" asked Stanley.

"Roast lamb is one of my favorites," said Janet as they turned into her drive just a few blocks from the restaurant. "You coming in?"

"If I'm invited." Stanley winked.

Janet punched him on the shoulder.

"YOU NEED TO write the Gulf Shores date on your calendar?" said Stanley.

"I wouldn't forget something like that." Janet smiled.

"You are unique." Stanley looked at his watch as he put his arm around her. "I'm lucky to have found you."

"What makes you think I didn't find you first?" said Janet as she slid closer running her fingers through his hair. Their lips met.

Stanley leaned toward her as she eased down on the couch.

Like a whirlwind, the galloping wedge of the William Tell Overture pried loose their embrace. Stanley sat up and reached for his cell phone.

"Why didn't you turn that thing off?" asked Janet.

"I'm sorry. I'm on call. Anything could happen in Cuba and—" He spoke into phone. "Hello. Stanley here." Janet, inches away, listened.

"Hi, Uncle Stanley," came the familiar voice over the phone. "Hope I didn't disturb you. Are you coming before I have to go to bed, so we can talk about the meeting tomorrow?"

"Certainly, Sweetheart . . . what? . . . yes . . . I know it's after nine . . . yes, bye, now."

Stanley pressed the "end" key on his Nokia. "I'm sorry. I guess I'd better go."

"Will you have that darn phone with you in Gulf Shores?"

"I hope not." Stanley laughed. "You'll pick me up at the airport in Mobile?"

"Yes. On the seventeenth. You be sure and let me know which flight you'll be on."

Stanley took her hands and drew her to him. He looked in her moist eyes. She was trembling. She calmed at his touch. "I love you, Janet."

He said it. He finally said it. In Gulf Shores, he'll have to prove it. "I love you, too, Stanley." She responded to his embrace. Their lips met and joined, no longer strangers. Magic words had bonded them.

After a long moment, Stanley disengaged and moved back a step. "I've got to go." He hurried toward the door and opened it.

Janet followed and watched as he walked down the drive to his car. "I'll see you at the airport," she whispered, not caring whether he heard or not.

"Dammit," said Stanley out loud as he pulled out and turned toward Orchard Hill. He looked back to wave, but Janet had already closed the door. *Dammit, to hell. My cell phone isn't the only thing I'm turning off in Gulf Shores. There's bound to be a mute-button somewhere on my damned Baptist Puritanism.*

46

ON SATURDAY MORNING, Susie, Emma, Paco, Katasha, and Jeremiah met with Stanley under the sycamore tree, to hear about his trip to Cuba.

"This is Paco, Uncle Stanley. He's the one I wrote you about," said Susie.

"*Hola, Paco. ¿Cómo estás?*" Stanley greeted him.

"*Muy bien, Señor Estanlee. ¿Y usted?*" Paco beamed. In Orchard Hill, he seldom heard his native tongue spoken outside his home.

"*Muy bien.*" Stanley turned to Susie and Emma. "And how are you?"

"*Muy bien,*" replied Susie. "I understood everything. I learned some Spanish in Mrs. Haley's class."

"She must be doing a good job," said Stanley. "Shall we continue our talk in Spanish?"

"No! Please don't!" said Emma. "We only learn a little bit in class."

"And who is this young man?" asked Stanley.

"This is Jeremiah," said Susie. "He's my friend." She blushed.

"Glad to meet you, Jeremiah," said Stanley then turned to Susie and winked.

"And this beautiful young lady?"

"I'm Katasha."

"I'm pleased to make your acquaintance."

"Tell us about Cuba, Uncle Stanley," said Susie.

"What do you want to hear?"

"Tell us about your last trip," said Susie.

"It was quite different from my other trips."

"See, I told you, Susie!" said Emma. "I told you Reverend Gaylor showed us a postcard from Cuba. Said it was from a friend. It was you, wasn't it, Mr. Hannah?"

"You got me," said Stanley. "Reverend Gaylor and I are friends. I wrote her from Holguin."

Emma looked at Susie and winked. Susie smiled and glanced at Stanley. She had the impression Uncle Stanley was reading her mind. She quickly looked away. The pause lengthened.

Paco broke the silence. "We wrote a prayer for class about Cuba, *Señor Estanlee*. You can tell us what there is going on? Has anything change?"

"Yes, please tell us what's happening in Cuba," pleaded Katasha. "I'll write everything down."

"Okay, let's see. I know. I'll tell you first about my arrival in Holguin." Stanley described the welcome given him at the airport by Mr. Paz who had seen that all his medical equipment and medicines made it through customs. Then he added, "But the strangest part of the trip . . ." Stanley paused.

"What Uncle Stanley?" Susie asked.

"Well, I'll tell you if you promise not to talk about it."

"We promise," chorused the quintet.

"That afternoon in the office of Mr. Paz a most unusual man awaited me."

"Who?" asked Emma.

"The man was President Fidel Castro."

"*¿Presidente Castro? ¿El presidente de Cuba?*" asked Paco.

"Yes, Paco, the president of Cuba."

"What did he want with you, Uncle Stanley?"

"That's what I want to tell you. I still don't understand it all. After President Castro introduced himself, he ordered drinks and began to talk about the economic embargo the United States had imposed on his country. He—"

"Were you afraid?" interrupted Susie. "Oh, I'm sorry. I didn't mean to stop you."

"That's fine. Yes, I was frightened and told him so. He assured me I had nothing to fear, that he simply wanted to share some important information."

"Why did he want to do that, Uncle Stanley? You don't work for the government, do you?"

"No, I don't. President Castro said he decided to contact me because of my humanitarian work in Cuba. Wanted me to pass on the information to some influential friends I have in Washington."

"What kind of information he have for you?" asked Paco.

"President Castro talked about the embargo, the CIA, and Brothers to the Rescue whose planes were shot down by Cuban fighters several years ago. He talked about the Helms-Burton Act that made the embargo even harder on his people. Then he dropped a bombshell."

"Did you get hurt, Uncle Stanley?"

"Not a real bombshell, Susie," said Stanley. "He dropped a verbal bombshell. He told me he wanted an orderly transition to democracy. Now, that's all I can tell you. Can't give away state secrets."

"*Caramba!*" exclaimed Paco. "What did he tell you, *Señor Estanlee?*"

"You'll have to wait and see. It may come out on the news."

"Wow!" said Emma. "We said a prayer in school about Cuba."

"And you're part of it, Uncle Stanley," said Susie.

Susie said, "We've written prayers for school about lots of things. We think some of them are coming true."

"Janet . . . er . . . Reverend Gaylor has told me about your prayers. I also read something recently in the paper."

"Are our prayers really coming true, Uncle Stanley?" asked Susie.

"Stranger things have happened," said Stanley. "Prayers are like dreams. You have to believe in your dreams. If you believe they will come true, that's the important thing."

"We believe it, Uncle Stanley. We believe it and we see it happening. It's so much fun!" said Susie. "And we're helping people."

"Don't lose faith in your dreams, your hopes, and your prayers. You can make things happen. Now, let me see what I have in my bag for my favorite niece and her friends. Emma, here's a large map of Cuba you can use in your class at school."

"Thank you, Mr. Hannah," said Emma as she began to unfold the map. "Can you show us where Hole . . . where you saw President Castro?" She turned the unfolded map toward Stanley.

"Right here." He placed a finger under a city name. "And way over here is Havana." He slid his finger across Cuba to the western end of the island. "President Castro came all the way from Havana to see me in Holguin."

Stanley reached in his bag and extracted a rolled paper. "Katasha, here's a poster of people at the Hemingway Marina in Havana."

Katasha opened the poster and exclaimed, "There are African-Americans like me! Thank you, Mr. Hannah."

"Paco, here are some postage stamps commemorating Pope Paul's visit to Cuba."

"Jeremiah, here are some brochures from the Cayo Coco tourist resort. Let's see the map, Emma. Right there is Cayo Coco, on the northeastern coast of Cuba, straight up from Holguin."

"Wow! Look at that beach! Thank you, Mr. Hannah."

"And, Susie, here's a book of poetry by Excilia Saldaña, a Cuban poet. It's about a little girl's questions to her grandmother. She reminds me of you."

"Have you read it, Uncle Stanley?"

"Every word. I'll show you one of my favorite poems." Stanley flipped through the book. Most of the pages were black with white print and drawings. "Here it is. Paco, you read it."

Paco took the book and read,

"*¿Por qué existe el odio, abuela?*"

"*Porque a esa pobre palabra, de niña, nadie le dijo: 'Eres bella`.*"

"Oh! That sounds so pretty," said Emma. "What does it say? Please, tell us what it says!"

Stanley took the book back from Paco.

"The little girl asks, 'Why does hate exist, grandmother?'

"Grandmother answers, 'Because when that poor little word was a child, no one said to her: You're beautiful.'"

"Maybe next time I'll bring each of you a book of poems. Now, let me see what else I've got. Here's something for all of you. It's a bag of *Chicle* from some children in Cuba. *Chicle* is chewing gum. Don't chew it in class."

"We'd never do anything like that, Uncle Stanley," said Susie with a grin.

"No, never," said Emma, as they burst out laughing.

47

Barbara called Forbe's direct line from her office in Atlanta. "Jimbo, this is Barbara. I'll be back in Alabama tomorrow and I want to talk to you."

"Business or personal?"

"Business—but I'll not rule out some personal."

"I have a bone to pick with you, Barbara."

"Then we'll have a two-way conversation. You busy tomorrow afternoon?"

"I'm always busy but I'll work you in—for old times' sake."

Barbara could not interpret the undercurrent in Forbe's voice. "I have an appointment in Orchard Hill tomorrow morning," she said. "I'll see you at the Capitol after lunch."

"Any time will be fine. Ask for Dick Little when you get here. See you tomorrow."

"See you."

Forbe hung up the phone and closed his eyes. He thought about the School Prayer Amendment. It had worked. He was governor of Alabama. No politician could get church-going Alabamians excited about poverty, justice, tax reform, or education funding. But prayer was another matter. Religion ran deep in Alabama. Run a campaign pro-prayer, pro-Ten Commandments, anti-evolution, or anti-gambling and you were a sure winner. The Prayer Amendment had worked—or had it? And the break-up with Barbara? Problematic.

THE FOLLOWING MORNING, Barbara found Stanley at the Wedgwood Restaurant in Orchard Hill.

"It's good to meet you at last, Stanley," said Barbara. "Irene Haley told me you were in town and would be willing to talk with me. I hear you have a Cuban connection."

"Yes," replied Stanley. "News does get around. Would you like a cup of coffee or a soda? Mr. Wedgwood makes the best coffee in Orchard Hill."

"I'll try the coffee. Cream and sugar," said Barbara.

Stanley motioned for a waiter and gave the order.

"Did you have personal contact with Fidel Castro?"

"We talked," replied Stanley.

"You may be interested in some reports I got off the wire before coming over this morning."

"I got a call on my cell phone a while ago but did not get a lot of detail," Stanley said.

"Fidel Castro has resigned and called for national elections."

"Yes. He talked to me about that possibility."

"That's not all." Barbara continued. "A Cuban transitional government is in the hands of the Catholic bishop of Santiago de Cuba, and Fidel Castro has announced himself as a candidate in the campaign for president."

"That is news! But it'll be hard to do."

The waiter sat two steaming cups of fragrant smelling coffee on the table along with cream and sugar. Stanley waited while Barbara prepared her coffee then did the same to his own.

"One more item," continued Barbara. "The expatriate Cuban community has been invited to participate in the elections."

"I can't believe it!"

"And the U.S. has agreed to lift economic sanctions."

"Right on!" Stanley jabbed a fist into the air. "I couldn't be more delighted."

Stanley's reaction amused Barbara. "I'd like to quote you about your Cuban connection."

"Sure," said Stanley.

Barbara asked him several more background questions about his relief work in Cuba and his interview with Castro. Then she said, "Let me focus on the subject I'm writing about currently. Cuba is related to it. You are aware that I'm doing a series for the *Journal-Constitution* on the results of the Alabama School Prayer Amendment."

"I've read the articles. Don't you think you've gone a little far in your conclusions?"

"I'm not sure I've gone far enough. Did you know there was a school prayer in Orchard Hill about the Cuban situation?"

"Yes. My niece told me."

"That would be Susie Holland. I interviewed Susie and her friend, Emma Wedgwood. I think there's a connection between their prayers and what's happening in Cuba."

"People have been praying for Cuba for many years. What makes you think their school prayer has something to do with what's happening there?"

"Journalists have a sixth sense. I've done extensive investigating in Orchard Hill and Montgomery. These kids are making music. There's magic in what they're doing."

"I don't know if I believe in this type of magic, but I'll have to admit it's a compelling case. How can you be so sure the unusual happenings are connected to Orchard Hill?"

"I've been asking around other schools in the state. No prayers like these are going on anywhere else that I can determine. What's happening in Orchard Hill is unique."

"You'll have lots of skeptics."

"And I'll have lots of believers. One of them will be the governor of Alabama. He's tottering on the edge right now.

When I get through with him this afternoon, he'll have no doubt that some school kids in Orchard Hill have changed the direction of his state. I will be surprised if he doesn't take drastic measures."

"What kind of measures?"

"Wait and see. The governor, bless his heart, is running scared. He doesn't know if it's God or the Devil after him. By the way, you sound like one of the skeptics. Do you believe in prayer?"

"Of course, I do. Religion harbors many mysteries. Prayer is one of them. Thanks for the news about the changes in Cuba."

"Don't mention it. Those are not the only changes going on. Watch the news about Alabama." Barbara slid her pad and pen into her satchel.

"You seem pretty self-confident."

"So confident, I'm having trouble with my objectivity. Thanks for your time."

"I enjoyed meeting you. I'll get the coffee." He reached for the ticket.

Barbara plucked it from his fingers and stood. "This one's on me." She turned and walked toward the cash register.

48

Dick escorted Barbara into the governor's office and started to leave.

"Hang around, Dick. I may need your advice. Good afternoon, Barbara." Forbe stood and shook her outstretched hand, then motioned her to a couch in the sitting area. "Glad you could make it."

"Me too, Jimbo." A red knit top and short black skirt hugged Barbara in all the right places.

Forbe looked away for a moment then spoke. "Let's get to the point. You keep tying the Orchard Hill prayers to some isolated events related to my state government, creating the illusion there's a connection. Some of the fanatics in this state are getting worked up. You seem to forget that this is the Bible Belt."

"I'm not creating anything, Jimbo. My paper's reporting the news."

Dick entered the conversation. "Barbara, no one would get excited about a couple of coincidences if you weren't making a big thing out of it. You're editorializing."

"It's more than a couple of things. The kids in Orchard Hill have written nine or more prayers since the passing of the Prayer Amendment. Would you like to hear what events took place after those prayers were recited by the children in their school?"

"Go ahead," said Forbe. "But it's not going to change my mind about anything."

"I've arranged them in chronological order. I won't bother

you with all the dates, but keep in mind that the apparent answers to these prayers occurred in most cases shortly after the prayers were recited."

"Get on with it. I'm listening."

"Last fall, the class prayed for Tom Brandon, a local resident with colon cancer. A few days later, he was operated on and immediately recuperated."

"Happens all the time," Dick said. "Doctors operate. People get well."

"That's right," agreed Forbe. "Go on."

"A few weeks later, they prayed for a local coach by the name of Tidwell and for your wife, Governor. Tidwell returned to his responsibilities at the school without having an announced heart transplant. You know the outcome of your wife's illness."

"I told you before, a lot of people prayed for Betty."

"Spontaneous remissions happen every day," said Dick, "with or without somebody's prayers."

Barbara ignored him and continued. "Shortly after your legislative session got underway, your own party killed some of your pet bills and passed school computer legislation. Computers were the subject of a school prayer a few weeks earlier."

Forbe shrugged. "I don't know what got into those damn politicians."

Barbara continued, "Did you hear about some student harassment because of the Prayer Amendment?"

"Yes. We got reports from several schools. I put my PR people on it," said Forbe.

"Did you know that the kids prayed that some homosexuals would join Tabernacle Baptist Church? Aren't you a member there?"

"I was there when that bunch came in. None of them joined."

"It's not because they haven't tried," said Barbara.

"Go on."

"A Cuban boy goes to the Orchard Hill school. The kids got interested in Cuba and prayed for the lifting of the embargo. Do you know that the embargo has just been lifted?"

"I saw it today on CNN," said Dick.

"I've been too busy to watch the news," Forbe said.

"Castro has resigned and elections are scheduled."

"It's about time."

"I saw you a few weeks ago fixing toilets in Orchard Hill. Did—"

"Hell, yes, I knew. Some kids there told me they prayed I'd come. I later saw it in the *Journal*. Why the hell did you have to write about that?" Forbe pulled out his handkerchief and wiped his forehead.

Barbara ignored the question. "School repair in Alabama cost your state a fortune. Where did the money come from?"

"Out of my damn pocket!"

"The children also prayed for sick people—"

"Gave me a nightmare. I might tell you about it sometime."

"There's more," replied Barbara. "The kids prayed that innocent prisoners would be set—"

"I know about that," Forbe interrupted. "Every damn inmate in the nation is trying to get transferred to an Alabama prison!"

"I've been told about one more prayer. The children heard you were upset about the direction your governorship has taken. They prayed that God would help you make the right decisions."

"Even I've been praying about that." Forbe placed his palms together, touched his chin, and looked upward in a mock attitude of prayer. Then he stood and faced the window, his back to Barbara and Dick, and he thought, *I want you off my case, Barbara Willis. I'm going to get you off now.*

"Those kids deserve recognition for what they're doing,

Jimbo. What are you going to do about it?"

Forbe took a deep breath and turned around. "Get some coffee, Dick, but not that stale piss from your office. Go get a thermos at Barnie's."

Dick gestured with his hand. "That's way out at the Montgomery Mall."

Forbe replied, "You won't find good coffee any closer. No hurry. Take your time." As the door slammed shut behind Little, Forbe shrugged at Barbara then walked over and touched a button on the intercom.

"Yes, Governor?"

"Judy, hold my calls." Then he looked across at Barbara. "What the hell are you trying to prove?"

Barbara jumped to her feet. "What the hell are you talking about?"

"I'm talking about this story. I'm talking about your presence in my office."

"If my memory hasn't failed me, I believe when I called you told me to come on over."

"Sit down." Forbe pointed to the chair in front of his desk. He sat in his chair across from her, putting the desk between them. His face tensed. He enunciated each word. "Why have you been pushing this issue?"

Barbara crossed her legs and leaned back. "It's called an assignment."

"Sounds to me more like a crusade."

"What are you getting at? Are you angry at me?" Barbara's forehead creased.

"You seem to be trying to convince me of something."

Barbara took a deep breath. "There are things you need to know."

"You're not my fucking psychiatrist."

Barbara recoiled but did not answer.

"I hear you've been out with Dick," said Forbe.

Barbara uncrossed her legs and leaned forward. "So that's what's bugging you. The rest was just bullshit." She paused. "What if I have? It's none of your damn business."

"It is my damned business. You've got one hand on Dick's shirt buttons and the other on my zipper."

Barbara sprang to her feet and drew her satchel back. "You son of a bitch! Who do you think you are? St. Jimbo of the Chastity League?" As she threw the bag, Forbe ducked. It glanced off his head taking his toupee with it.

Forbe regained his composure. "I didn't mean that the way it sounded."

"Then how the hell did you mean it?"

"Are you using Dick to make me jealous?"

"Maybe I am. Maybe I'm not." Barbara sat back down.

"I thought it was over between us."

"That's never been very clear."

"We need to make it clear. Keeping this matter hanging isn't good for either of us."

Barbara closed her eyes for a moment then opened them and looked at Forbe. "I don't want to give you up, Jimbo. I thought you realized that a few weeks ago in Atlanta. Didn't that mean anything to you?"

"Hell, yes. But I can't go on. It's over now, Barbara. I'm sorry I didn't have the guts to make a clean break. I've been unfair to you."

Barbara dropped her face into her hands. Forbe looked away.

Finally, Forbe spoke. "You've got to help me follow through. It's up to both of us."

Silence surrounded them once more. Neither made eye contact with the other. Finally, Barbara spoke. "It will be one of the most difficult things I've ever done. I care about you."

"Would you care about me if I weren't governor, or mayor, or something like that?"

Barbara leaned forward, her eyes moist. "Now you *are* being unfair. I care about you no matter what you are."

"And I care about you, Barbara, but the next time—it's hard for me to say this—the next time you want an interview with me, please *send another reporter*. I cannot deal with you on a professional level."

Barbara teared, placed her face in her hands again, and sat very still for a long time. Then she looked at Forbe. "Okay, Jimbo, I'm leaving for the last time. But before I go, I want to ask you a personal question."

Forbe stared at the floor but said nothing.

"Look at me!" demanded Barbara.

Forbe looked.

"Have you ever talked to Betty about us?"

Forbe slowly moved his head back and forth.

Barbara spoke again. "Don't you think it's about time you did?"

Forbe opened his mouth to speak but Barbara put her finger to her lips. Then she rose, walked around the desk, and kissed his bald spot. Without another word she retrieved her satchel and left.

Forbe watched her walk out the door and ease it shut behind her. He leaned forward, propped his elbows on the desk, and rested his forehead on the heels of his hands. He closed his eyes and sat for a long time, deeply involved with his troubled thoughts. His office clock chimed the hour, then the quarter, then the half.

A bump at the door startled him. Dick entered with a thermos and three mugs. "Where's Barbara?" he asked.

"She remembered another appointment she'd forgotten. Said to give you her regards. She'll call you later."

Dick slammed the thermos and mugs on Forbe's desk. "Jimbo, the next time you need to be alone with someone, please tell me. Don't send me halfway to the moon to get coffee. I'm not your dammed gofer." He turned and stomped out.

Forbe sat in stunned silence. He thought, *If that don't beat it all. I'm a screwed up son of a bitch.*

He sat for a long time with his chin cupped in his hands, his eyes closed, his elbows on the desk. He tried to think about his good times with Betty, but another face and form kept squeezing between them. He thought about the Prayer Amendment and the crisis in his government. The clock chimed the hour again. He opened his eyes and looked at a snapshot of Betty that occupied a small space beyond his blotter. She wore a bright yellow dress and a straw hat and stood in front of a church. *God, she was beautiful then—and now.* He meshed his fingers and rubbed the sides of his chin with his thumbs. Tears left trails on his cheeks. He looked at the Alabama Great Seal on the wall across from his desk. The State of Alabama sat in the midst of four states—Tennessee, Georgia, Florida, and Mississippi—pressing in from all sides except for a corridor between Florida and Mississippi to the Gulf of Mexico. He thought about his situation. Suddenly, he sat up straight, *I'm not locked in. There's always a way out.* He reached over and pushed Dick's key on the intercom.

"Yes, Governor."

"Dick, I'm sorry about this afternoon. I've got a lot on my mind."

"Don't worry about it, Jimbo. I was a little short myself."

"Listen. I've got a very important matter to deal with. Call a meeting of the cabinet for tomorrow morning. I also want the senate and house majority and minority leaders in the meeting. Ten sharp."

FORBE SAT ON A stool at the kitchen bar and looked at Betty, "Honey, a cup of coffee and a couple of Famous Amoses is all I want. I'm going to bed early. I've got a tough decision to announce tomorrow." He laid his head on his crossed arms.

"Would you like to talk about it?" asked Betty as she ran water into the kettle and set it on the stove.

Forbe spoke without raising his head. "I don't want to burden you with it, but it's a decision that can make or break my administration."

"Might help you to talk about it." Betty watched the blue flame then removed the kettle when it started to whistle. She looked at her husband before she spooned the gourmet coffee into the grinder. He was sound asleep.

49

"Cuba? We're going to Cuba?" said Forbe to the uniformed officer at the door of his cabin.

"That's right," said the officer. "We have a shipload of used toilets for the people of—"

Clanging bells cutoff the conversation. "All hands on deck! All hands on deck!" came an authoritative voice over the ship's speaker.

Forbe looked at the officer and raised his voice. "Why, I know you. I'd recognize you anywhere. You're Barbie."

"Yes. And I'm also the captain of this ship—your ship, Mr. Forbe."

"Fire!" shouted the voice. "Fire aboard! All hands on deck! Man the hoses!"

"Let's go," said Barbie. "On deck!"

"But I'm naked," said Forbe. "I can't go out there naked. Let me get some—"

"No time." Barbie grabbed Forbe's hand and dragged him along the gangway and up the stairs.

"Captain! Captain!" An officer saluted as Barbie and Forbe burst out onto the deck.

Barbie returned the salute, listened, then said to Forbe, "The fire equipment has failed."

"Failed?" said Forbe. "How can the equipment fail? I just bought this ship."

"Anything can happen on this ship, Mr. Forbe. The equipment has failed."

"What now?"

"We can sink the ship to put out the fire or we can sail on to Cuba and let the ship burn. It's your call, sir."

"Sail on! Sail on!" said Forbe.

"Sail on!" echoed Barbie to the first mate.

Flames leaped through the deck. "God, save us!" cried Forbe. "Oh, God, save us. Put out this fire!" Forbe stopped shouting and listened. "Thunder! I hear thunder." The ship began to pitch. Waves crashed over the deck. Lightning flashed across the sky. Raindrops pelted Forbe's naked body. He reached for his handkerchief. *No handkerchief,* he thought. *Without my handkership I can't—*

A towering wave crashed into the boat. The deck tilted. Forbe slid toward the edge. "Help me, Barbie!"

"Not me! Not me!" Barbie dodged Forbe's flailing arms and began to slide in the opposite direction—up the listing deck. "Grab yourself, Mr. Forbe. You are your only hope. Bye, bye."

Forbe watched as Barbie slid over the edge above him and disappeared. Another wave crashed cross the deck. Forbe threw his hand to his head. His toupee was gone.

"Help! Help! Hel—"

"Jimmy, Jimmy, wake up! Wake up!" A familiar voice sounded above the roar of the sea. Forbe opened his eyes and released his grip on Betty's shoulder.

Betty sat up in bed. "I'll have bruises, Jimmy. Are you all right?"

Forbe shook his head and looked at the clock. It was 4 a.m. "How'd I get to bed?"

"You walked, dear, with a little help. Did you have another nightmare?"

"No. Yes. I don't know."

"Tell me about it. Maybe your dream means something."

"Dreams are dreams. They don't mean anything."

"Maybe God is speaking to you through your dreams."

"It sounded more like the Devil."

"Do you want a cup of coffee?"

"I need something stronger than that. How about a Cuba libre?"

"At 4 a.m? I'll make some coffee."

Betty pivoted her feet to the floor, rose and started toward the kitchen. At the bedroom door she turned. "You dreamed about Cuba?"

"I was on the way but didn't get there. It's sometimes hard to get where you want to go."

"You want to talk about it?"

"I sure as hell don't want to dream about it again. Let's have that coffee and talk about this prayer stuff." Forbe looked at Betty, her trim figure silhouetted through her night gown by the dim night light near the sink. His eyes moistened. "And . . ." He paused. Tears formed on his cheeks.

"Yes?"

"Let's talk about—"

"Talk about what?" said Betty as she turned and flipped on the light in the kitchen.

"Let's talk about Gulf Shores. It's about time we had a vacation."

"Oh," said Betty. "I'd like that."

50

FORBE LOOKED AROUND the room at the cabinet and the party leaders. He avoided eye contact with Senator Patrick Little, his nemesis. Patrick, Dick's brother, had authored and pushed the school budget bills through the legislature. Now serving his fifth term in the Senate, he was highly respected by both parties.

Dick called the meeting to order and asked if there were any pending matters to be discussed.

"Yes, there is," snapped the Senate majority leader. "Rucker is still on the kill list of the federal administration. More bases are sure to be added. You met with the local committee, Governor. What's being done?"

"We're still awaiting a committee report."

The House majority leader spoke. "There are rumors of healthcare reform that could affect employment in all of our districts. Has that committee made a report yet?"

"I'm still waiting," answered Forbe.

"We need more teachers in our schools to bring the teacher-to-student class ratio in line with the national average," said Senator Little. "We expect bi-partisan support for the bill I will introduce next week."

"Are the gambling bills dead, Governor?" asked the Senate majority leader. "I hear that the Concerned Cooperating Christians lobby is accepting millions of dollars from Georgia, Florida, and Mississippi gambling interests to block their passage. Strange bedfellows."

"We're getting positive fallout from the school budget legislation, Governor," said the House minority leader. "I support Patrick's new education bill."

"Where's the money going to come from?" asked the State Finance Committee chairman.

Forbe barely heard the questions and the debate that followed them. *I'm so tired*, he thought. *This job, it kills you slowly.* He would let them have their say—get things off their chests. Everything paled beside the magnitude of what he was about to say. Only one matter occupied his mind. The state had one problem. When the trivia ceased, he would lay it on the table.

After an hour's debate, he raised his hands for order and asked the cabinet members and political leaders to indulge him a few minutes.

"Please don't interrupt. Let me finish before you ask any questions."

Forbe looked around the table, this time gazing into the eyes that were focused on him. He wondered how each man might react to what he was about to say. He wondered about his next term. *Next term? Would there be a next term? Do I want a next term?* His marriage to the political future of the state had begun with the promise of a glamorous honeymoon but had become a ghastly nightmare. Puzzled at first about why his program had been frustrated at every turn, he now knew the answer. He once again panned his cabinet and the political leaders of both parties who sat in rapt attention awaiting his words.

"My fellow colleagues," he began. "You, too, Patrick."

Ripples of nervous laughter rolled around the table.

Forbe pulled out his handkerchief and wiped his forehead. "I come from a religious family. I was raised to go to church and, as a Baptist, to respect the religious convictions of other people that can't be converted to mine."

More nervous laughter.

"I was elected guvnah of this state because I projected an image of one who stood for Christian family values enshrined in the School Prayer Amendment. 'Let's get prayer back into the schools,' I said. Swept into office by the good people of this great state, I set out, with your help, to solve Alabama's problems. I have accomplished absolutely nothing."

"Wait! wait!" A senator protested.

"Don't sell yourself short!" Another pleaded.

Forbe held up his hands. When the noise subsided, he continued. "Following the successful passing of the Prayer Amendment bill—thanks to all of you who brought about its approval and ratification in a statewide referendum—my administration's legislative program went down the drain. Democrats presented a new legislative agenda to which you Republicans, against my wishes, gave enthusiastic assent. Ensuing legislation wrecked the state budget—cut government salaries back to national averages, raised teacher salaries up to national averages, and apparently there is more to come. But legislative excess is not all that bothers me." Forbe paused and took a deep breath.

"A few weeks ago, I became aware of unusual prayers in a small school in the east Alabama town of Orchard Hill, in Tallapoosa County." Forbe noticed chins drop and eyebrows arch around the conference table. "I have gleaned information from reliable sources and I have analyzed that information. I have concluded that school prayer is responsible for killing my legislative program and devastating the economy of the state of Alabama. Don't read me wrong. Some good things have happened but the bad far outweighs the good."

"Governor, are you feeling okay?" asked the Senate majority leader.

Forbe ignored the question. He pulled from his coat pocket some pieces of folded newsprint and laid them on the table in front of him. Using the *Atlanta Journal-Constitution* news articles as a guide, he traced the chronology of the prayers from Orchard Hill and the extraordinary series of events that he believed had wreaked havoc on his state. Then he carefully folded the papers and placed them back into his coat pocket.

"My fellow colleagues, I have given much thought to my next course of action." Forbe paused and wiped his forehead. "What I must do is crystal clear to me although I have very mixed emotions about it. Today, I am calling for a special session of the Alabama legislature for one and only one purpose: to repeal the prayer amendment!" The words thundered from his mouth.

Incredulous voices rose in unison from around the table.

"What did you say, Governor?"

"Would you repeat that?"

"Are you crazy?"

"I said, repeal the fu . . . frigging prayer amendment! Get the state prayer out of our schools."

"Get it out? Are you nuts?" asked the senator from Dothan.

"Roll it back! Kill it! The voters of the United States repealed prohibition. The voters of the State of Alabama can repeal prayer—prayer in the schools, I mean."

"Pardon me, Governor, but with all due respect, I must say that you are out of your mind," said the representative from Evergreen. "The Concerned Cooperating Christians in Alabama will crucify us. We'll never be re-elected. They've got three million members nationwide and I think two million of them live in Alabama."

Forbe raised his hands for calm. "If we don't get those prayers stopped in Orchard Hill and God knows where else, it won't matter whether we're ever re-elected. There won't be anything left to govern."

Patrick Little rose. The shouts and comments diminished

and then ceased. "Governor, I would like to clarify my under-
standing of what I am hearing. You've probably already answered the question I am about to ask, but I would like to hear
you answer it again. Why did you campaign for governor on the
School Prayer Amendment?"

That self-righteous S.O.B., thought Forbe. "Senator Little, the
School Prayer Amendment got me elected as guvnah of this
state."

Patrick began softly and ended with a loud, forceful inflection. "Did you believe school prayer would have any value
beyond getting you elected?"

Forbe paused and took a deep breath. "I never considered the
value of school prayer beyond what it was designed to do,
namely, get us elected to office. Whether or not prayer worked
was of no concern to me . . . *then*. It was a campaign strategy.
Don't act like you don't know what I'm talking about. You all
made promises to get re-elected. Even you, Patrick."

"So, now that you are convinced that prayer does work, you
want it out of the schools," Patrick said.

"I wouldn't put it that way."

"Then how would you put it, Governor Forbe?"

"The official Alabama Prayer for the schools was designed to
be a benign, inoffensive spiritual exercise. If the kids had stuck
with the official prayer, nothing significant would have happened. But the kids in Orchard Hill had the bright idea that they
could improve on my prayer. We've had lots of problems since."

"I've read the articles in the *AJC*," said Patrick. "The children
believe their prayers have been answered. They think they have
seen improvements in their schools and communities."

"Whatever improvements they claim to see are nothing
compared to the devastation they are causing this state. Strange
and unsettling things have happened since they started tamper-

ing with the official prayer. We're out of money, Patrick. We can't pay for everything. Our economy is in ruins."

"In other words, the kids got serious about their praying and it may be affecting your pet projects and programs," continued Patrick.

Fuck you, Forbe thought. "We've got to shut that prayer down," he said, pausing to swallow, "before Alabama goes bankrupt. Those kids are out of control."

Patrick sat down. "Thank you, Governor. Your words have been troubling but quite revealing."

Forbe again addressed the assembled politicians. "I need your support to repeal the Prayer Amendment."

"You actually intend to go through with this?" asked the Senate majority leader.

"I have no choice. Do I get your support or not?"

The Senate majority leader stood. "Governor, many of us have watched the deteriorating economic situation in the state. Whether it has anything to do with school prayer directly, we're not sure. But your call to repeal it has merit, on whatever grounds. We'll support you if you will help us neutralize the Concerned Cooperating Christian voter guides."

"Governor Forbe," said the House majority leader, "we'll support it as long as the House does not require a roll-call vote."

"Hear! Hear!" voiced several others. "No roll-call votes."

"My party will support the repeal," said Senator Little. "Many of us were never in favor of mixing religion with public education in the first place."

After a few procedural questions had been cleared up, the meeting adjourned. Forbe had Dick leak the contents of the meeting to the press, then called Betty to pack clothing for their much-needed vacation at Gulf Shores. Under no circumstances did he plan to be in Montgomery when the shit hit the fan.

51

THE ANGRY CROWD chanted, "GOD, YES! FORBE, NO! GOD, YES! FORBE, NO!"

"Several hundred men, women, and children had gathered on the capitol steps. Hand-lettered placards nodded and waved above the assembly. Most made reference to Forbe. "THE END IS NEAR—FOR FORBE," read one. "FORBE GO HOME, LEAVE GOD ALONE," read another. One sign said, "WWJD? IMPEACH FORBE!" Several professionally printed placards carried references to "CONCERNED COOPERATING CHRISTIANS FOR PUPIL PRAYER." Soon a pitch pipe sounded over the PA system and the crowd intoned, "Sweet Hour of Prayer."

Following the song, a speaker rushed to the mike. With tie loosened and sleeves rolled up, he shouted to the crowd. "Gimme a 'J'!"

"J!" roared the crowd.

"Gimme a 'E'!"

"E!"

"Gimme a 'S'!"

"S!"

"Gimme a 'U'!"

"U!"

"Gimme a 'S'!"

"S!"

"And whadaya have?"

"Jesus! Jesus! Jesus!" thundered the multitude.

"Give Jesus a hand," the speaker cried.

The crowd applauded.

"Lift your hands to heaven and praise Jesus."

Emma jumped up from the couch. "There's Brother Johnny Carroll!"

"Where?" asked Susie.

"There, right behind the man at the microphone."

"God says we must pray for our government leaders," said the speaker. "Where are our leaders?"

"Running from God!" roared the crowd.

"We elected James Forbe governor of the state," the speaker continued. "What should we do now?"

"Impeach him!" roared the crowd.

"Sounds like they're going to throw peaches at him," said Susie.

"No, silly. It means to fire him."

"I knew that." Susie laughed. "I wanted to see if you did. But why do they want to fire the governor?"

"Let's listen and find out. Look! Brother Johnny's about to speak," said Emma.

"All we, like sheep, have gone astray,' Isaiah 53:6," said Brother Johnny. "One of our own has strayed from the fold."

"He's talking about sheep," said Emma.

"Brother Johnny talks a lot before he says anything," said Susie. "Just listen."

" . . . and Governor Forbe has turned against God," continued Johnny. "He wants to drive God from the schools."

Susie disagreed. "He's a good governor. He helped fix our school."

"The repeal of the Prayer Amendment is an affront to Almighty God. Call your senators and representatives." Johnny stepped back from the mike.

"Throw Forbe out!" shouted a voice.

"Throw him out!" echoed another.

"THROW HIM OUT! THROW HIM OUT! THROW HIM OUT!" the crowd took up the chant.

The scene cut to a studio announcer. "This is the Concerned Cooperating Christians Network. You have just witnessed the massive turnout of the CCC on the Alabama state capitol steps protesting the repeal of the Prayer Amendment. The last speaker was Brother Johnny Carroll, a worker in God's vineyard and minister to the senior citizens of our great state. Brother Johnny needs your donations. God used him to get the Prayer Amendment passed and he needs your support again. Call the number on your screen and pledge your dollars for Brother Johnny and his divine ministry."

"I didn't know Brother Johnny needed money," said Emma.

"Neither did I," said Susie. "Why don't we try to get him some."

"Great! Let's include Governor Forbe in the prayer. I don't think the last one got through."

"We'll take it to school tomorrow and see if Mrs. Haley will let us do it again."

Dear God: The TV said that Brother Johnny works for you. When's the last time you gave him a raise? They're raising money for him on television. If you could chip in, I'm sure he would appreciate it. And while you're at it, please give the governor a hand. Some of your people are out to get him. Not thy will but our will be done. In your name we pray, Amen.

52

Brother Johnny could not believe what the attorney was saying. He had been notified by the law firm to appear for the reading of a last will and testament. He had never been present for one before. "Would you repeat that statement about the $253,000?" he asked. No Bible verse seemed to apply.

"Yes. Mrs. Vera Ogletree has passed away and in her will has left the sum of $253,000 for your ministry."

"Aunt Vera from the Valley of the Shadow Rest Home?"

"Yes, Aunt Vera—that's what everyone called her—has left the aforementioned sum to your ministry. She loved you dearly."

"I thought she was destitute," said Johnny.

"Mrs. Ogletree was a wealthy woman who, at the age of ninety-six, had outlived all her descendants. She outlived her husband—may he rest in peace—and all her brothers and sisters. She had one daughter who never married and died about twenty years ago. She left all the after-tax proceeds from her estate, which she liquidated when she entered the rest home, for your ministry to the elderly."

"'Surely goodness and mercy shall follow me all the days of my life,' Psalm 23:6," Brother Johnny quoted from his book of divine wisdom. *God has smiled upon me. I must serve him faithfully. I have to finish the mission he is calling me to do.*

53

FORBE PEELED THE shell from another Maine lobster tail while Betty struggled to extract the succulent meat from a snow crab leg.

"Here, let me help you," offered Forbe.

"Why can't I do it? The meat always parts and stays buried in the shell."

Forbe placed the crab leg in the shell cracker, cracked it, and removed whole sections of the delectable flesh. He laid it on Betty's plate.

"You don't have a politician's touch," he laughed. "A politician can extract blood from a turnip. By the way, do you know the couple seated near the window over there to your right? Don't look now, but check them out. They act as if they've recognized me."

"I'm not surprised. After all, you are the governor of Alabama, and the two state troopers seated behind us are a sure giveaway."

"You're probably right. I sure hope it's not another damn reporter, or one of them Jesus freaks."

Betty stole a glance. "He looks familiar."

"Oh, hell! They're coming this way," whispered Forbe. "Act like you don't know them!"

The troopers stood and situated themselves between Forbe and the approaching couple.

"But we do know them—at least him," Betty said. "Isn't that your roommate from college?"

Forbe motioned for the troopers to let them pass.

"Well, I'll be damned. Stanley!" Forbe rose to greet the pair.

"Hello, Jimmy," said Stanley as he extended his hand. "It's been a long time."

"You S.O.B!" Forbe ignored Stanley's hand and threw his arms around him—chest high. He pushed back and looked up. "You bastard! Without the beard I didn't recognize you."

Upon release from Forbe's grip, Stanley hugged Betty. "It's nice to see you both. You look good. "

Betty turned toward Janet and extended her hand. "And this is Mrs. Hannah, I presume?"

"Not yet," said Stanley. "This is Janet Gaylor, minister of the Unitarian Universalist church in Orchard Hill."

"Pleased to meet you."

"Yes, glad to meet you, too," said Forbe as he took her hand. "Orchard Hill, did you say? In Tallapoosa County?"

"Yes," replied Janet. "The great city of Orchard Hill."

"I'd like to talk with you, "said Forbe. "Why don't you join us for drinks, er . . . coffee at the Gulf Park Resort Restaurant? Do you know where that is?"

"Yes," replied Stanley. "We'd be delighted to. How about 9 p.m.?"

Forbe nodded.

"Good, Enjoy your meal. This restaurant is the best eating place in town."

"We always come to the Gulf Shores Steamer when we're here," said Forbe. "No body broils seafood as well as they do."

"What will you have?" asked Forbe as the four sat down in the lounge.

"I'll have a Heineken," replied Stanley.

"Make that two," said Janet, "mine dark."

"That'll be two Heinekens and . . . two decaf coffees . . . naw . . . scratch one of the coffees and bring me a Scotch and soda," said Forbe.

"Scratch the other decaf and bring me a glass of Zinfandel." Betty looked at her husband and winked.

"I didn't know Baptist ministers drank," said Forbe.

"I don't *drink*," replied Stanley, "but I do have an occasional beer."

"By the way," said Janet, "I'm curious about your nickname? Stanley called you 'Jimmy', yet all I hear is—"

"Jimbo?" Forbe smiled. "I was known as 'Jimmy' in college. But when I first entered politics, a friend suggested that I take on a more distinctive nickname."

"Why 'Jimbo'?" asked Janet.

"Bubba was already taken." Forbe laughed and everyone joined in. "If Alabama were Catholic, Bubba would be the patron saint."

"Saint Bubba," said Stanley and everyone laughed again.

"My middle name is Bogue—my mother's maiden name. So my friend started calling me Jimbo and it stuck."

"Pardon my overactive curiosity, but I thought you wore a toupée," said Janet.

"I did," said Forbe. "But times are changing. Betty likes me better without it. Says I look more like me. To tell you the truth, I *feel* more like me."

"What brings you two to Gulf Shores?" asked Betty. "My, but you look good!" She glanced at Stanley then at Janet.

"Rest and relaxation. Life in Washington can get hectic."

"Are you still in religious work?" she asked, and again cut her eyes toward Janet.

"Yes, but not pastor of a church. I burned out when I was at Tabernacle Baptist. You may have heard of my leaving."

"Yes. I heard one side of the story. I'd like to hear yours one day. Have you and Reverend Gaylor known each other long?"

"Janet and I have been friends for about a year and Gulf Shores seemed like a good place to work on our relationship."

Janet looked at Stanley and smiled.

"We're also here for R and R," said Forbe. "Montgomery is a mad house these days."

"The announced repeal of the Prayer Amendment?" asked Stanley.

"You've heard about it?"

"Who hasn't? That was a shocking move for the Bible Belt."

"It's was a shocking thing for me to do." Forbe turned to Janet. "A reporter convinced me it all started with one of your kids."

"One of my kids?"

"She said that a kid from the Unitarian church in Orchard Hill started the add-on school prayers. Did you have something to do with it?"

"No. I wish I could take credit for that. To my knowledge, those prayers were the sole responsibility of the children who took them to class—a girl from my church and her friend from the Baptist church."

"I've seen some of the prayers. They're clever."

"Not clever. They're simple. It's difficult for us adults to think simply. We complicate matters. Children think with their hearts," said Janet.

"It's hard to believe that children thought up those prayers. I commissioned an expensive and highly educated committee of politicians and preachers to write the official prayer."

"Innocent simplicity is a virtue," said Janet.

"We certainly don't have much of that left in Montgomery," Forbe said.

Betty looked at her husband then burst out laughing. Stanley and Janet followed before Forbe joined in.

"Here are your drinks, folks. Is there anything else?" said the waiter as he placed the tray on the table.

Forbe waved him away and looked again at Janet. "I've got to know something. I am confident that the Prayer Amendment will be repealed. Attached to the repeal is a provision that will prohibit the overt exercise of religion in public schools. Do you think that will stop the children? You think they'll quit praying at school?"

"Hopefully not," said Janet. "Probably, yes. Someone will discourage them. We're so quick to rob children of that which is most precious to them—their innocence, their natural spontaneity, their uncluttered spirituality."

"Why are you so sure it's the prayers that did you in?" asked Stanley.

"The simple logic of cause and effect. I know what's going on in the legislature. I read the *Journal* articles. I even talked with the reporter who did the stories. The legislative actions followed those prayers, in some cases by a matter of days."

"Do you think all the prayers have been answered?" continued Stanley.

"I've seen enough to convince me, but I've got mixed feelings about it. Betty was the subject of one of their prayers and look at her now—almost back to normal. Isn't she beautiful?"

"She always was," said Stanley smiling. "I never understood what she saw in you."

Forbe smiled. "You haven't changed, you son-of-a-gun. Were you about to say something, Janet?"

"Maybe you misread your party. Perhaps the senators and representatives have always wanted the reforms they voted for."

"Whatever the reason," said Forbe, "I've come to the conclusion that religion and secular education don't mix. When you play around with religion, you are sure as hell going to get burned."

"I'm tired," said Betty. "Why don't we continue this conversation tomorrow?"

"Me, too," said Forbe. "We have some things to talk over."

"Perhaps we could have breakfast together," said Stanley.

"I'd like that," said Forbe. "My political neurons are firing. Maybe they'll make connection by breakfast."

"Let's meet at our place," said Janet. "Roger's Castle by the Sea."

THE FOLLOWING MORNING, Forbe and Betty were already in the dining room when Stanley and Janet walked in.

"Stanley proposed!" shouted Janet across the restaurant.

Heads turned and breakfasting vacationers applauded as Janet and Stanley walked to the Forbes's table.

"Congratulations," said Forbe as he took Stanley's hand. "I had a feeling something was in the works."

Betty hugged Janet then both reached for table napkins to blot their eyes.

After they were seated and had ordered, Forbe said, "Betty and I did a lot of talking last night after you left. I see lots of things more clearly now."

"You look more relaxed," said Stanley.

"I am relaxed. We did some personal housekeeping and also talked about the future."

"We've come a long way," said Betty. She leaned toward Forbe and squeezed his hand.

"I have often overlooked one of her qualities that would have been very helpful to me in my work—her intuition. She knows me better than I know myself. Do you know that she can read me like a book?"

"But you seldom let me tell you what the book said."

"She accused me of wetting my finger to see which way the wind was blowing then steering my craft in that direction."

"It's difficult to sail against the wind," said Janet, "but it can be done."

"I've got a lot of sailing to do," said Forbe.

"By the way," said Janet, "Did you ever hear anything else from that reporter, Barbara Willis, of the Atlanta paper, who broke the Prayer Amendment story?"

"No." Forbe looked at Betty then at Janet. "She's out of the picture now."

The waiter brought their order and left.

Forbe sipped his coffee, then said, "I've really been an ass. Those kids weren't out to get me or wreck the state. It was something you said last night, Janet, that made me think— innocent simplicity. Those kids were doing what they thought was right. And it was right, dammit. They were trying to help me and the state and I didn't see it—even when I learned they led the school to pray for Betty. It doesn't matter whether their prayers did it or not. The important thing is that total strangers cared and it happened. I want to invite Susie and Emma to the Capitol for a joint session with the Legislature."

"Jimmy, what a wonderful idea!" Betty threw her arms around him, almost tipping his coffee. "You've come so far since all this started."

"But I'm not there yet. I can't make it by myself. I need some new blood in my administration."

Stanley said, "That's a decent thought. You have anybody in mind?"

"Yes, I want you to join my staff."

"Me? The notorious Reverend Doctor Stanley Hannah?"

"Yes, you, my friend, Stanley Hannah. Alabama needs you."

"I've never been involved in politics."

"Don't tell me Baptists don't do politics."

"I won't go there, but I still don't think I have the kind of experience you need."

"I know more about you than you think. Although I don't know the details, I am aware that you had something to do with the recent thaw in the U.S. relations with Cuba. That counts. And your humanitarian work."

"What would the job involve?"

"You would replace Dick Little," said Forbe. "He plans to resign soon to prepare his run for the office of lieutenant guvnah in the next election. First thing I'll do is send you on a trade mission to Cuba—get something coming and going through the Port of Mobile."

"You're pulling my chain," Stanley said.

Forbe said, "You and I got along pretty well in college. I could use you in an advisory capacity, as my chief-of-staff. Sometimes I see things narrowly, black and white. You would bring a broader perspective to the state-house—help me see the whole picture. I might even ask you to run my reelection campaign."

"No! Not that! But the other interests me. I like what I hear."

"Then you'll accept?"

Stanley looked at Janet, then at the ebb and flow of waves on the beach a few yards away. Seagulls walked and chattered and a pelican skimmed the waves in search of breakfast. Then he looked back at Janet. She looked him directly in the eye. Her eyes glistened. He looked back at Forbe.

"I need a little time to think about it. I love my work with the Baptist Alliance for Progress. I'll let you know as soon as possible."

"Let's take a walk, Jimmy," said Betty as she finished her coffee. "The day is young and we've still got talking to do."

54

"WE ARE GATHERED here this day to pray for the government of the State of Alabama." The pastor of Tabernacle Baptist Church spoke from the state capitol steps. CCCN, the Concerned Cooperating Christians Network, broadcast the service.

"Looks like everybody's praying for the government," said Susie.

"We shall pray around the clock until God hears our prayers," the pastor continued.

"Why do they pray around the clock?" Susie sipped an orange soda as they watched the TV in Emma's room.

"Maybe they don't know which time zone God's in," said Emma.

The booming voice continued. "Send a representative . . ."

"I got to go to the bathroom," said Susie.

"Me, too," said Emma. "You use that one and I'll go down-stairs."

". . . pretend to tell God what to do," came the familiar voice of Brother Johnny as Emma and Susie returned to the room.

"God knows what he must do. But we must lift the right petitions to the throne of grace so that our prayers will not be amiss. 'Ye ask, and receive not, because ye ask amiss,' James 4:3.' Here are our petitions: Number one: Exile Governor James Forbe from the State House. Number two: Afflict any senator or representative who votes to repeal your Prayer Amendment. Number three: Disturb the lawmakers until the Ten Commandments is the law of the State of Alabama."

"I thought he wasn't going to tell God what to do," said Susie.

"God can still turn him down," replied Emma.

"What if he doesn't?"

"Reverend Gaylor says it will probably be repealed whether God has anything to do with it or not. She suspects God never wanted it in the first place."

"If God didn't want it, how did it happen?"

"I don't know."

"If the amendment is repealed, will we have to stop praying?" asked Susie.

"Reverend Gaylor says that prayer is private, and the law can't stop us from doing it."

"Just the same, Emma, I got a feeling that something bad is gonna happen."

"This is a sad day for our great state," said a new speaker. "The forces of evil want to remove God from the places of learning."

"God sure gets moved around a lot," said Susie.

The speaker continued, "Fornication and illegitimate births will increase."

"What's hornication?" queried Susie.

"It's practicing marriage without a license," said Emma.

"And illiterate births?"

"I think it's having babies before finishing school."

"Alabama will never be the same. If this state's bold experiment with prayer in the schools comes to a tragic end, Alabama will return to the dark—"

Emma pressed the remote and the screen went black.

"Let's go climb the sycamore tree. I'm tired of television."

"There are other programs."

"Maybe we'll have our own television program some day," said Emma.

"That'll be great. We'll have a kids-only show."

"We won't be kids forever."

"Will we think like grownups when we grow up?" asked Susie.

"I hope not. Grownups say the darndest things."

Susie said, "We'll always think like kids. Here, give me a lift. I'm not used to climbing your tree."

Emma saddled her hands and boosted Susie to the lowest branch. "We'll think like kids even when we no longer act like kids. And, we'll write prayers for everything. It'll be great."

"I'm scared," said Susie.

"We're not four feet off the ground."

"Not about that. I have a tickling in my stomach that won't go away."

"It'll go away when we write another prayer."

"A prayer about what?"

"About our schools."

"But we must have about the best schools in the nation now," said Susie.

"And they are about to get better," said Emma.

"How?"

"How about Olympic games for high school students. Prizes will be scholarships to college. We'll be going to college some day."

"That's a good idea!"

"Where will they get the money for scholarships?" Emma wondered out loud.

"How about the money colleges get from football games and stuff," Susie blurted out.

"God will appreciate that suggestion," said Emma. "We'll

write the prayer as soon as we get out of this tree."

"And take it to school tomorrow." Susie jumped to the ground followed by Emma. They raced for Emma's house.

55

BROTHER JOHNNY READ, again and again, the *Journal-Constitution* text of one of the children's add-on school prayers.

In the privacy of his home, Johnny half prayed and half preached. "This is utter irreverence. It's an abomination to the Lord. It's a sacrilege. 'All manner of sin and blasphemy shall be forgiven unto men: but the blasphemy against the Holy Ghost shall not be forgiven unto men,' Matthew 12:31. The governor is lost, but, with God as my helper, I can save those poor, innocent little kids. I must help them get it right before it's too late. Dear merciful God, I pray that they will listen to me."

Brother Johnny made plans to visit Orchard Hill the following Sunday. He did not know who the children were and reluctantly dialed the pastor of the Unitarian church who had been quoted in the paper.

"Hello, this is Janet Gaylor."

"Hello, Rever . . . ah . . . Miss Gaylor. This is Brother Johnny Carroll. Do you have a moment? It's a matter of great importance."

"Why, certainly, Brother Johnny. It's been quite a while since we last talked. What's on your mind?"

"I'm calling about the school prayers those children are lifting up to Almighty God. I'm concerned for the welfare of the little ones. 'Jesus said, Suffer little children, and forbid them not, to come unto me, for of such is the kingdom of heaven,' Matthew 19:14."

"And, what is the nature of your concern, Brother Johnny?" asked Janet.

"I have learned that the prayers are written by little children from different religions—some un-Christian religions."

"I believe the correct word would be 'non-Christian,'" Janet said.

"I want to get to the bottom of this problem, Miss Gaylor. Are there Jewish and Roman Catholic children in the schools in Orchard Hill?"

"Yes. And there are Baptist, Methodist, Pentecostal, and Unitarian Univeralist. What is the problem?"

"Satan, Miss Gaylor. '. . . for Satan himself is transformed into an angel of light,' Second Corinthians 11:14."

"The children wrote the prayers, Brother Johnny, without help from anyone."

"That's the problem," replied Johnny. "Those dear little children, unlearned in the ways of Almighty God, are not qualified to do something so sacred and transcendental as write prayers."

"What's the problem with the children's prayers? We've had no complaints from the teachers, parents, or pastors in Orchard Hill."

"'I would not have you ignorant, brethren,' Romans 1:13. Have you seen the prayers? Have you read them?"

"Certainly. They are beautiful, simple, and full of childlike faith. Didn't Jesus of Nazareth say, '. . . unless you change and become like little children, you will never enter the kingdom of heaven'?"

"Yes, Miss Gaylor, he did. But God also depends on the shepherds of his flock to keep his lambs on the straight and narrow path."

"I read somewhere in the scripture, Brother Johnny, that

Jesus said, 'I praise you, Father, because you have hidden these things from the wise and learned, and revealed them to little children.'"

"Miss Gaylor, you are misusing the holy Word of God again. Please tell me who the children are so I can warn them."

"What are the errors that have you upset?"

"I simply cannot believe you have not detected the blasphemy in the last lines of the prayers?"

"Oh, you mean the inversion of words 'not thy will but our will be done'?"

"Yes, yes, those are the words. Now you know why I must talk with the children—get their prayers on track."

"I'm sure you mean no harm, Brother Johnny. But I believe it best to leave the children alone. God reads their hearts, not their lips."

"I'm sorry to have bothered you, Miss Gaylor. I've got to go. Goodbye." Johnny slammed the phone on the hook. Satan was trying to discourage him, but God was stronger and would lead him to the children who needed him.

UNABLE TO REACH the Reverend Doster of the Orchard Hill Baptist Church on the phone, Johnny sped along the highway to catch the pastor at the Sunday service. He broke the speed limit going through Dadeville, and a patrol car pulled him over.

"But officer, I'm on a divine mission. I must obey the laws of God."

"And I must enforce the laws of Alabama, Brother Johnny."

"Won't you forgive me just this one time?"

"I'll let God forgive you while I write this citation. May I see your driver's license?"

Delayed by the officer's lecture, Johnny arrived just minutes before the service ended. As he slipped into the back pew, he thought, *Satan put that trooper in my path. But God will prevail.*

The hymn of invitation ended, the benediction was pronounced, and Brother Johnny acknowledged greetings from several of the church members who knew him. As the last person left the church, Johnny approached the pastor.

"Well, hello, Brother Johnny."

"How are you today, Brother Doster? I'm sorry I arrived late."

"How can I serve you, Brother Johnny?"

"I have been very . . . uh . . . impressed with the school prayers of the little children and would like to talk to you about them." Johnny edited his words.

"Come have lunch with me and we'll talk it over. One of the children attends this church."

"Oh, that won't be necessary. Besides, I've already eaten," Johnny lied. He caught his breath. He could not believe he had lied. It was a white lie and he was on a divine mission. God would surely forgive him. *All sin is equal in the eyes of*— but he cut the thought out. "Which of the children goes to your church?"

"The Holland girl, Susie. She was here with her parents this morning."

"Do you know the other children?"

"Orchard Hill is a small place, Brother Johnny. Everybody knows everybody. I believe Susie's friend, Emma, helps her write the prayers. They're like two peas in a pod."

"Are there any more?"

"Several kids have helped in the project, but those two are the main ones."

"Don't let me keep you from lunch, pastor. I must be going." Johnny turned to leave.

"You're sure you won't go with me? We eat well on Sundays. Besides, you won't find anyone to talk to until after lunch."

"No, thank you. I must be going," said Johnny.

The engine fired quickly on his new Chevy Suburban. He hoped God would forgive him for spending so much of Aunt Vera's money on new transportation but his old Cutlass had died and he had to get around. And with the SUV, he could help transport the old folks to the baptisms.

He headed for the restaurant he had seen on the bypass coming into town. His stomach growled.

The Wedgwood Restaurant filled with families in their Sunday best. Johnny surveyed the dessert section at the beginning of the serving line. After selecting fried chicken, mashed potatoes, and okra from the steam table, he found a seat at a booth facing the wall in the corner of the dining room. He removed the plates from the tray and turned to place the empty tray on the caddie behind him. Upon catching sight of the Baptist pastor and family in the serving line, he pivoted toward the wall and ate his meal in silence, praying for anonymity.

Johnny remained in the corner until the restaurant had almost emptied. In the directory at the phone booth outside, he found the name Holland. There were several Hollands. He inserted a quarter and dialed the first one. A female answered the phone, "Hello."

"Hello, I'm Brother Johnny, minister to the elderly. Are you the mother of Susie Holland?"

"No. I have all sons," replied the lady.

"Do you know those Hollands? The ones with the daughter?"

"No. I'm afraid not," came the voice. "They don't go to my church."

"Thank you," said Johnny. He depressed the cradle switch, inserted a quarter and dialed the next Holland.

"Hello."

"Hello, young lady. May I speak with your momma?"

"Hello. I no young lady. I young man."

"Young man, please call your momma to the phone!"

"Hello. My momma in the toilet."

"Then call your daddy to the phone. Say, 'Daddy! Come to the phone!'" instructed Johnny.

"Hello. My daddy come home drunk. He sleep now."

There was a pause on the line. Johnny feared the child would hang up. "Momma! Here man on phone."

Johnny took a deep breath.

"Hello! Who's there?" A female voice spoke.

"This is Brother Johnny Carroll, minister to the elderly. Are you Mrs. Holland?" asked Johnny.

"Yeah. What you want?"

"Could I speak with Susie?"

"There's no Susie here. That's my brother-in-law's daughter, but she's quite young. Are you sure you have the right name?"

"Yes, yes. I have the right name. Could you give me their phone number?"

"Certainly. It's . . ."

Johnny scribbled the number on the phone book, thanked Mrs. Holland, and hung up. The number corresponded to the last Holland in the H section: Zachary J. Holland. He looked at the address, removed the handset, and dialed the new number. A man's voice answered, "Hello."

"Hello, I'm Brother Johnny, minister to the elderly. Are you Mr. Holland?"

"Yes, how can I help you?"

"I minister in the homes for the elderly in this area. Do you mind if I come by and chat with you a few minutes?"

"We don't have any family members in the homes, but sure, come on over. Why, I've seen you on television. Do you have my address?"

"Sycamore Street," said Johnny. "If you will give me instructions, I'm sure God will help me find it." As Johnny stepped outside the booth, he felt a cool breeze brush his sweat-washed skin. The sun still beat down without mercy but clouds were forming in the west.

56

Jimmy and Betty Forbe dragged into their hotel room.

"Seems like we've walked and talked all day," said Betty

"We needed it," said Forbe. "All that salt air and seafood has gotten me excited."

"What time is it?"

Forbe stretched. "About bedtime. I think I'll take a shower."

"Me, too," said Betty. "You go ahead. I'll get mine later."

Forbe showered and dressed in his new silk pajamas. While Betty was in the shower, he shaved and splashed on his face the after shave Betty liked best. He walked back into the bedroom, turned down the cover and stretched out on the bed. He switched on the TV and flipped through the channels stopping on HBO. A commercial ended and the screen read, "Returning to Night-life in Amsterdam." A female stripper danced into the audience throwing her clothing into the faces of male patrons. Within moments she was totally naked. Forbe looked toward the bathroom then turned the TV off.

Betty entered the room, dressed in the new gown she had bought for the trip. Her eyes drooped.

"The shower was good," she said, "but I'm still tired. We walked for miles." She dropped onto the bed.

Forbe moved over and kissed her. "My, but you're beautiful. I don't know where I would be if it weren't for you."

"You were not a bad catch," said Betty. "But you do lack a sense of self-girth."

"More of me for you to love." Forbe smiled and kissed her

again, this time lingering. She responded with her lips but not with her body.

Forbe pulled her closer. "This is like a second honeymoon."

"I'm tired," said Betty. "I'll feel better equipped for this tomorrow."

"We leave tomorrow."

"I know. The truth is that I still hurt. Just give me a little time."

Forbe said, "I feel so close to you."

"And I to you," said Betty. "In so many ways."

"Could we cuddle a bit?" Forbe moved his hand down her thigh. "I'm as horny as a unitar . . . uh . . . unicorn."

Betty caught his hand. "Darnit, Jimmy, not tonight!"

"But I feel I really need to . . . uh . . ."

"Then why don't you go sneeze?" said Betty as she rolled over and turned out the light.

A few minutes later, Betty asked, "Are you still awake?"

"Yeah," moaned Forbe.

"About *that*, why don't you ask me again in the morning."

"I'll do it," said Forbe. "I'm sorry about things before. I . . . I love you." He closed his eyes and slept. No turbulent dreams interrupted him. He slept long and hard, the sleep of the just.

"TENSIONS ARE MOUNTING again in the Middle—"

Stanley changed the channel. ". . . Israeli troops moved—"

"Is that all there is on TV?" said Janet from the bathroom. "Surely there's something better to do."

Stanley pressed the channel-button once again then reached for the program guide on the table beside the bed. "—dent Bush has sent his personal envoy to the regi—"

Suddenly, the TV went silent. Janet turned and faced Stanley, the power plug dangling from her hand. "We've had enough war and tension. Let's major on peace, tonight." She lay down on the bed beside him, clad only in a semi-transparent gown.

Stanley, in his cotton percale pajamas, turned to face her. Janet began to unbutton his pajama shirt. Stanley eased out of it and slipped off his pajama bottom.

"Oh, Stanley, you're—"

The William Tell Overture charged into the room and circled the bed.

"Dammit, dammit, dammit," said Stanley as he sat up looking for the cell phone. "I thought I left that thing in the car. Let me answer it." He started to swing his feet to the floor.

Janet grabbed him. "Let the music play, Lone Ranger, and come to me. Tonto can wait."

57

Brother Johnny Carroll pulled into the drive of a large, white frame house on Sycamore Street in Orchard Hill. Another large house sat next door with a huge sycamore tree in the backyard. He thought of Zacchaeus who climbed up in a tree like that to see Jesus. The door of the house opened as he walked up the steps.

"Welcome, Brother Johnny. It's nice to have you visit us," said the middle-aged, balding man who extended his hand. "I'm Zack Holland."

"Thank you for inviting me over. I hope it's not a bad time."

"Not at all. You're in time for coffee or a Coke. Come on in. Looks like it's coming up a cloud."

Johnny peered at the western sky, now dark and threatening, and thought of the Biblical storm on the Sea of Galilee. Then he turned and entered the spacious living room of the turn-of-the-century home. A large, white Bible adorned a coffee table in front of the couch and a tapestry of the Last Supper hung on the wall. The furniture was modern.

"This is my wife, Karen," said Zack, gesturing toward the trim woman who entered the room wearing an apron.

"How do you do, ma'am. I'm Johnny Ca—"

"Yes, I've seen you at the rest home in Dadeville," Karen interrupted. "Our W.M.U. visits there occasionally to chat with the residents. I heard you preach on TV, too. You really know the scripture. Would you like some coffee or would you prefer something cold?"

"Iced tea will be fine, or anything cold."

As Karen left the room, Brother Johnny laid down the Biblical foundation for his visit. "Mr. Holland, the Bible says, 'Hear my prayer, O God; give ear to the words of my mouth,' Psalm 54:2. I'm here today to talk about the school prayers in Orchard Hill. I believe your daughter, Susie, helps write them."

The darkening sky sucked the sunlight from the living room. Zack turned on the floor lamp beside his chair.

"The prayers have been getting some notoriety lately," said Zack. "We had a reporter here a few weeks ago and it came out in the *Atlanta Journal-Constitution*. What do you think about that?"

"Yes, I read about it in the *Journal*. I would like to talk with your daughter about what I read."

"She and her friend, Emma, are around somewhere. Exactly why do you want to talk to Susie?"

"I saw the prayers, Mr. Holland. I'm concerned about the content of the prayers, especially the ending. Have you noticed anything unusual about the ending of the prayers?"

"Can't say that I have," replied Zack, "except for that switching of words 'my will, thy will' or something like that. The children are young. They were bound to get something wrong."

"That's it! That's what I'm concerned about, Mr. Holland. Those words. A prayer is a very sacred thing. God says, 'Ye ask, and receive not, because ye ask amiss, that ye may consume it upon your lusts,' James 4:3. We must be careful how we pray."

"The *Journal* reporter thinks the prayers are being answered," said Zack. "Perhaps God isn't concerned about misplaced words."

"There's more than misplaced words, Mr. Holland. There's blasphemy. God has sent me here to put it right. May I talk with Susie?"

"I don't think that would be a good idea, Brother Johnny.

Susie is a bright and perceptive child. I'm sure she meant no harm—"

"Oh, certainly not," agreed Johnny. "An innocent mistake."

"These children are very enthusiastic about what they are doing. I'd hate to see them discouraged," said Zack.

"Oh, I wouldn't do that. I carefully follow the Word of God. God says, 'I will teach you what ye shall do,' Exodus 4:15. May I talk with Susie?"

"Oh, I suppose so. But be tactful. Susie believes she's doing something good."

Karen entered the room. "Can you gentlemen stop long enough for refreshments?" She placed a tray with coffee and iced tea on the white Bible.

Johnny lifted the tray and slid the Bible to the side before placing the tray on the table. "It's a habit I have. I can't stand to see anything come between us and the Word of God."

Zack looked at his wife. "Call Susie, honey. Brother Johnny would like to meet her."

"She's over at Emma's."

"Then call them both." He turned to Johnny, "Will that be okay? Susie might feel intimidated by herself."

"Of course. I'd love to talk with both of them."

As the two men sipped their drinks, two laughing girls burst through the front door.

"It's getting cloudy and windy," said Susie. "It's going to rain cats and dogs." Suddenly, she saw the visitor. "Oh, I'm sorry. I didn't know there was somebody important here."

"Come on over, girls. This is Brother Johnny Carroll."

"Hi, Brother Johnny. I've seen you on television. How exciting!" said Susie.

"You must be Susie. You favor your daddy." Johnny turned to the other girl. "And you must be Emma."

"Yes, sir. I'm Emma Wedgwood. I live next door. I saw you on television, too."

"Brother Johnny is interested in your school prayers," said Zack. "He wants to help you make them better."

"Good! We could use some help," said Susie. "Don't you think so, Emma?"

"Sure. But we never thought about asking a grownup to help us."

"God has sent me here today," said Johnny, "to help you see that with one little change, the prayers would be much, much better."

Thunder rumbled in the distance. The lights flickered.

"That's good," said Susie.

"Very good," said Emma.

"Do you have copies of the prayers?"

"The ones printed in the paper?" said Susie. "I cut the articles out. You want me to get them?"

"No, that's okay. I have them here." Johnny pulled some papers from his vest pocket and carefully unfolded them on the coffee table, careful not to cover the Bible.

"My copies ain't falling apart," said Susie. "I'll get 'em."

"No, that's all right." Johnny laid his hand on the coffee-table Bible. "First, I want to talk to you about the Word of God. 'For the word of God is quick, and powerful, and sharper than any two-edged sword,' Hebrews 4:12." *Darn*, thought Johnny. *That's the verse my alcoholic daddy beat us over the head with.*

"We like Bible stories, Brother Johnny," said Susie. "We studied in Sunday School how the Jews were a proud people but always had trouble with nasty genitals."

"GGGGentiles, my child. Gentiles," Johnny sputtered. He looked toward Mr. Holland who smiled but remained silent. Johnny continued, "We must be careful how we quote the Word of God."

"Can I ask you a question, Brother Johnny?" asked Susie.

"Sure, honey. Anything you wish."

"Is God really invisible or is it a trick?"

"You shouldn't talk like that, child! 'Many shall come in my name, and shall deceive many,' Mark 13:6. God doesn't do tricks. He doesn't deceive us. He really is invisible and is with us in this room at this very instant."

"I thought God was everywhere," said Emma.

"Oh, he is, child. He is everywhere at once."

"He must be spread pretty thin," said Susie. "Have you ever seen God, Brother Johnny?"

"I see him every . . . I mean, I hear him speak every day. Nobody can see God."

"Reverend Gaylor says we can see him in the poor and the sick. She says we can see him in little children," said Emma.

"My pastor says we see him in the stars and the rain and the sunshine," added Susie.

"I meant we can't . . . God is . . . I'm not sure you'd under-stand . . .," Johnny stammered. "I would like to talk to you about the Bible and prayer."

"You girls let Brother Johnny talk," said Zack. "Save your questions for Sunday School."

"Okay," said Susie.

"We're listening," said Emma.

"Do you children remember when Jesus was about to be crucified and prayed in the Garden of Gethsemane?"

The thunder rumbled closer.

"Yes, sir," replied both girls at once.

"It's when He told God He didn't want to go through with it," said Emma.

"Oh, dear, dear," said Johnny. "He didn't say that. He said, 'not as I will, but as thou wilt,' Matthew 26:39."

Susie spoke. "What if God had—"

Johnny interrupted. "God wants us to pay close attention to his Word and not ask too many questions. 'Foolish and un-learned questions avoid, knowing that they do gender strifes,' Second Timothy 2:23. That's God speaking."

The thunder rumbled closer and more often until it formed a continuous backdrop to the conversation. Karen walked over and looked out the window.

"Are your car windows rolled up, Brother Johnny? It's going to rain any minute."

"Yes, thank you, Mrs. Holland. My car's fine. Now, children, the Bible says, 'If any man shall take away from the words of the book of this prophecy, God shall take away his part out of the book of life,' Revelation 22:19. When we use the Word of God, we must be very careful to use it right."

"Yes, sir," said Susie.

"I agree," said Emma.

"About your school prayers, did you write them yourselves or did someone help you?"

"Someone helped us," said Susie.

"Who helped you, my child?"

"God helped us," responded Susie.

"God and friends in our school," said Emma.

"God helped, did he? Oh, dear. How did he help you?"

"He helped us see some things that needed to be done," said Emma.

"And we wrote prayers about them," said Susie.

"You wrote the words, well . . . yes . . . I see. I'd like for you to look at the words. Look at these words, right here at the end of all the prayers." Johnny turned the news article toward the girls and pointed to the closing lines of one of the prayers.

Susie read aloud. "Not thy will but our will be done. In your name we pray, Amen."

"Those are the same words Jesus used in the Garden," said Emma.

"Not exactly," said Johnny. "It should say, '*Thy* will be done,' not "*our* will be done.' That's the trouble with the world today; we want *our* will and not *God's* will."

"Oh," said Emma. "I see, but I don't think it makes much difference."

"But it does, my child. We should want God's will to be done."

"Our will *is* God's will," said Susie. "We wanted computers for school, sick people well, and other good things, like God does. Doesn't God want good things to happen?"

Johnny finished his iced tea then looked at Mr. Holland and shook his head. Then he turned back to the girls. "We must get the words right, my dear children or we might offend God."

"Does that mean to hurt God's feelings?" asked Susie.

Johnny nodded yes.

"We'd never do that," said Emma.

"You might do it inadvertently," said Johnny.

"What's that mean?" asked Susie.

"You might offend God without wanting to."

"Is it easy to offend God?" ask Emma.

"Well, ah . . . er . . . I don't think so. But we must pray in a way that is not confusing. Other people who hear you might not understand."

"We weren't praying to other people," said Emma.

"That's right, honey," said Johnny. "Now wouldn't you like for me to show you how to pray like God wants us to pray?"

"I guess so," said Susie.

"Might as well," replied Emma.

Johnny raised both hands, palms up, toward the ceiling. "God be praised! Blessed be the name of Jesus!" Turning back toward the girls he said, "Be sure to end the prayers with the words, 'not *our* will but *thy* will be done.' Do you understand?"

Lightning illumined every crevice of the room. Seconds later, thunder chased the bolt across the sky.

"Yes, sir, Brother Johnny. I understand," said Susie.

"Me, too," replied Emma. "Can you write it down for us so we won't forget?"

"Certainly, my children. Praise the Lord!" He reached for the scratch pad Zack offered and wrote the words, tore off the page, and handed it to Emma.

Johnny directed his words to the children once again. "Watch me very carefully, my dear little ones. I will show you how to know God's will. May I use your Bible, Mr. Holland?"

Johnny went over his simple procedure, then asked, "Do you think you can do that the next time you want to know what God wants you to do?"

Johnny did not hear the children's response. A bolt of lightning split the sky. Thunder resealed it with a resounding boom that brought Susie and Emma to their feet. Lights blinked and expired. Wind howled across the eaves and torrents of rain beat on the windows. The news article fell to the floor.

Johnny, disturbed by the storm but confident that his divine mission had been accomplished, left for Montgomery over the protests of the Holland family. "Jesus will calm the storm," he told them, and ran for his van.

"May God be praised," he said aloud to himself as his new chariot turned toward the storm. "He which converteth the sinner from the error of his way shall save a soul from death, and shall hide a multitude of sins,' James 5:20."

As Brother Johnny Carroll strained to see the road through

the driving rain, blinked with each flash of lightning, trembled as the thunder rolled, he said to himself, "God must be angry tonight. I'm glad I'm on His side."

His thoughts wandered back to his childhood as he drove through the storm, in his new SUV, looking neither right nor left, his eyes locked straight ahead.

58

KAREN HOLLAND RETURNED to the kitchen to prepare by candle-light the evening meal of left-overs. Zack Holland picked up the Sunday edition of the *Atlanta Journal-Constitution*, turned to the sports section, and read it by the dancing flame of the candle Karen had brought to the living room.

Susie and Emma carried a candle upstairs to Susie's room to write a prayer for their Monday morning class at Alberta Jones Middle School. There was a war going on somewhere else. They couldn't pronounce the name of the country.

"I don't know what to say." Emma watched the prancing shadows on the wall and began to cluck. She saw Susie make a face. She stopped clucking.

"Let's do what Brother Johnny told us," said Susie. "It'll be lot easier."

"That's right. We won't have to waste so much time trying to figure out what to say."

"I won't have to write anything down," said Susie.

"Brother Johnny said God would lead us. You got a Bible up here?"

Susie picked up her white, imitation-leather King James Bible, the one the church had given her when she was baptized. She fanned the pages with her eyes closed, and let the Holy Book fall open on the table, like Brother Johnny had taught them to do. Emma, with eyes likewise closed, placed her finger on the open page. They opened their eyes. In the trembling light, they both looked at the passage where Emma's finger pointed. The

Bible had fallen open to the book of Lamentations. Emma's finger rested on verse forty-four of chapter three. As Emma positioned her finger under the verse, Susie read, "You have covered yourself with a cloud so that no prayer can get through."

Emma looked at Susie, paused, then fidgeted with her hair. "That doesn't sound good. Let's do it again. Let me drop it this time." She picked up the Bible, closed her eyes, and with her thumbs fanned the pages back and forth. She let it fall open again on the table. The candle faltered. The shadows wavered. At the top of the page, she saw the title, Philippians. "Okay, Susie, find a verse. Don't peep."

Susie felt for the Bible, then moved her finger around on the page and stopped on verse four of chapter six. "Read it," she said.

Emma leaned close to the page and read. "'Be careful for nothing; but in every thing by prayer and supplication with thanksgiving let your requests be made known unto God.' She straightened up and smiled. "I like that one!"

"Me, too, but . . ." Susie looked at Emma, shrugged and extended her hands, palms up. "Which one is right?"

"It's a tie," said Emma. "We'll have to do it again."

"My time to drop it," said Susie as she picked up the Bible, closed her eyes, and began fanning the pages. As she fanned, the flame fluttered and died.

Epilogue

EMMA, A LITTLE overweight, bra-less, wearing loose jeans and a tank top, dialed Susie on her cell phone from her back yard. "Come on over and let's talk about what we need to pack for Washington."

"Give me about ten minutes. I'm on the other line with Jeremiah. He's going to Israel this summer. Caio."

Emma pressed the disconnect. She looked at the decaying stump where the towering sycamore tree had once stood. Mr. Wade from the Forestry Service said the long drought had killed it. *If I'd only known*, she thought, *I'd have watered it every day. This place doesn't look the same without it. Everything's changed.* She sat on the Wal-Mart lawn swing, shaded by a canvas canopy, oblivious to a freight train lumbering through Orchard Hill.

Shortly, Susie, tall and slender, hair cropped, wearing shorts and a T-shirt, came walking around the corner of the house into Emma's back yard. She stopped in front of Emma and crossed her arms across her chest. "Why the long face?"

"I've been thinking about how everything's changed since we were in middle school. With the sycamore gone, this yard looks like a desert."

Susie looked around and gestured left and right. "Come on. You still got oak trees around front and the new maples back here." She pointed to herself. "It's us that have changed. The sycamore probably died from loneliness when we quit climbing it."

"I know. But I keep thinking how things used to be," said Emma.

"Cheer up!" said Susie. "Think about how things are going to be."

Emma patted the seat beside her. "Sit down and tell me about it."

"We are going to Washington, D.C. Can you believe that Governor . . . I mean, Senator Forbe is in Washington and we're going to be his pages?"

"Barely," replied Emma. "If it hadn't been for his Prayer Amendment, we might not be going at all."

"I thought he was going to have us locked up at the time. *He* sure did change. Helped finance our new James B. Forbe High School."

"Did you know he's trying to get us college scholarships now that Auburn and Alabama managed to get the High School Olympic Games repealed?"

"I hope he's successful," said Susie. "I don't think my parents can manage to pay my tuition at Samford University and I certainly don't want to work—not with all those boys around."

"We can save the money we're going to make in Washington." Emma rubbed her thumb and fingers together. "We'll have a wad."

"Not the way I spend it," said Susie. "I'm taking two empty bags to Washington to bring back everything I'm going to buy."

"We're lucky to be going. Mr. Forbe barely got elected Senator. You remember how Brother Johnny campaigned against him?"

"They call him Doctor John Carroll now since he got that ornery degree," said Susie.

"You mean *honorary*."

"Whatever." Susie shrugged. "Now Senator Forbe wants us

to help him get Washington straightened out. You think we can do it?"

"Alabama's not straightened out yet. Since they hired Brother Johnny as head of the Concerned Cooperating Christians, he's been pushing for constitutional reform and wants to replace the Alabama Constitution with the Ten Commandments."

Susie stopped the swing. "Can that be done?"

"He's trying." Emma pushed the swing. "At the pledging-in ceremony of the new Alabama Chief Justice, Les Forcytte, Brother Johnny said that Alabama's laws will soon flow from Mount Sinai. You remember when used to call it Mount Cyanide?"

"Yeah. But it was a *swearing-in* ceremony, wasn't it?"

"Brother Johnny said that the third commandment prohibits swearing," said Emma. "They've got the Ten Commandments hanging everywhere, in the courtrooms, in the schools, in the state liquor stores."

"I don't know what we can do about the Ten Commandments," said Susie. "They've been around for a long time."

"I think we'll learn some new tricks in Washington. We taught Mr. Forbe a few things back when he was governor and he'll probably teach us a few things in Washington."

"We can always fall back on prayer," said Susie. "It worked before."

Emma stopped the swing this time and looked at Susie. "Do you really believe our prayers had anything to do with all that stuff six years ago?"

"We thought so at the time."

"But some things we prayed for didn't happen—at least not the way we thought they should."

Susie smiled. "I learned that the hard way. You remember when Brother Johnny showed us how to let the Bible fall open?

I tried that once with a school book to find out what I needed to study for the test. I almost flunked."

"It seems to me that asking God to do everything for us is a cop-out."

"I wouldn't go that far," said Susie. "I pray as if everything depended on God—He likes that—and then I work like the devil as if everything depended on me."

"Susie, I like your metaphors."

"My what?"

"Never mind."

Susie started the swing. "I've got some fresh news for you. Did you know that Uncle Stanley and Aunt Janet are in Cuba?"

"Both of them?"

"Yeah. He's been named Ambassador to Cuba and told Momma on the phone that they dined with ex-president Fidel Castro at a restaurant overlooking the Hemingway Marina in Havana."

"Wow!" Emma said. "Now I *know* I want to be a Unitarian Universalist minister. Maybe I'll marry an ambassador to some exotic country. By the way, I've got some news about Governor Dick Little."

"What's he done?"

"Listen." Emma stopped the swing and lowered her voice. "You remember Ms. Willis, the reporter?"

Susie leaned close. "Yeah. What about her?"

"You know what she told Mrs. Haley, who became our new principal after she got that administrative degree at Auburn?"

"Of course not. That's what you're going to tell me, isn't it?"

"Don't get sassy!"

"If you don't tell me, Emma Wedgwood, you'll bust."

"Okay. Mrs. Haley came to talk with my mother about why I wouldn't say the Pledge of Allegiance, and I overheard them talking about Ms. Willis and Governor Dick Little. She's his girlfriend now. Mrs. Haley said that Ms. Willis told her that the governor's name sure doesn't describe him very well."

Susie looked at Emma with a waiting-for-the-punch-line expression.

"Susie, think!"

Susie threw her hand to her mouth. "Oooooh! Emma, I can't believe you said that."

"I can't believe Mrs. Haley said that."

"And I can't believe you wouldn't recite the Pledge of Allegiance."

"I did recite it," said Emma. "But I changed a word."

"You left 'God' out."

"No, no. I changed a different word that I thought would make everybody happy. My home room teacher was standing behind me one morning when I changed it and I didn't know she was there."

"That's not the first time that's happened. How does your version go?"

"I thought you'd never ask." Emma stood and instead of crossing her heart, thrust her fist into the air as she recited, "I pledge allegiance to the flag of the United States of America and to the Republic for which it stands, one nation *by God*, indivisible, with liberty and justice for all."

"Emma! No wonder the principal came to see your parents. You could get arrested by the Homeland Security Police!"

Emma reached for Susie's hands and pulled her up from the swing. "Come on. Let's start packing. You got any extra bras? I think pages have to wear them with all those senators around."

Acknowledgments

A special thanks to:

My readers who had the patience to read this novel during its earliest stages. Most were kind enough to be encouraging and the rest critical enough to give me valuable suggestions which influenced the manuscript. my wife Judith Hale, Nadine Cooper, Janet Jackson, Mark Causey, Diana Renfro, Mary Alice Tucker, Francis Tucker, Barbara Taylor, Billy Harrison, Barbara Baldwin, Jan Hinnen, Gerald Johnson, Bob Sanders, Catherine McLain, and Todd Crider.

My classmates in the Novel Writers' Workshop at Auburn University, and its instructor, Mary Carol Moran, who midwifed this novel and helped me edit the manuscript before I gave it to the publisher. The East Alabama Writers' Group also provided valuable insights and suggestions.

My Alabama politicians who unknowingly provided the idea and most of the raw material for the novel.

About the Author

Born in Bowdon Junction, Georgia in 1937, the first of six children of a saw-miller and a farm girl, Dennis Hale grew up in the South. When he was four, his family moved to Opelika, Alabama, and after high school, Hale attended Auburn University and Clarke Memorial Junior College in Mississippi, before earning a B.A. at Samford University in Birmingham—where he married Judith Greene of Chattanooga, Tennessee—and a Masters degree at the New Orleans Baptist Theological Seminary in Louisiana.

During his seminary days, his involvement in minor civil rights activities in south Mississippi drew the attention of the Mississippi State Sovereignty Commission—called the "Mississippi KGB" by *Time* magazine—which investigated him and his wife. Two years after the investigation, the Hales left Mississippi, and moved to Spain for the next 25 years, working as fraternal representatives to Spain's Baptist Evangelical Union where, along with multi-faceted ecclesiastical activities, they reared three daughters and saw Europe.

Hale's writing has spanned four decades—first writing mostly sermons, letters to Mississippi's U.S. senators, some poetry, and promotional articles published in the national journal of Spain's Baptists. His first book, religious non-fiction written in Spanish, was published in 1991.

Hale retired in 1999. He now works as a freelance Spanish interpreter/translator, and serves as minister of a small Unitarian Universalist church near his home in east central Alabama. Hale was encouraged by placing first in a South-wide short short story competition and produced *The Prayer Amendment*.